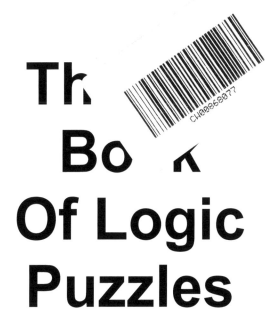

The Book Of Logic Puzzles

Edward J. Harshman

Illustrated by Myron Miller

The Big Book of Logic Puzzles

by Edward J. Harshman

About This Book

This book is a merging of puzzles from my books *Fantastic Lateral Thinking Puzzles, Mind-Sharpening Lateral Thinking Puzzles, and Clever Lateral Thinking Puzzles*, with the addition of several puzzles that were intended for a separate, fourth, book, but until now were never published.

My second book (*Mind-Sharpening Lateral Thinking Puzzles*) was written during my convalescence from a spinal-cord injury (broken neck). Typing that manuscript was difficult and painful because of bad coordination of my hands and some muscle spasms. Critical readers will observe more attention in this book to disabled and seriously injured people than is present in most similar books.

To prevent unduly long sections, there are several on crime, travel, home, and office.

Scientific aptitude is helpful, but definitely not necessary. Some puzzles are pure entertainment, and some are entertaining and provide useful information too. Have fun!

Edward J. Harshman

Credits

Some puzzles were previously published in:

Fantastic Lateral Thinking Puzzles
Mind-Sharpening Lateral Thinking Puzzles
Clever Lateral Thinking Puzzles

Thanks due to:

Sheila Harshman, my wife
for help with the cover and various other things

Claire Bazinet,
for editing assistance with some of the puzzles

by Edward J. Harshman

Sources:

"Appendicitis"
Adapted from "I Wish I'd Said That!" by Art Linkletter, Doubleday 1968.

"Boat-Bashing"
Adapted from an actual sale of a boat to a film crew, as told to the author by Frances Newell.

"Caught Red-Handed"
Adapted from "Those Were the Days" by Edward R. Hewitt, Duell, Sloan and Pearce 1943.

"Collecting Backwards"
Adapted from "Up Yours!" by George Hayduke, Paladin Press, 1982.

"Half-Jaundiced"
DeGowin and Degowin in "Bedside Diagnostic Examination."

"Happy with the TV AD"
Adapted from "Hardcore Hayduke" by George Hayduke, Paladin Press, 1993.

"He Didn't Mean to Kill"
Presented January 1986 at the Nevele Hotel, near Ellenville, New York, in a different form.

"The Ice Water"
Derived from the actual in-school-dishwashing experience of Richard Harshman, my father.

"I Is Good at Grammar"
Adapted from "Riddles, Riddles, Riddles," by Joseph Leeming (Franklin Watts, 1953).

"The Length of a Year"

The second analysis is adapted from "Science Puzzlers," by Martin Gardner (Scholastic Book Services, 1960)

"Magazine Subscriptions" adapted from "Steal This Book" by Abbie Hoffman, Pirate Editions 1971.

"Miracle Cures" adapted from "Encyclopedia of Jewish Humor" by Henry Spalding, Jonathan David Publishers, 1969.

"No Place for Women"
Credit Jimmy Hatlo, in his comic strip "They'll Do It Every Time", for this observation.

"No Littering Summons"
Adapted from a similar puzzle in Your Move, by David L. Silverman: McGraw-Hill 1971.

"Not for Ransom"
Credit "Forgive? Forget It" by Michael J. Connor, Paladin Press, for the principle that forcing money on a crime victim makes the victim's story less credible.

"Nothing Done" and "Wrong Again" based on actual construction errors based on losing count of floors climbed, as explained by Mary Harshman, my mother.

"Positions, Everyone!"
Source: The Worst-Case Survival Handbook by Joshua Piven and David Borgenicht, Chronicle Books 1999

"The Roundabout Taxi Route"
Adapted from "Fun Fare," a compilation of selections from Reader's Digest, 1949.

"Secret Fuel"
Adapted from "Sweet Revenge" by George Hayduke, Paladin Press, 1989.

"Spoken by the Book"

by Edward J. Harshman

Attributed to Mark Twain.

"Sweet Coffee"
The premise is adapted from "More Games for the Superintelligent," by James F. Fixx (Popular Library, 1972).

"Tied His Own Ankles"
George & Helen Papashvily, Yes and No Stories, Harper & Brothers 1946

"Underpopulation?"
Ultimate Resource 2, by Julian Simon, Princeton University Press, 1996

Contents:

by Edward J. Harshman

The Big Book of Logic Puzzles

by Edward J. Harshman

Puzzles

Strange Actions

Over the Wall

A man ran from his armed pursuers, looked around furtively, jumped for the prison wall, climbed to its top, and jumped down on the other side. Made it! Then he set about looking for a law enforcement person. Why, after his successful escape, did he do that?

Clues: 167 Answer: 333

His Plans for Her

A man called the workplace of a woman whom he had not seen or heard from in about five years. He politely asked if she worked there, confirmed that she still did, and learned her telephone extension. He did not want to talk to her, leave a message, or even give his name. He did not intend to harass her or anyone at her workplace then or ever. He had no other reason to call her workplace. What was he planning?

Clues: 195 Answer: 324

She Paid to be Seen

A burlesque dancer arranged a private session with a man. Alone with him, she undressed completely. He adjusted special lighting, looked her over, and was happy with what he saw. After she got dressed, she paid him. Why?

Clues: 167 Answer: 314

She Didn't Like His Picture

A single man in the USA located a single woman in Asia, and he wrote a friendly letter to her. She wrote back and asked for a picture of him. He sent her a picture of himself that matched her request, and she was very offended. Why?

Clues: 215 Answer: 343

Forgiven Break-In

While the homeowners looked on in horror, a man broke into a house, ran upstairs, smashed a window, took what was most important to the homeowners, and ran outside. When he came out, he encountered police officers with whom he cooperated, handing over what he took. But the officers did not want to prosecute. Why not?

Clues: 216 Answer: 351

by Edward J. Harshman

Her Unromantic Reply

A man and a woman stood facing each other. The man embraced the woman passionately. "I feel so happy and romantic," he told her. "I feel like throwing up," she replied. She had felt fine before he joined her. Why was he not offended?

Clues: 237 Answer: 359

He Wanted the Copy

In the days of videocassette recorders and before DVD's became common, a man bought a copyrighted pre-recorded videotape for much more than the cost of a blank tape. He copied it and threw away the original. He knew of video stores that bought similar tapes, used; but he threw away the original videotape without even trying to sell it. Why?

Clues: 261 Answer: 367

The One-Penny Contribution

A charity volunteer knocked on the door of a rich man's house. The rich man opened the door, heard about the merits of the charity, and said, "Wait here." He returned about a minute later with a penny, which he gave to the volunteer. The charity soon afterward wrote an enthusiastic letter of thanks to the rich man. Why?

Clues: 215 Answer: 373

He Voted

Ellery was a thoughtful citizen and a registered voter. When an election came near, he studied the candidates' positions, records, and platforms. Then he went to the polls. He studied the ballot. Lee, his favorite candidate, the one who he thought could do the best job and whose political beliefs most closely matched his own, was listed on the ballot. But Ellery deliberately voted for Ramona, another candidate. Why?

Clues: 238 Answer: 378

Truckin' Through the Intersection

Chris and others from his workplace went to a busy intersection and, using a stopwatch, carefully observed the timing of its traffic-light cycle. Then Chris bought a battered old pickup truck and drove it through the intersection numerous times. When he could no longer do so, he was happy. Why?

Clues: 167 Answer: 334

The Teacher Hit Mary

Mary behaved badly in school. She interrupted her class and kicked the boy next to her, and her teacher made her stand in a corner. The previous evening, the teacher had been to a faculty meeting in which the principal had announced that corporal punishment was no longer permitted. The teacher had previously spanked Mary for similar conduct the previous week, but this time made her stand in a corner instead. After a few minutes, however, the teacher picked up a book and hit Mary on the arm with it. This incident was reported to the principal, as required by the school board; but no action was taken against the teacher. Why not, given that the principal was strongly against corporal punishment?

Clues: 196 Answer: 304

Destruction

Burning Down the House

A man inherited some land, took out a mortgage, and had a house built. Several years later, he paid off the mortgage. About a month after doing so, he set fire to the house and burned it to the ground. He did not file an insurance claim, and he instead canceled his fire insurance just before burning down his house. Why did he burn down the house?

Clues: 262 Answer: 314

Burning Down the House Again

The man who burned down his house soon got another piece of land with a house on it. He made sure that the previous problem could not recur. He befriended the fire marshal, some money passed under the table, and this house burned down too. There was no fire insurance for it. The man was happy. What happened?

Clues: 237 Answer: 324

Burning Down the Building

An old apartment building caught fire. Most apartments were damaged badly, and many people were left homeless. An investigator arrived from the fire department. A shady man pulled him aside into a dark corner of the building and handed him five hundred-dollar bills. "It would be better for both of us," said the shady man, "if something went wrong with the investigation. Lose the papers, or whatever." The investigator looked at the money and protested, "But the landlord will want to file an insurance claim and need our report." "He won't mind," the shady man replied. "Be nice to other fire victims and don't ask questions." The investigator pocketed the money and conveniently forgot the case. Why did the landlord not get upset?

Clues: 281 Answer: 343

Hates to Break Windows

Tina was trapped in a burning building. She knew about emergency procedures, felt the only door to the room, found it hot, and left it closed. The room started to fill with smoke. She lay on the floor, breathing through a handkerchief. She crawled to the window and looked out. The window was solid glass, not designed to be opened. She saw no one outside who would be hit with flying glass if she broke the window. But she did not break the window even though the room was getting more and more full of smoke. She did not even try. Why not?

Clues: 294 Answer: 351

by Edward J. Harshman

He Crashed Deliberately

A man was driving a car. He suddenly swerved and deliberately crashed into a parked car. Despite having no collision insurance, he easily got reimbursed for damage to his car. Why?

Clues: 196 Answer: 359

He Didn't Mean to Kill

A man was driving a car, with one passenger. Suddenly, a drunk driver crashed into his car. Police arrived, and an ambulance was called. The man was badly hurt, and the passenger was killed. The drunk driver was obviously at fault and was easily convicted of driving under influence, reckless endangerment, and causing bodily injury. But the prosecutor, despite being furious at the drunk driver, did not even bother to press charges relating to the dead passenger. Why not?

Clues: 216 Answer: 367

Mess on the Rug

Diana, a fastidious housekeeper, deliberately spilled powder on a rug and walked on it. Why?

Clues: 168 Answer: 374

17

The Car Won't Run

Keith deliberately cut several wires under the hood of a car, thereby disabling it, while expecting to own the car shortly thereafter. Why?

Clues: 238 Answer: 334

Waste

Bewildering Bargain

A woman went to a drugstore to buy some toothpaste. She found her favorite brand and compared the prices and the cost per ounce of various sizes. She wanted the best possible value for her money. But she nevertheless deliberately chose the size that had the greatest cost per ounce. Why?

Clues: 196 Answer: 315

He Overpaid

Rick was about to graduate from college. He had obtained a credit card to start building a credit rating, and he always made at least the minimum payment. He often paid the balance in full. One day, he received a statement showing a total balance of $149.73 but sent a check for over $2000. Why?

Clues: 239 Answer: 359

Do Away with Diamonds

A shopping center had a jewelry store that sold diamonds. Nearby was another store whose employees used to tell people to throw diamonds away. Why was that a sound recommendation?

Clues: 262 Answer: 325

Cheap Silver

A woman had some silver that she did not want. She did not sell it. She did not give it away. She paid someone to take it. Why?

Clues: 168 Answer: 379

Money in the Mailbox

A man walked down a city street. He opened his wallet, took out most of the money, and put the money in a mailbox. He did not first put it in an envelope addressed to anyone; he just put loose dollar bills into the mailbox without even counting them. Why?

Clues: 239 Answer: 304

Finance

It's Not a Gamble, Son!

A rich couple went to a casino and played for a while. They reported that they lost over a hundred thousand dollars, but were not particularly upset. "Go to that casino," they told their son. "Doing so will make you rich." The son, who was not a gambler, did not understand. But he went there, and sure enough he became rich. What happened?

Clues: 282 Answer: 343

He Made a Killing

Scott watched the political scene carefully. When the time was right, he invested in some commodities for which no formal national or international exchange, similar to the stock market or over-the-counter market, exists. As he expected, his investment paid off; he made a 40% profit in about three months. He discussed his investment strategy with his friends Roger and Nancy. "You really made a killing!" Roger said enthusiastically. Scott laughed. Nancy turned pale and almost fainted. Why did Nancy react as she did?

Clues: 216 Answer: 374

The Fifty-Pound Losses

Andy, Bertie, and Charlie were chatting. "I lost fifty pounds," said Andy happily, pinching a loose flap on his too-big trousers. "That diet sure worked well." "I lost fifty pounds, too," said Bertie sadly, "but I got them back." He was obese. "I lost fifty pounds in less than a minute," said Charlie gloomily, "and I will never be the same again." What are they talking about?

Clues: 168 Answer: 351

Unequal Values

Jack and Mack each paid a substantial and equal sum of money for something that they believed to be of value. One year later, Jack had received nothing for his money. Mack, conversely, because of his purchase had received goods and services worth many times what he had paid. But Jack believed that he was better off than Mack after considering the intended effect of the goods and services that Mack received.   What did they originally purchase?

Clues: 197 Answer: 334

Sam Skiptown

One Bad Check

Sam Skiptown, under pressure from creditors, wrote a check and handed it to one of them. The creditor accepted it, but crossly returned the next day because the check was not good. Sam had enough money in the account to pay the debt and had not stopped payment on the check. Why was the creditor unhappy?

Clues: 261 Answer: 315

Another Bad Check

After the previous incident, Sam was coerced by his creditor into writing another check in payment for the debt. This time, the creditor handed Sam a pen and watched him write the check in ordinary ink. The check proved to be useless, even though Sam had not stopped payment on it. Explain.

Clues: 217 Answer: 367

Crime

The Witnessed Break-In

Standing in front of a house, a man wedged a tire wrench between the front door and its frame. With some effort, he jimmied the door open. A police officer watched, but did not interfere. Why not?

Clues: 169 Answer: 304

The Victim was Arrested

Three men, after making careful plans, broke into a house and took hundreds of thousands of dollars in cash from it. The owner of the house was arrested, but the three men were not. What happened?

Clues: 240 Answer: 325

Carried Away

A man encountered a woman he had never seen before, tore off her blouse, cut through her bra, and took her away with him. Her husband did not try to stop him and, though disconcerted, was grateful. Why?

Clues: 169 Answer: 379

Afraid of the Bar

Bill and Linda met for their first date at an expensive restaurant. He was 30 years old, stood six feet four inches tall, wore a business suit, and drove up in a new luxury sedan. She was 24 years old, stood five feet six inches tall in her high heels, wore a cocktail dress, and drove up in a year-old convertible. They recognized each other in the lobby, and the headwaiter told them that there would be a 15-minute wait for their table and suggested that they sit at the bar and have a drink there. Bill had previously offered to pay all expenses and nodded encouragingly. Linda politely declined, saying that if she went to the bar she could get arrested and sent to prison for a long time. Why did she prefer to wait in the lobby, given that she was telling the truth?

Clues: 284 Answer: 343

Just Like Prison

A prisoner was talking to a visitor. "The time spent here is more important than what we do, as long as we don't cause trouble," said the prisoner. "Nothing that we do will have any economic value to anyone." "Just like me," replied the visitor. "The laws against assault and battery don't apply here," continued the prisoner. "If someone tries to beat you up, the police won't interfere. You just have to be tough." "I'm used to that; official position of the police department not a quiet slacking off," said the visitor. "And the food is poor. We have to eat what they serve us, however bad it is. Some people are trying to get the food better, but it's all politics." "That's my life, too," replied the visitor. "And they inspect us all the time, to keep us from having weapons," continued the prisoner. "Same with me, every morning," replied the visitor. "Did you commit a crime?" asked the prisoner. "No," replied the visitor. "Can you change your lifestyle to a nicer one?" continued the prisoner. "I wish I could, but it's against the law," replied the visitor. Why is the visitor subjected to prison-like living conditions?

Clues: 217 Answer: 334

Shoplifting Backwards

Shoplifters usually attempt to smuggle merchandise out of a store. When might a shoplifter smuggle merchandise into a store?

Clues: 240 Answer: 315

Arrested for Shopping

A man walked into a supermarket, took a jar of food off of the shelf, walked to the checkout counter, and offered to pay for the jar. He had not concealed anything. The cashier secretly signaled a security guard, who arrested the man. Why?

Clues: 197 Answer: 360

Legal Conspiracy

Mugsy and Butch hunched over a table in a dingy basement. They drew floor plans of a bank and sketched its burglar alarm. They heard a car approach. Butch got up, looked out the dirty window, and recognized the car as belonging to an off-duty police officer. The car stopped, and the officer got out and knocked on their door. "Hello, Rocky," Mugsy greeted the officer. Rocky surveyed the plans, told them a few more ideas on how to break into banks, and wished them luck. "There's a thousand for you if this works," Mugsy promised him. Their work paid off handsomely soon after, and sure enough Mugsy gave Rocky the thousand dollars. But no crime was committed. Explain.

Clues: 170 Answer: 351

How Did *That* Happen?

by Edward J. Harshman

The Trained Athlete Loses

Frank, a track star, competed against George, who had a weak heart. George soon was two jumps ahead of Frank and eventually beat him. How?

Clues: 263 Answer: 325

Shoot That Eagle!

Three men, each carrying a rifle, walked through the forest. Suddenly, one of them shouted, "A bald eagle!" and pointed. A bald eagle was, in fact, flying slowly overhead. The three men took careful aim, and one successfully shot it. A local bird-watching society later found out about the men and was appreciative. Why?

Clues: 282 Answer: 304

There's a Fly in my Soup!

A man was in a restaurant and ordered some soup. "There's a fly in it," he protested when it was brought to him. The waiter took the soup and went to the kitchen, returning with soup that had no fly in it. "This is the same soup that you brought before," protested the man. He was right. How did he know?

Clues: 240 Answer: 367

The Four-Mile Conversation

Two men stood next to each other and started walking. After a while, one of them had walked 3 miles and the other one had walked 4 miles. But they conversed easily with each other while walking. How?

Clues: 197 Answer: 343

The Five-State Golf Drive

Joe was boasting about his golfing. "I can hit my golf ball with my putter so effectively that it will pass through at least five states before it stops moving." Moe replied, "That's easy. Put it on a chute that coils around the corners of Utah, Colorado, New Mexico, and Arizona...No, wait, that's only four states. What are you talking about?" Joe is right. What is he talking about?

Clues: 294 Answer: 383

Beat the Water Shortage

During a severe water shortage, emergency regulations prohibited car washing. One woman, however, managed to wash her car in full view of police authorities and was not arrested or fined. Why not?

Clues: 170 Answer: 379

Strange Bedroom

David got out of bed, washed up, got dressed, ate breakfast, walked outside, got into his car, drove 300 miles, left his car, went inside, ate supper, got undressed, and went to bed. His bedroom was the same as when he left it before driving. But he was 300 miles away from his earlier location; he did not drive in a circle. How can this be?

Clues: 263 Answer: 351

Hurried Funeral?

A man died on March 5th of a certain year and was buried the previous day, March 4th, of the same year. What happened?

Clues: 298 Answer: 325

The Unwelcome Strike

A union member received word of a new contract and was pleased with it. He got a raise and good job security, and he was satisfied with his union negotiators. Nevertheless, when he next went to work, in front of over a thousand witnesses, he called a strike. Everyone else at his workstation stood idly while a manager angrily protested. But the union member was immune from retaliation despite his action and the many witnesses to it. Why?

Clues: 217 Answer: 315

Mysterious Captions

Years ago, during the days of analog TV broadcasts and videocassette recorders, Eric and Bessie gave their son Robert a television set for Christmas. A few months later, they visited Robert and were happy to see their granddaughter Susan watching that television set. Susan was watching a movie; and because she was learning to read, she enjoyed the closed-captioned subtitles that appeared on the screen to match the dialogue. "I didn't know that the set had a closed-caption decoder," said Bessie, surprised. "Me neither," added Eric. "It doesn't," replied Robert. And no decoder was connected to it or added to it. Explain.

Clues: 241 Answer: 360

No Side Effects

To reduce your risk of death from a heart attack, you can take heart medicine, adjust your diet, get appropriate exercise, and lose weight. Drugs often have side effects, such as fatigue, skin rashes, or dizziness. But what can you take that, having taken them, you never need to take again for years, that have no side effects, and that not only help prevent death from heart attack but also can prevent death from fire?

by Edward J. Harshman

Clues: 294 Answer: 305

Sweet Coffee

You have three cups of coffee. You have twelve lumps of sugar. How do you put an odd number of lumps into each cup while putting all of the sugar into the three cups?

Clues: 170 Answer: 334

Heavy-Footed Harry

Harry wears economical shoes. They are solid steel. They are easy for him to use and maintain. He does not even bother taking them off at night. Why not?

Clues: 198 Answer: 374

The Stubborn Door

A boy walked to a door, turned its knob, pulled it open, walked through it, and closed it behind him. He then walked down a hall, came to another door, turned its knob, and tried to pull the door open. It would not move. He noticed that the door had a lock, and he took a key from his pocket. He put the key into the lock, and it fit and turned the lock. But whatever he did with the key, he could not pull the door open. Then someone told him something that enabled him to open the door easily. What did the boy learn?

Clues: 263 Answer: 315

She Hated Leftovers

Sally was planning a picnic. She wanted to serve hot dogs and hamburgers and decided to supply 10 hot dogs and 6 hamburgers. Hot dogs come 10 per package, hamburger and hot dog rolls each come 8 per package, and hamburger meat can be bought in any quantity. Sally wanted as little leftover material as possible. What did she do?

Clues: 218 Answer: 367

Does This Bulb Work?

To tell a good incandescent light bulb from a burned-out bulb, you can screw it into a socket and test it. Or you can shake it and listen for the rattle of a broken filament. But Cal used to tell if his incandescent light bulbs worked just by looking at them. How?

by Edward J. Harshman

Clues: 241 Answer: 385

Hank and Frank

Truckers Went Separate Ways

Hank and Frank were old buddies, worked for the same trucking company, and drove 18-wheelers along an interstate highway in the same direction and about a quarter of a mile from each other. They turned on their citizens-band radios, began talking, and happily learned from an oncoming sports-car driver that the highway had very little traffic and no obstructions for at least a hundred miles. Hank and Frank, who were headed for the same place, decided to maintain radio contact for the rest of their trip. But something happened that made Frank insist on not doing so, even though he enjoyed Hank's camaraderie. The incident had nothing to do with stopping, maintaining, refueling, or repairing the truck. What happened?

Clues: 295 Answer: 335

Truckers Were Arrested

Hank and Frank later encountered each other at a restaurant about halfway along a turnpike. "Hey, Hank! Good to see ya!" shouted Frank, slapping him on the back. They sat together and had a great time eating lunch. As they got up, Hank dropped his map and some papers. Frank helped him pick them up. Then they got into their trucks and drove away. When they tried to leave the turnpike, they were arrested. They had driven safely and had not wanted to commit a crime. What happened?

Clues: 172 Answer: 361

Truckers and No Toll Money

After getting their arrests straightened out, Hank and Frank were soon on the road again and heading in the same direction on the same highway. They stopped at a restaurant for lunch and chatted. Hank got into his truck and drove away. Frank followed closely in his truck. They approached a toll barrier. Hank told Frank on his CB, "I don't have any money for the toll." Frank was not surprised and told him how to go through the toll booth without paying. How? And why was Frank not surprised?

Clues: 198 Answer: 380

In the Office

Two Copies, Not One

"Here is a hundred-page document," said Alice to the clerk at the copy shop. "I want two copies of it." The clerk looked over the document and checked the count, which was, indeed, exactly one hundred pages. Later, Alice returned for the document. She retrieved the original and one hundred additional sheets of paper. She was satisfied and paid for the two copies. Why?

Clues: 282 Answer: 344

by Edward J. Harshman

Was Her Job At Risk?

Benny was happy with Jenny's work. Jenny, conversely, was happy at her job. Why did Benny, therefore, run an advertisement for someone to replace Jenny?

Clues: 218 Answer: 326

The Nine-Penny Ruler

Lillian was a very eccentric secretary. She tried to balance nine cents on the end of a ruler, but failed. Then she mailed a letter, boasting that she saved far more than the nine cents that had fallen into her hand. What was the motive for her fussing with the nine cents?

Clues: 198 Answer: 305

Don't Break the Scale

Lillian finally got a postage scale that weighed, to approximately the nearest ounce, up to two pounds. Then she had to weigh a package that weighed more than two pounds, but probably less than four pounds. How did she do that?

Clues: 171 Answer: 379

The Clock was Right

"It's getting late. Thirteen o'clock," said Al, a weary computer programmer. "No such time," replied Joan, another weary programmer, who looked at the clock. "I see why you think so, though." The clock worked perfectly. What time was it really?

Clues: 282 Answer: 374

The Misleading Telephone Message

Martin called a store and got a recorded message: "The number you have reached (store's number) has been changed. The new number is (store's number again). Please make a note of it." He called the telephone company, and the repair service staff said that the number had not been changed and that the telephone line was working. Martin had dialed correctly, and the repair service report was accurate. What happened?

Clues: 300 Answer: 300

by Edward J. Harshman

He Followed Instructions

A student was sent to the principal's office for one hour of detention. As was customary, the principal's secretary instructed the student to do minor tasks during that hour. The secretary ordered the student to get a specified folder from a file cabinet. The student followed instructions that were posted on the cabinet, but was immediately scolded by the secretary for making unnecessary noise. Why?

Clues: 241 Answer: 335

He Hated Bad Attitudes

Percy got a job and got along well with everyone except the payroll clerk, who seemed to have an unpleasant attitude. Percy's supervisor and his other co-workers were friendly, and he was basically happy with his job.

37

After about a month, Percy threatened the clerk. "Give me a hard time once more, and I will fill out one government form that will give you major complications and you will have no recourse whatever." The clerk's attitude did not change, and Percy carried out his threat. Sure enough, the clerk had problems with the payroll checks thereafter. What did Percy do?

Clues: 264 Answer: 360

But I Said....

They Love Each Other

"I love you," said Pat. "I love you," said Mary to Pat as she embraced him. "So smart you are. It's hard to believe your parents never said a word all their lives." Mary was right. And Pat's parents never said a word, but were normal in every way. How can this be?

Clues: 198 Answer: 383

Wrong Answers are Plentiful

Many adjectives end with the letters F-U-L. "Hopeful," "plentiful," and "wonderful" are examples. There is one word, however, of which the last four letters are F, U, and two L's in that order. What is the word?

Clues: 171 Answer: 368

Vowels in Order

A teacher asked his class if there is any English-language word in which the vowels occur. A student raised his hand and answered, correctly, "Unquestionably." The teacher asked if there are any words in which the vowels all occur and are in alphabetical order. One mischievous student answered in a supercilious, disrespectful, manner, saying that there is one but teasingly not saying what it is. Another student, when asked if there are any such words, respectfully but firmly refused to say yes and refused to say no. Why did the teacher give credit to those two students for answering his question properly?

Clues: 242 Answer: 344

Give Them a Hand

"Give me a hand," said Bill, who was struggling with a tall figure. Instead of coming to Bill's aid, Charlie passed something to him that was neither a weapon nor helpful in a fight. "Thanks," said Bill, not at all surprised or upset by what Charlie gave him or Charlie's apparent lack of concern.   What was happening?

Clues: 264 Answer: 351

I Is Good At Grammar

Little Johnnie was sitting on the living room floor, leafing through a picture book. His mother and father were in the kitchen. Johnnie shouted a question that his father could not understand. The mother began to shout a reply, "I is...." The father interrupted her, grumbling about her setting a bad example with her speech. The mother insisted that she was using good grammar and finished her reply to Johnnie. What did the mother say?

39

Clues: 171 Answer: 305

Weird Words

The words "begins" and "chintz" have an unusual property, completely unrelated to their meaning. What is that property?

Clues: 218 Answer: 315

Travel

Child Driver

"Look at me! I'm driving!" exclaimed the six-year-old, who was gripping the steering wheel of the family car as it traveled along the highway at over a mile a minute. His mother sat next to him, but was unconcerned. What was happening?

Clues: 283 Answer: 324

Full Speed Ahead

A man was driving a car and saw a traffic light, red, at an intersection he was approaching. Of course, he slowed down. But then he suddenly sped up, even though the traffic light still showed red. He was not trying to evade someone behind him, he did not hear an emergency siren, and no police officer waved him through the intersection. He also was an ordinary safe driver, anxious to avoid an accident. Why did he speed up?

Clues: 219 Answer: 305

by Edward J. Harshman

This Car Loves Hills

A man was driving a car and started to back into a curbside parking space. The passenger next to him said "Don't park there." The driver asked, "Why not?" The passenger replied, "Because that's not on a steep hill." Why did the passenger not want the car parked on level ground?

Clues: 172 Answer: 316

She Paid Easily

Cooper and Cecily were in a car and encountered a tollbooth. Cooper, who was driving, handed Cecily his wallet and asked her to take out money to pay the toll. She did so. She also rolled down her window and paid the toll. Why did she not pass the money to Cooper, who was in the driver's seat?

Clues: 264 Answer: 344

Loves Being Stranded

Herbert was test-driving a used car. The car stalled. Herbert said, "I am happy that the car stalled. If it hadn't, then expensive repairs might have been needed." Why?

Clues: 283 Answer: 326

41

The Crooked Headlight

A man was driving a car along the road at night. He suddenly pulled over and deliberately misaimed one of his headlights. Then he started driving again. Why?

Clues: 242 Answer: 368

The Bicycle Bolt

Edith was working on her bicycle and needed a new bolt for it. She asked her son to go to a hardware store and get one. She carefully wrote out the shaft length, thread size, length of threaded section, inner and outer diameter, and size and shape of the head of the bolt. The son went to the hardware store and got a bolt. Edith glanced briefly at the bolt and apologized to her son; he would have to exchange it. The specifications accurately described what was needed, and the bolt fit them perfectly. Why was Edith unhappy?

by Edward J. Harshman

Clues: 242 Answer: 335

The Inferior Car Rental

Sally was planning a long trip. She retrieved her car from a repair shop that she trusted, and was told that her car was in fine condition after its preventive maintenance. It was fully paid for, and its registration and insurance were intact and fully paid-up. The next day, Sally started her trip in another car, a rented one. The rented car was smaller and less comfortable than her own car and not better than her car in any way. She did not need any special features of a car, such as a trailer-towing hitch, four-wheel drive, or a large trunk. But she nevertheless rented the car instead of using her own car. Why?

Clues: 173 Answer: 374

His Car Was Identified

Nick and Dave were just leaving work at an ambulance dispatcher station. "We're off tomorrow, right?" said Nick. "Right," replied Dave. "What do you say we meet in the shopping center parking lot, get in the car I just bought, and head out to the lake?" suggested Nick. "Let's do that," agreed Dave. Nick had just bought a used car, which he mentioned to Dave but without describing it in any way. It had license plates that were unfamiliar to Dave and were not new. It had no parking stickers or other identifying marks of any kind. Nevertheless, Dave identified it easily when he drove to the shopping center parking lot. How?

Clues: 199 Answer: 316

Snow on the Windshield

Melanie lived alone in a two-family house. Her landlady lived in the other half of the same house. One day, after two inches of snow had fallen, a blizzard emergency was announced. Melanie had parked her car on the street well before the snow started to fall, and because of the emergency she had to find another place to park her car. She called her landlady. "May I park my car in your driveway until the snow emergency is over?" she asked. "Please do. That will save one carlength of snow shoveling later," came the reply. Melanie got into her car and drove it into her landlady's driveway. But she did not bother to clean the snow off of her windshield before driving. Why not?

Clues: 219 Answer: 305

The Traffic Ticket

Paul was moving across the country. He put all of his belongings into his car and started driving. After a while, he drove onto a highway, which had light traffic. He passed a sign that said "No TRAILERS," but he was not towing a trailer. A police officer made him pull over and gave him a summons. He was not speeding or driving too slowly, his registration and license were in good order, he had not been involved in an accident, his lights worked well and were properly used, he had not evaded a toll, he was driving safely, and he was not wanted for a previous moving violation or other infraction. Paul accepted the summons and paid the fine. Why was he told to pull over?

by Edward J. Harshman

Clues: 173 Answer: 361

The Happy Cabdriver

Square City was a brand new city that was laid out on a coordinate grid. Streets ran east and west and were named North First Street, North Second Street, etc. if north of Center Street and were named South First Street, South Second Street, etc. if south of Center Street. Avenues ran north and south and, similarly, were named East First Avenue, East Second Avenue, etc. if east of Center Avenue and were named West First Avenue, West Second Avenue, if west of Center Avenue. A real estate speculator arrived in Square City and flagged down a taxicab at East Fifteenth Avenue and North Twentieth Street. He wanted to go to Center Avenue and Center Street, noted the lack of a meter, and asked the driver the fare. "We cabbies get paid by the distance traveled. Fifteen blocks plus twenty blocks, at a quarter per block, $8.75." The speculator insisted that the distance was excessive, offered a good tip in return for a more direct route, and got enthusiastic thanks from the cab driver even though the speculator paid less than $8.75 when the trip was finished. Why?

Clues: 243 Answer: 344

The Roundabout Taxi Route

Melinda was in a hurry. She ran to the corner of a busy city intersection and flagged a taxi. She wanted to get to her destination as quickly as possible. Why, therefore, did she order the driver to circle the block several times?

Clues: 265 Answer: 326

Saved by the Convertible

Milton was badly hurt in an auto accident. He had been driving his convertible, seat belt fastened (no shoulder strap), and hit an oil spill. His car had spun sideways and hit an overturned truck, and another car had also spun sideways and slammed into his car. Now, he was in the hospital. His left arm was broken in several places, both his legs were broken, he had had emergency surgery for internal bleeding, he had received blood transfusions, and he was on a respirator. But he was going to recover. His wife visited him in the hospital. After a while, she said to him, "I hope our next car will not be a convertible. They aren't safe." Milton wrote on a notepad, "Ask paramedics." His wife reviewed the report from the rescue crew that delivered him to the hospital, and she then went to the ambulance dispatch center. She found the paramedics who had rescued her husband from the accident and asked them about the safety of a convertible. One of them shook his head. "Lady," he told her, "if he had been in a hard-top instead of a convertible, then he might have died on the spot. Being in a convertible may have saved his life." Explain.

Clues: 199 Answer: 335

by Edward J. Harshman

Hot Car

Lucy was driving in slow city traffic on a hot July day. She was perspiring heavily and was extremely uncomfortable. Why did she turn on the car heater, which made her feel hotter and more miserable?

Clues: 172 Answer: 352

At Home

Find Bingo!

"Bingo has escaped!" shouted Jimmy, seeing the empty hamster cage. "Close the window!" "Hamsters can't climb like that," replied Peter, looking under the bed. Jimmy ran to the window and closed it, and he and

Peter began searching. Why did Jimmy want the window closed?

Clues: 243 Answer: 352

Dangerous Safety Glass

Impact-resistant or shatter-resistant glass is recommended or required, for safety, in car windows, shower-stall doors, and other places. Where is it more dangerous than ordinary, easily broken, glass?

Clues: 283 Answer: 306

The Unpowered Outlet

Alex plugged a lamp into an outlet. The lamp did not work. He plugged another lamp into the outlet. The second lamp also did not work. He checked all of the circuit breakers, and they were all on. He confirmed that no outlets in the room were connected to wall switches. The outlet, nevertheless, gave no power. How did he eventually supply power to the outlet without calling an electrician or doing the equivalent electrician work himself?

Clues: 173 Answer: 316

Steamed Up

Alice was sitting in her uncomfortable apartment. The weather was hot and humid. If she turned down the air-conditioner thermostat, the apartment got cool, but clammy and unpleasant. If not, the apartment was uncomfortably hot. Then she had an idea that made the apartment very comfortable in a few hours and did not involve repairing the air conditioner, waiting for cool weather, or using a fan. What did she do?

Clues: 243 Answer: 361

Won't Stop Ringing

Rita stood at the front door of a house. She put her finger on a button, and a bell started to ring. She took her finger off of the button, and the bell continued to ring. What was happening?

Clues: 174 Answer: 383

Doesn't Need Hot Water

Dora put a cup of water into a microwave oven that was known to work perfectly and did not need testing. She set the timer and turned on the oven. Predictably, the water got hot. Dora then took the water out and poured it down the drain. She was not trying to clean the drainpipe. What was she doing?

Clues: 199 Answer: 328

Perfectly Efficient

Electrical and mechanical devices have various efficiency ratings. A gasoline engine, for example, may convert 20% of the energy from its fuel to mechanical energy. An electric motor may convert 80% of its electrical energy to rotational energy. What device is 100% efficient?

Clues: 244 Answer: 306

Fix That Clothes Washer!

Big Zeke had some land in an undeveloped area and built a house on it. There was no commercial power available, so he got a generator. The generator ran beautifully while he used power saws to cut lumber to size, and he was surprised at how his electric drill worked as well as ever but never seemed to get as hot as when he used it previously. When the house was finished, he turned on electric lights and vacuumed the sawdust off of the floor. He was pleased. Then, he got a clothes washer. The main motor, the one that moved the agitator and did the spin cycle, worked well. But the timer motor burned out. He replaced the timer motor, and the replacement burned out too. What was the problem?

Clues: 174 Answer: 344

The Mail is In!

In the era before online purchases, Little Oscar had mailed an order form for something the previous day. Now he was constantly pestering his mother to let him check the mail. He looked out the window at the mailboxes of their apartment complex and shouted, "The mail is in! The mail is in!" His mother looked out the window and did not see a mail carrier or a mail truck. Oscar was in another room earlier and did not see or hear the mail truck. Oscar knew that the mail had been delivered only by what he saw by looking out the window. He did not see people walking away from the mailboxes with mail. Why was Oscar certain?

Clues: 221 Answer: 368

by Edward J. Harshman

The Mail Must Go Through

A ferocious dog was in a front yard, fastened to a stake by a 30-foot chain. The front door was 45 feet away from him. A timid mail carrier surveyed the scene and asked a neighbor to accept and deliver the mail to the front door. The neighbor did so, noting that despite the chain and stake the mail carrier would be in danger. Why?

Clues: 266 Answer: 374

The Brighter Bulb

Two electric old-fashioned incandescent light bulbs, identical 100-watt bulbs, are screwed into a lamp. Their sockets are connected in series, not in parallel. The wiring that connects their sockets to the power source is arranged so that current must flow through

51

both bulbs, instead of through either bulb as for most lamps. The lamp is switched on. Both bulbs glow equally brightly, of course. Then one bulb is unscrewed and replaced with a 25-watt bulb. The bulbs no longer glow equally brightly. But which bulb is brighter?

Clues: 295 Answer: 336

The Cold Fire

John and Joan were at home, in their new house. The day had been warm, but this night was cold. They built a fire in their fireplace, but were soon colder than they would have been if they did not build a fire. What was wrong?

Clues: 219 Answer: 316

Another Cold Fire

John and Joan had the necessary repair made. Later, on a cold evening that followed a warm day, they built a fire in the fireplace. They had shut off the central heating entirely. They were soon colder than they would have been if they had used no central heating and not built the fire. What was the problem this time?

Clues: 265 Answer: 352

The Doctor Is....

by Edward J. Harshman

The Critical Student

A medical student was interested in further medical education and went to an interview at a teaching hospital. The student got a tour and sat in on a lecture that was for medical school graduates at the hospital. The lecturer discussed achalasia, a condition in which swallowing food is painful because the valve into the stomach does not open properly. The lecturer mentioned the appropriate kind of drugs to treat the condition and listed several drugs of that kind, with frequencies and strengths of doses. The lecturer said that most patients with achalasia are not helped by the drugs, and then asked for questions. A few sensible questions about specific drugs and their frequencies and strengths of doses followed. Then the lecture continued. The medical student knew that the most common reason for drugs not to work is that the patient does not take them. The student had previously known absolutely nothing about achalasia. Why did the medical student become dissatisfied with the hospital?

Clues: 176 Answer: 380

But the Patient Followed Orders

A patient went to a doctor for a known and common ailment and scrupulously followed the doctor's advice. At a followup visit, the doctor was angry and said, "You have overdone my instructions. If you don't stop exceeding what I told you to do, then I will hit the ceiling!" The patient, not angry, replied, "Doctor, if I continue getting results from the treatment at the same rate as before, then in less than a year I will hit the ceiling myself." What was the ailment?

Clues: 200 Answer: 326

She Easily Went Home

A woman consulted a physician about a sore throat. The physician examined her, said "Heart attack," and called an ambulance. Doctors at the emergency room noted the electrocardiogram tracings and confirmed a massive heart attack that was certain to require a lengthy hospital stay. But the woman was walking around easily the next day and thought nothing of being at home. What happened?

Clues: 244 Answer: 336

The Sun, The Earth, And Other Things

The Length of a Year

The earth takes about 23 hours and 56 minutes to rotate fully on its axis, as seen from distant stars. Defining a day as equal to this time period, how many days (to the nearest 1/4th) are in a year?

Clues: 174 Answer: 306

Where's the Sunshine?

At noon in the continental USA, the sun is due south (except during daylight savings time, in which case the sun is due south at 1:00 P.M.). Right? Wrong, almost invariably! Why?

Clues: 285 Answer: 361

Approximately Seven Days Per Week

Is the probability that January 1 falls on a Sunday, December 25 on a Friday, July 4th on a Saturday, or that any other specified date falls on a particular weekday for a randomly chosen year exactly 1/7th? Can you prove your answer?

Clues: 220 Answer: 316

Brighter at Night

Because the sun shines by day but not by night, most places are lit at least as brightly by day as by night. Exceptions exist, such as nightclubs and other structures that are principally used at night and are especially lit for that purpose. What structure is more brightly lit by night than by day but that is not intentionally lit especially brightly at night?

Clues: 175 Answer: 345

How Can This Be?

He's All Wet

A man stood outdoors under an umbrella. It was a large umbrella, large enough to cover him completely; and there was no wind. He was not standing in a pond or other body of water. So why was he thoroughly drenched?

Clues: 200 Answer: 353

One Way to Liberty

To reach the inside of the head of the Statue of Liberty, which stands in New York Harbor, you climb many flights of stairs. When you have almost reached the head, you climb a spiral staircase. While on that staircase, you can look outward and see the inner walls of the statue in all directions; you cannot see a separate staircase next to the one that you are climbing. You are on a staircase that is too narrow for people to go in both directions. Having reached the top, how do people get down?

Clues: 244 Answer: 369

Short Swing

Ned, a Little League baseball player, watched the coach open a long box and take out some baseball bats. "That's a big box," said Ned to the coach. "I know," replied the coach. "It has to hold a lot of bats." "At home, we have a bat box that's only a foot long," continued Ned. "That doesn't make sense," said the coach. "None of these bats would fit in it." But it does make sense. Why?

Clues: 267 Answer: 326

The Switch of Mastery

The family was sitting around, reading and relaxing. "This monster is master of all he surveys," said little

Matthew, looking up from a comic book. "That's nothing," replied his mother. "If I flip this switch, we will all be master of all we survey." How?

Clues: 285 Answer: 285

Safe Landing

Vick, a seven-year-old boy, was in the park with his mother. He climbed to the top of a three-hundred-foot tree. Then his mother called him. "Vick, come here!" she shouted. He jumped from the top of the tree, landed uninjured on the ground, and ran to his unconcerned mother. How did he land without hurting himself?

Clues: 245 Answer: 305

Hold Still!

A professional photographer set up his camera on a tripod, adjusted the aperture, set the exposure speed, and mounted the flash. Then he had his model pose and focused the camera. "Hold still," he said. "The exposure is for one full second." Why, if a flash was used?

Clues: 295 Answer: 336

A Gift To Share

Laura won a prize in a fund-raising raffle. It had been donated by a local business, a women's clothing store. "Great!" she exclaimed happily on hearing of her win. "I know just the person to share it with!" What was it?

Clues: 175 Answer: 385

Spoken By The Book

After a singularly dull lecture that followed a formal dinner, a man walked up to the lecturer and said, "Strikingly unoriginal. I have a book that has every word of your speech in it, and most people here do, too." The lecturer was enraged and demanded proof. He got it. How?

Clues: 200 Answer: 317

Rope on its End

A rope is an object that supposedly can be easily carried, but not be stood on end. Can it be stood on end?

Clues: 220 Answer: 345

The Will

A man died, leaving four grown children. His will left 1/5 of his estate to be divided equally among all law-abiding male offspring, 3/5 of it to be divided equally among all female offspring, and the balance to be divided equally among his grandchildren. His offspring were Pat, Leslie, Terry, and Evelyn. Pat had joined the Navy. Leslie gained local notoriety for getting many women pregnant. Terry got a job in a hospital and married a nurse. Evelyn had been convicted of murder and was in prison. After the estate was settled, Evelyn's son had inherited exactly twice as much as anyone else who had inherited. Explain.

Clues: 245 Answer: 362

Ski Through The Tree

The tracks of two skis were visible in otherwise virgin snow. They led directly to a tree; then the tracks passed the tree—one on each side of it! How were the tracks made?

Clues: 221 Answer: 383

Half-Jaundiced

Jaundice is a sign of liver impairment that makes the whites of a person's eyes, and the skin of a Caucasian person, turn yellow. One hospital patient had a jaundiced appearance in one eye, but not the other. Why?

Clues: 175 Answer: 353

No Sale

In the days before the do-not-call registry, a telephone solicitor, trying to sell magazine subscriptions, dialed a number chosen at random from the telephone book. A circulation manager for the magazine answered the telephone. The telephone solicitor had made sure not to call the circulation manager, but kept reaching the manager anyway even after trying the number several times. Explain.

Clues: 268 Answer: 327

Trials of the Uninvited

John was making lunch when his friend Ron arrived, unexpectedly bringing along his two kids and their nanny. Soon, the men, unconcerned, were sitting in the kitchen eating steak sandwiches, while the kids, unfed, played outside under the nanny's watchful eye. When the hungry kids started to chew on strands of grass, the nanny didn't stop them. Why not?

Clues: 247 Answer: 369

Dismaying Decisions

by Edward J. Harshman

Time in Reverse

A man wanted a clock for the wall, the traditional kind with an hour hand and a minute hand; but he wanted its hands to move counterclockwise. Why?

Clues: 177 Answer: 375

Strong Enough Already

Willie entered an exercise program, and when he finished it his arm was more than a hundred times as strong as when he started it. He told his friend Spike, a professional boxer, about the program. Spike thanked Willie for the information, but said he wasn't interested in entering the program. Why not?

Clues: 176 Answer: 307

No Place for Women

High-heeled shoes, girdles, stockings, and other articles of women's clothing have been attacked as deriving from male-dominated society. What characteristic of some women's clothing boutiques can be similarly attacked?

Clues: 265 Answer: 317

Self-Destruction

One approach to reducing health care costs is to discourage self-destructive behavior. Smoking, driving without seat belts, and certain other activities are identified as needlessly risky; and social pressure has built to make them less and less desirable. One form of self-destructive behavior, however, receives little public attention. It can lead to reconstructive surgery, but people who receive the surgery often do not stop the behavior and need the surgery again. Oddly enough, the health care administration establishment is biased against having this particular self-destructive behavior identified as such. What is it, and why does the health-administration establishment not want it recognized?

Clues: 201 Answer: 336

Tricky Tactics

Mowing the Pool

Helen had a swimming pool, surrounded by a small lawn and encircled by tall trees, next to her house.

Every week during the summer, her son first mowed the lawn. Then he pushed the lawn mower around the concrete deck that surrounded the pool, although no grass grew there. Why?

Clues: 205 Answer: 380

The Terrified Mother

A young mother wheeled her baby, in a carriage, through a park. A man looked at the baby and admired it. "What a lovely baby," he said. "Thank you," she replied, smiling gently. A few minutes later, a woman saw the baby and gushed, "What a beautiful boy! I'd love to take him home with me." The mother screamed in terror, snatched her baby, and ran. Why?

Clues: 177 Answer: 383

She Cheated

A history teacher gave an essay test. To one question, two students, Sherry and Mary, gave identical answers. Their handwriting gave no clue as to who had copied from whom. Nevertheless, the teacher found Mary guilty of cheating. How?

Clues: 222 Answer: 345

Wet in the Winter

Weird Winnie does her laundry in a coin-operated laundromat near where she lives. During the summer, she uses a washer and a dryer for each load of laundry. But during the winter, she uses only the washer and takes her wet laundry home to dry. Why?

Clues: 245 Answer: 327

The Upside-Down Newspaper

A timid-looking man sat on a bench in a city park. He held an upside-down newspaper and was reading intently. Why?

Clues: 201 Answer: 362

He Held His Liquor

Randy and Andy were at a table in the back of a bar, each holding a bottle of beer. They finished their beer, and Andy got up and walked over to the bartender. He returned with two full beer bottles, handed one to

Randy, and sat down. Again, they drank until their bottles were empty. Again, Andy walked over to the bartender and returned with two full bottles. They repeated this process until they had each finished about ten bottlefuls. Randy was, predictably, drunk. Why was Andy nearly sober?

Clues: 267 Answer: 352

Hot Jewelry

Elsie was planning to go away for about a month. She wrapped her good jewelry in a blanket and put it in her self-cleaning oven. Why?

Clues: 178 Answer: 307

Picking Good Apples

Cora, Flora, and Nora went for a walk in the woods and encountered a tall apple tree. It had wonderful ripe apples; but someone must have been there just before them, for all of the good apples were too high for them to reach. Some worm-infested apples could be easily picked, and more bad apples lay on the ground. How did the ladies gather some good apples?

Clues: 285 Answer: 317

Tied Up In Knots

You have two ropes, a thick one and a thin one. You want to tie one rope to the other rope. If they were the same size, then you would be able to use any of several knots. Unfortunately, they are of different sizes. How do you do it?

Clues: 201 Answer: 369

Zelda Was Cured

Zelda, who had a one-month-old baby, was five feet eight inches tall. Although she told her doctor about suffering from low-back pain, the doctor simply blamed the loose ligaments that result from childbirth and was not very helpful. When she told her husband about it, he promptly did something that greatly reduced her pain and that required neither drugs nor exercise. What did the husband do?

Clues: 222 Answer: 345

Old-Time Digital

"This is a CD player," said an electronics store salesman to an old woman. "It gives excellent sound because the signal is recorded digitally. That means that the individual tones that were recorded are specially encoded, so that you don't hear any background noise. They will sound just the same when you play the disk as it did when the original music was recorded." "I don't see the advantage," she told him. "Well, it's relatively new," he continued. "In the old days, all recordings were analog, which means that they picked up background noise and sounded worse after being played often." "Nonsense!" she retorted. "If digital recordings are what you say they are, then I've been using them since I was a little girl!" Explain.

Clues: 246 Answer: 375

Catch The Dollar

Hold a dollar bill near one narrow edge, with the other narrow edge pointing down, in your right hand. Put your left hand about six inches below your right hand—thumb and fingers separated—ready to catch the bill when you drop it. Let go of the bill. You can easily catch it with your left hand. If you have someone else try to catch it, by holding his hand six inches below your hand, and you drop the dollar without warning, then he will probably miss it. Unlike you, he needs time to react to your having dropped it. How can you drop a dollar so as to make it nearly impossible for him to catch by using his thumb and fingers in a pincer grip, as described above?

Clues: 178 Answer: 362

Rainy Walk

Ima Boyd Breyne lived in a suburban development and had two parrots. She enjoyed walking in sunny weather, and her parrots enjoyed sunlight too. But she took them outside only during heavy rain. Why?

Clues: 178 Answer: 337

Tiresome Questions

Two suburban neighbors stood, talking, at the small fence that separated their lots. "How tall is your son now?" asked Marla. "He keeps growing, of course," replied Carla, "and I can't really say; but this morning

by Edward J. Harshman

he stood next to my husband's new truck and was just as tall as its right front tire." "How tall is that?" continued Marla. "I don't know, and I can't even tell you what kind of truck it is," replied Carla. Marla wandered around the fence and up Carla's driveway, and she then asked Carla to lend her something. Soon, both of them knew how tall Carla's son was. How did Marla figure it out?

Clues: 267 Answer: 307

One Must Eat

Still Hungry

A man and a woman entered a restaurant. They sat down, studied a menu, and ordered several dishes. They were presented with a bill and paid it. Then they left, as hungry as when they entered. Explain.

Clues: 178 Answer: 332

Pleased With Pork

Later, a Jewish man who observed rigid dietary restrictions went into the restaurant, sat down, and studied the menu. He noticed that pork was served and was pleased. Why?

Clues: 286 Answer: 352

Eggs-Asperated

Bill and Jill were about to serve lunch to their children, and they had a bowl full of eggs. "Which of the eggs are hard-boiled?" asked Bill. "I don't see X's marked on any of them." "I don't bother doing that," replied Jill. "After all, if an egg spins easily, then it is hard-boiled. If it just wobbles a little when I try to spin it, then it's raw." "That's usually true, but it doesn't help us now!" Bill said, crossly. Why?

Clues: 202 Answer: 317

Safe at Home

Safe from the Fire

Somehow during the night, a fire started in the kitchen. Flames quickly spread to the only stairway in the house, making it impassable. Husband, wife, and four children were asleep in the house, in their bedrooms. The wife smelled smoke and jumped up. Within a minute, everyone was outside. How did everyone get to safety?

Clues: 246 Answer: 337

Sprayed at the Lawn

Henry had a lawn sprinkler installed and connected to a timer. He wanted the lawn watered daily for half an hour late in the day, but not so late that he would see the spraying when he got home from work. For a few weeks, the sprinkler worked perfectly. But one day, after he parked his car in the garage and started walking to his front door, the sprinklers turned on and drenched him. What happened?

Clues: 179 Answer: 380

Sprayed at the Lawn Again

Henry adjusted the sprinkler timer and was happy for a couple of weeks. But then, in the middle of the week, he parked his car and walked across the lawn as before and again was sprayed as the sprinklers turned on. Why?

Clues: 269 Answer: 369

A Shocking Problem

Louie and Lucy were in their basement, working on their household wiring. "We need a twenty-foot extension cord," said Louie. He unwound twenty feet of 2-conductor 16-gauge wire from a spool and cut off the piece of it. He stripped the insulation from both ends and handed one end to Lucy. Then he took a plug and fastened it to one end. Lucy worked on the other end. "Ready?" asked Louie. "Yes," answered Lucy. "Let's plug it in and test it," said Louie, putting the plug into an outlet that was connected to a wall switch. As soon as Louie flipped the wall switch, a circuit breaker tripped. What was wrong?

Clues: 296 Answer: 386

Carpeted Laundry Room

A year previously, Marjorie had paid a builder for a luxury apartment that had not yet been built. The builder had promised to finish the shared areas of the apartment building and to give her an apartment that was structurally complete, but not to finish the interior of the apartment itself. The builder had, by this time, fully kept his promise about the apartment; and Marjorie was discussing its interior with an architect. She explained: "I want the laundry room to have deep carpeting." "That's risky," replied the architect. "The washer and dryer are against the wall. Suppose the clothes washer breaks down. The first thing the repairman will do is pull it away from the wall and ruin the carpeting, right?" "Not the way I plan it," countered Marjorie. Why not?

Clues: 179 Answer: 308

Nothing Done

When the plans were finished, Marjorie and the architect engaged a contractor to put the panel in the laundry room wall and to lay the carpeting. Marjorie spoke to the contractor: "I'm on the eighth floor. The elevators do not work yet, and there are no floor numbers on the stairway landings. Be sure that your workers count the floors very carefully, because a workman lost count a month ago and remodeled the wrong apartment by mistake." "Dashed impertinent," replied the contractor. "I'll send round some chaps who are especially good at arithmetic." The contractor did so, and sent a bill for work done a month later. When she received the bill, Marjorie walked up the stairs and found that nothing had been done to her apartment. What had happened?

Clues: 224 Answer: 327

Wrong Again!

On realizing the cause of the error, the contractor was furious and used very strong language to explain the error to the foreman. Then he was hired to remove a wall from another apartment in the same building. "The fifteenth floor," the apartment owner told him; and the owner provided a floor plan with the wall clearly identified. But when the foreman and his crew arrived at the fifteenth floor, they encountered painters who were painting the wall that they had planned to remove. What happened?

Clues: 202 Answer: 317

Fix The Furnace

Chilly Chester had called for someone to fix the forced-air furnace. The outdoor temperature was below freezing, and the indoor temperature was about 60 degrees Fahrenheit. When the repairs were complete, Chester walked over to the wall and turned the thermostat to its highest setting. He did not hear the expected sound of the blower motor or feel the draft of air through the vents. Why did the forced-air system blower not react when Chester turned up the thermostat?

Clues: 179 Answer: 337

She Kept Her Cool

Alexis wanted air conditioning for her large living room. She went to a thoroughly reliable store with her living room measurements and was asked to buy an air conditioner with a specified BTU rating. "Unless the temperature exceeds 90 degrees, this air conditioner will cool the room well for you," the sales person had told her. She knew that such high temperatures existed, but were rare. "I'll take one air conditioner of that rating, and another of half that rating, for the same room," she decided. Why?

Clues: 248 Answer: 345

Can't Turn It Off!

Wendy noticed light coming from her bedroom lamp, and she wanted the bedroom dark. She tried turning the lamp off, but light continued to shine. She unplugged the lamp, but it continued to provide light. Explain.

Clues: 269 Answer: 352

Hazard In The Code

Building codes are designed to prevent hazards. What common building code provision, if followed exactly, prevents one hazard but permits another?

Clues: 286 Answer: 362

The Bumpy Street

Homeowners along a block got together and grumbled about poor city services. One of them noted the unrepaired potholes in the neglected street and agitated about getting the city to resurface the street. Most of the other people agreed. One homeowner, however, objected. Why?

by Edward J. Harshman

Clues: 180 Answer: 308

More Travel

Belligerent Bus Driver

Cal drove his pickup truck behind a school bus and was angry. Not only did the bus move slowly, but the driver stopped to chat with every child's parents as he picked up the children on the way to school. Cal was late for work, and the bus driver knew it. "Let me pass, will ya? I'm late for work!" Cal finally shouted. The driver put his hand out the window and made an obscene gesture. Cal finally had enough. When the bus next stopped, and another chatting session started, Cal got out of his truck, slammed its door, and... what did he do that allowed him to pass the school bus legally?

Clues: 222 Answer: 327

Bad Directions

Ethan was going to visit some relatives about forty miles away, whom he had not seen for a long time. He called them and got driving directions, carefully writing them on a piece of paper. They were very clear and told him to get onto a big highway for most of the trip, later leaving it and driving onto Main Street for about a mile before turning off of it and into their driveway. After he hung up, he thought for about a minute and made some additional notes. When he started the trip, he carefully took the piece of paper with him and followed its instructions. But he promptly got lost. Why?

Clues: 369 Answer: 369

Stolen License Plates

A few months earlier, Steve had paid a hundred dollars for custom (vanity) license plates. Now someone had stolen them. Steve got an anonymous letter offering two hundred dollars in exchange for a promise not to prosecute. He made the promise, and he got the two hundred dollars. When he went to the auto registry to get another pair of custom license plates, the clerk did not know why anyone would offer so much for relatively new license plates that could never be used on a vehicle. Steve did not know, either. Do you?

Clues: 180 Answer: 318

I Brake for Snowdrifts

Randy was trying to free his car from a snowdrift. His rear-wheel-drive car was stuck. When Randy tried to drive away, one rear wheel spun and the other stayed still. Sandy, who sat next to him, asked if the brakes were off. "Of course, stupid!" replied Randy. "We couldn't possibly go anywhere if the brakes were on." "Well, put them on and try it one more time before I get out and push," replied Sandy. Randy, bewildered, shook his head. But Sandy grabbed the parking-brake lever and pulled it. Then Randy, to his surprise, drove away. What happened?

Clues: 202 Answer: 337

No Help

Two men were hiking in the woods. One of them fell and broke his leg. The other wanted to go get help, but both men knew at once that he could not. Why not?

Clues: 286 Answer: 375

Lost Again

After the man's leg was fully recovered, he and his wife and son went for another walk in the woods. The sun went down, and they gingerly continued walking. "Now what are we going to do?" demanded his wife. "You know stars, but the sky is overcast and we can't see them." "They predicted clear skies, didn't they?" he retorted. "I know which way is north!" announced their son brightly. How?

Clues: 223 Answer: 346

Two Triangular Journeys

Two explorers set up camp at a different latitude and a different longitude from each other, but less than a day's journey apart on foot. The first day, one of them traveled one mile south, one mile east, and one mile north and ended where he started. The second day, the other one traveled one mile south, one mile west, and one mile north and also ended where he started. Where were they?

Clues: 181 Answer: 308

You Have To Stop

A road that has a stop sign usually has it at the side, so that a driver will see it, stop, and proceed when safe. When might a stop sign be in the center of a road?

Clues: 269 Answer: 327

Mystery Gate

Some people approaching a five-star beachfront hotel are surprised to see an imposing iron gate blocking a roadway between it and a nearby residential street. Yet it is easy to drive to the same hotel by another route without encountering any gates or security checkpoints. Why is the gate there?

Clues: 223 Answer: 384

by Edward J. Harshman

There Goes The Sun

Edgar the Explorer set out to explore the distant areas of the earth. One evening, just after sunset, he set up camp. He looked at his trusty compass, and from it he inferred which ways were north, south, east, and west. But the next day, the sun appeared to rise in the west. He looked at his compass again, and the sun was apparently just above the horizon, in the west. Edgar decided not to go anywhere that day, and he watched the sun travel across the sky and appear to set in the east. He never did figure out what happened. Can you?

Clues: 247 Answer: 355

Miracle Shopper

Dolores was sitting in her living room when she realized that she needed groceries. She left the room, went outside, and was soon well on her way to a supermarket about half a mile away. Once there, she bought about twelve pounds of food. Then she brought it home and put it away in her kitchen. She had broken her leg a month earlier, and she did not get into a car or other conveyance to drive or be driven to the supermarket. No one helped her with this shopping trip. Explain.

Clues: 180 Answer: 362

Towing the Car

Police will predictably tow cars if they are illegally parked, obstructing traffic, improperly registered, or encumbered by unpaid parking tickets or other legal actions. When do police move a car that is legally parked and does not have a history of unpaid tickets?

Clues: 296 Answer: 380

Two In The Woods

Two people entered the woods for a walk. Later, two people left it. No one else was in the woods when they entered it, and no one entered it while they were walking. Nevertheless, one of the two people who left it was soon on the telephone and mentioned a third person who was in the woods. Explain.

Clues: 203 Answer: 318

by Edward J. Harshman

More Crime

Legally Castrated

A doctor castrated a fully-grown male patient. The patient did not give informed consent for the surgery, had no testicular or other tumor, and had not been charged with rape or any other sex crime. The surgery was done in the USA. It was completely legal. Why?

Clues: 247 Answer: 338

Unsolved Robbery

Two men were talking. The first man said, "You know that bank robbery two months ago? I understand that the police never caught the robber and don't even have any leads." The other man replied, "So I've heard, but the man who did it will spend the next twenty years in prison." Why, if he wasn't even arrested for the robbery?

Clues: 270 Answer: 370

Death in the Pool

An expert swimmer dived into a swimming pool, from the diving board into the deep end of the pool, and promptly died because he did so. Why?

Clues: 286 Answer: 308

This Burglar Got In

A man fastened quarter-inch plywood over the windows of his house. He boarded over the back door, and he installed a deadbolt on the front door that operated only from inside. Other than the front door and the back door, there were no doors to his house. The house was conventionally designed, complete, and intact; there had been no storm damage or other unintended easy way to enter the house. But fifteen minutes later, a burglar was in the house without having broken in. How?

Clues: 298 Answer: 328

Death of a Hunter

Several men went hunting together. They were all familiar with horror stories about people who were shot because they were mistaken for animals, and they carefully wore bright red. None of the hunters was colorblind. They took their shotguns into a forest and waited patiently. After a while, a shot was fired. Because of it, one of the hunters died. Why?

Clues: 181 Answer: 318

A Matter of Survival

Mort raised himself up and peered up uneasily from behind the counter at his appliance store. Close to a hundred shots had been fired. Three armed robbers lay dead on the floor, revolvers in hand. Mort rubbed his hand gratefully along the quarter-inch steel plate that he had earlier fastened to the back of the counter. Holding his rifle nervously, he called the police: "I want to report an attempted robbery. Three bandits are here, shot dead, but two of them got away." Newspapers quickly covered Mort's heroic thwarting of the attempted robbery, going on to say that the police had no leads to the suspects who escaped. Why was Mort relieved, instead of fearing reprisal?

Clues: 203 Answer: 353

Silent Murder

The police went to an apartment building to investigate a murder and found the body on the living room floor, with the murder weapon, a shotgun, nearby. The time of the murder was narrowed down to a three-hour period, and the victim's neighbors were questioned. Both of the people in the adjacent apartment, separated from the victim's living room only by a thin wall, were home at the time of the murder. Separately questioned, they both denied hearing a gunshot. The police were not surprised. Why not?

Clues: 223 Answer: 375

Poker Assault

Eight men decided to play high-stakes poker together. They liked seven-card stud, and they mixed two decks of cards together. After a few hands were played, one of the men carefully picked up the cards, shuffled them slowly and stiffly, handed them to the player on his right to be cut, and took them back. After he had dealt one card to each of five players, three of the other men jumped up, grabbed him, threw him against a wall, and beat him up. Why?

Clues: 247 Answer: 386

Not For Ransom

A woman walked out of her house one evening and closed and locked the front door behind her. Suddenly, three masked men grabbed her and held her at gunpoint. They made her undress completely, unlocked her front door, threw all her clothes and personal belongings inside, threw her keys onto the roof, blindfolded her, drove her to a deserted and unfamiliar part of town, and released her. Just before releasing her, they gave her some money. It would seem that the men's motive was revenge for something the woman had done. But why, given that they were committing a serious crime and intended to cause the woman great distress, did they give her money?

Clues: 181 Answer: 346

Unexplained Theft

The back door of the house had a simple lock, and the burglar had no difficulty opening it. Doing so, however, tripped an alarm. The burglar quickly jumped clear of the house and ran as fast as he could, making a successful escape. At first, the homeowners were pleased that their alarm system had apparently averted a theft; but when they investigated, they noted that small valuables were missing from each of several rooms in the house. Explain.

Clues: 270 Answer: 308

Rats!

Nasty Nat went to a vacant lot and set and baited about half a dozen rat traps. The next day, he picked up the traps, each one having caught a rat. Then he carefully broke into a house and put the traps, with rats, in it. He was not motivated by revenge against the owner or occupants of the house. What was he doing?

Clues: 182 Answer: 338

Work-Related

Her Good Message

The office telephone rang. The secretary answered it. "No, he left the office an hour ago," she said to the caller. She was referring to her boss, who stood beside her. After she hung up and identified the caller, he was angry with her. "Why didn't you put me on? That was one of my important clients!" he demanded. She explained, and he suddenly ran out the door. Why?

Clues: 287 Answer: 346

Tea-ed Off

As the boss returned from the meeting, he noticed his secretary at the coffee maker. "Are you making coffee?" he asked. "No," she replied, as clear steaming liquid collected in the pot below. Continuing to his office, he thought, "Good. Tea would hit the spot for a change." He got out a bag of his favorite tea, filled his cup from the pot, let the bag steep for a few minutes as usual, took a large sip in anticipation—then made an ugly face and promptly spat out the brew! What was wrong?

Clues: 204 Answer: 328

He Knew His Materials

A newly hired young man at a building contractor's office was asked, as a joke, to buy a left-handed adjustable wrench, a can of striped paint, and a spool of pipe thread. Most newcomers to the trade would have either dismissed the request as a joke or tried to get the materials and looked foolish. But this young man filled the request perfectly. How?

Clues: 182 Answer: 363

Defying Gravity

Later, this same young man was painting, with an ordinary brush and ordinary paint of course. Something startled him, and he dropped the brush. It fell on the ceiling, not the floor. Why?

Clues: 224 Answer: 369

Too Heavy

A shipping clerk needed to send a piece of heavy machinery to a customer and preferred to use a trucking firm that was inexpensive and dependable. Unfortunately, this trucking company had a 75 pound weight limit per package. The machinery, packed for shipment, weighed 77 pounds and could not be easily disassembled for two separate packages. How did the clerk send the machinery using his preferred trucking company?

Clues: 248 Answer: 318

Unusual Office Buildings

Grand Central Station, a large railroad station in New York City, is a large railroad that has more than 30 platforms at which trains can stop and deliver or take on passengers. Underground tracks leave the station and head approximately northward under the street called Park Avenue. Above ground, for about half a mile north of Grand Central Station, Park Avenue is lined with tall and prestigious office buildings. Intersections in the area until recently followed a decades-old precedent: they each had only one traffic light. If you walk along that part of Park Avenue and carefully study the buildings on its west side, then you will observe a characteristic shared by many buildings there that can be inferred from this description and is rare in buildings everywhere else. What is it?

Clues: 270 Answer: 309

At the Science Lab

The Microscope

Why does the astronomer have a microscope in the laboratory?

Clues: 225 Answer: 338

The Universal Solvent

"I have a universal solvent," says the scientist. "What do you mean?" you ask. "Everything it touches dissolves and becomes part of it. That's why I call it a universal solvent," replies the scientist. "Nonsense! What can you keep it in?" you retort. But the scientist, many years in the future from now, really does have such a universal solvent. What does he keep it in?

Clues: 182 Answer: 353

Destructive But Useful

A universal solvent, especially the kind that the scientist discovered, is extremely dangerous. How does the scientist plan to use it?

Clues: 287 Answer: 375

Brian Braggart

Brian Braggart's Space Story

Brian Braggart, teller of tall tales, described his alleged adventure on the moon of a distant planet. "We put on our space suits, left the spacecraft, and explored the moon's surface. It had no atmosphere. But when we walked behind a mountain, we saw some little green moonmen. They greeted us in English, and we quickly made friends. They have well-developed legs, and one of them jumped three hundred feet up while describing lunar gymnastics. Their gravity is only about one tenth of ours. Then the moonman told me that my partner

89

said that he had radio trouble, and I looked at my partner and saw him. He and I went back to the spacecraft and repaired his transmitter." Assuming that space travel to a distant moon is possible and that intelligent life could be found there, disprove the story.

Clues: 271 Answer: 318

Brian Braggart's Fish Story

"Well, anyway," continued Brian after his first tale had been proved false, "I later went swimming in a large fresh-water lake. I wore a mask connected by a thirty-foot tube to a float on the water surface, and I swam along the bottom of the lake. Suddenly, I saw a shark!" Someone interrupted him, protesting that sharks are only found in saltwater. "As I was saying," Brian continued crossly, "I suddenly saw a big fish. I quickly took a deep breath and held it as I swam to the surface and to safety." Disprove.

Clues: 226 Answer: 363

Brian Braggart and the Equator

"Well, so that little adventure was all wet," said Brian after his second story was disproved. "But I went to Kenya and climbed a high mountain. I was right on the equator and spent a day there. Sure enough, the sun passed directly overhead. The weather was lovely. I called a friend, and he said 'Boy, are you lucky! Winter just began, and already we're under a foot of snow.'" Disprove.

Clues: 250 Answer: 309

Brian Braggart and the Ant

"Can I help it if my friend was exaggerating a little bit?" demanded Brian. "But back to me. On my travels, I went to a museum that had a giant ant, and it was perfectly preserved. Think of it! An ant that looked exactly like tiny, modern-day, ants, but entirely as large as a full grown human being!" Disprove.

Clues: 287 Answer: 370

Brian Braggart in Japan

"Bah, betrayed by an ant!" Brian grumbled. "But here's a place I've been, and I have the slides to prove it!" He commandeered a slide projector and put a slide tray on it. Flicking it on, and the room lights off, he began. Up came the first slide. "This is Tokyo. Note the tall buildings, the busy streets…." The next slide showed a lovely garden in the center of the city. Other slides showed more city scenes and the surrounding countryside. Brian gave his usual long-winded, but plausible, commentary. Finally, a slide showing a factory provoked a protest. "You've never been to Japan, and I can prove it!" How?

Clues: 296 Answer: 338

Bertha's Romance

She's Not Afraid

Big Bertha, a professional boxer, was being told about a blind date that someone had arranged for her: "He's a handsome six-footer." Bertha was skeptical. "The last six-footer I encountered," she replied uneasily," I killed with one blow. Not just knocked out. Killed." How?

Clues: 203 Answer: 346

He Won't Hear From Her

Bertha eventually met the man whom she had heard about. He proved to be six feet tall and very good-looking. They went to a nice restaurant and later to a nightclub; they had a wonderful time. Bertha particularly enjoyed his habit of looking only at her, especially as she spoke, and not letting his eyes wander to other women. "I had a wonderful time," Bertha heard him say at the end of the evening, "but I don't expect to hear from you again." Bertha, who liked him very much, was surprised and upset. But he was telling the truth. How did he know?

Clues: 249 Answer: 329

Dancing

Bertha's new friend sent her a brief note inviting her for dinner and dancing, and she accepted. Then, when she thought about him, she wondered how he could manage to dance. But he managed easily. How?

Clues: 183 Answer: 381

Finance, High and Low

Table That Investment Plan

A large for-profit corporation bought a controlling interest in a furniture manufacturer and changed the latter's policies. The furniture manufacturer lost money, but the corporate executives were pleased. Why?

Clues: 186 Answer: 330

Money and Laundering

To determine the cost per load of using laundry detergent in a clothes washer, you first determine the per-load wear and depreciation on the washer, then you add the electric and water expense, add the hot water heating expense if the detergent requires warm or hot water, and finally you add the per-load cost of the detergent itself and of any other laundry additives that you use. Right?

Clues: 204 Answer: 347

Not A Worthless Check

A man requested a check from someone else and threw it away without even trying to cash it. Why?

Clues: 226 Answer: 319

The Debt Was Paid

For almost half a year, a wholesale merchant had been trying to collect a debt from a small store. The merchant had written increasingly firm letters, but had received no response. Finally, he had had enough. He stormed into the store and demanded, "You see this invoice? Pay it now, or I'll take you to court!" "Has it come to this?" asked the store owner. "Yes!" roared the wholesaler. The store owner opened his safe, took out an envelope, and handed it to the wholesaler. The envelope was full of cash, exactly paying the debt. "But if you had the money, then why did you make me wait?" asked the puzzled wholesaler. Why indeed?

Clues: 250 Answer: 309

The Investment Scam

A group of investors pooled their money and bought into a high-growth mutual fund. A few months later, one of the investors received a telephone call: "This is Justin Peterson, of the Federal Bureau of Investigation. We believe that the fund in which you invested is a Ponzi scam. Please withdraw all of your money at once. Will you ask the other investors to withdraw their money, or shall I?" The investors all sent certified letters asking for their money back, but the fund manager had mysteriously disappeared with the money. "He was seen crossing the border into Mexico," reported Justin a few days later. "We will catch him within a month." But he was never caught. Why not?

Clues: 271 Answer: 353

The Counterfeit Money

A man had a large stack of counterfeit hundred-dollar bills. He entered a store and did not buy anything. Later, a clerk from that store was arrested for trying to pass counterfeit money. The man was happy. What happened?

Clues: 288 Answer: 363

The Noble Lawyer

In about 1890, when rents were low and protection for tenants was lower, a poor old widow was being evicted; she had no money and had not paid her rent. A public notice of eviction had been posted; and while the landlord's henchmen removed her possessions from her former apartment, townspeople gathered around to offer their support and perhaps to buy some household goods from her. The rich and avaricious town miser made the first purchase, a sugar bowl, and after paying for and taking the bowl insisted that the sugar in it belonged to him, despite her protest. The town lawyer, who was respected and beloved by all because of his honesty and fairness, offered to intercede in the miser's behalf. The miser accepted, and the lawyer expounded about the sugar's going with the bowl, citing statutes and precedents at length. The poor widow sobbed vigorously, staring at the lawyer with tear-streaked eyes. Had the lawyer turned traitor?

Clues: 183 Answer: 376

Batty Banditry

Robbing the Bank

Upon being tipped off that a large organization paid its employees on a certain day, and that its employees went to a specific bank to cash their paychecks at a certain time on that day, a gang decided to rob the bank at exactly that day and time. They would have been better off if they had robbed the bank on any other day or at any other time during that day than that one. Why?

Clues: 288 Answer: 381

Supposed to Kill?

A man drew pulled a gun, pointed it at another man who was known to be totally law-abiding, and pulled the trigger. Click! The gun wasn't loaded. Everyone present, which included at least ten people, was surprised and outraged. Why was the intended victim blamed for the incident?

Clues: 226 Answer: 370

by Edward J. Harshman

He Called the Police

A burglar broke into a house, intending to steal from it. While still in the house, he called the police. Why?

Clues: 183 Answer: 384

Welcome, Slasher

Bob, a fifteen-year-old boy with a record of violent crimes, approached a screened porch. Taking out a switchblade, he cut through every screen panel with large diagonal rips. A policeman drove by in a patrol car, saw what the boy was doing, and was pleased. Explain.

Clues: 250 Answer: 338

Smashed Taillights

Later, Bob picked up a tire wrench and smashed the taillights of a car that he had never seen before. Police officers witnessed his act and arrested not him, but the owner of the car. Explain.

Clues: 204 Answer: 329

No Ransom Demand

A man entered a government building and went through a weapons-detector search. Then he entered a government office and displayed a sawed-off shotgun. "Up against the wall, everyone!" he ordered. Then, after everyone complied, he called the police. When police officers arrived, he put down his gun and cooperated with them. He refused to defend himself in court and was convicted of assault with a deadly weapon and given a long prison sentence. "What's the point of taking people hostage if you don't make a ransom demand?" asked a news reporter. "I thought of making one," he replied, "but there just didn't seem to be any point to it." So why did the man act as he did?

Clues: 206 Answer: 356

Caught in the Act

A woman walked into a police station. "I want to report a pickpocket," she announced. A man staggered in behind her, his hand in her coat pocket. "Arrest that man!" she continued, pointing to him. He was arrested, tried, and convicted of picking pockets. Why did he enter the police station in a posture that obviously suggested his crime?

Clues: 297 Answer: 319

Slippery Sidney Slipped Up

Slippery Sidney rented a car for a month. He returned it and paid the rental fee. Three months later, he was arrested for attempting to defraud the rental-car company. What happened?

Clues: 251 Answer: 309

Honest Ivan

The rental-car company, after convicting Sidney, advised all personnel to watch for odometer tampering. Later, Ivan rented a car in central Florida. Two days later, it was badly damaged when a truck lost control and hit it on a thruway in Virginia. The odometer reading was too low to account for the trip from Florida to Virginia, but Ivan easily went free. How?

Clues: 271 Answer: 347

People Puzzles

Hearing them Quickly

"Hey, Pop! Can I have some money?" asked Dana. "The Electric Earsplitters are giving a concert here in town next week, and I really want to hear it." His father put down the television listings, turned off the TV, and firmly declined. "But that's my favorite group!" protested Dana. "I want to buy tickets real fast so I can hear them perform as soon as possible." "If hearing them as soon as possible is what's most important to you," replied his father, "then you won't need any tickets." Explain.

Clues: 227 Answer: 363

Happy that She Cursed Him

A man called the woman that he loved, and she cursed at him and hung up angrily. Why was he happy?

Clues: 251 Answer: 329

by Edward J. Harshman

A Crying Problem

Sandra had problems with her husband and was on strained terms with his parents. Nevertheless, one day she called them and chatted for about fifteen minutes. They thanked her for calling and told her that they felt better about her after talking. When she hung up the telephone, she burst into tears. Explain.

Clues: 272 Answer: 319

She Never Fixed Him Up

When Mitch started working in the small office, he was noted for his shyness. Anna, a co-worker, found out about his recent divorce and offered to set up a blind date for him. Eager to establish a new social life, he accepted her offer. But she never followed up on it, and he never met anyone else. Why did Mitch not mind?

Clues: 298 Answer: 339

Crazy Cars
and Tricky Transport

Response Team Right-of-Way

Unhappy about motorists' not yielding to emergency vehicles, the slow-witted ruler of a small foreign land passed a law that said, "All police, firefighter, and ambulance vehicles that use flashing red lights and a continuous siren shall have the right of way and need yield to no other vehicles. If failure to yield to such vehicles causes a collision, then the owner and driver of the aforementioned vehicles shall not be liable under any circumstances whatever." Soon afterward, there was a motor vehicle accident. The police dispatcher called for ambulances from nearby lands, but the ambulance dispatchers in those places at first refused to send help. Why?

Clues: 183 Answer: 310

The Test Question

Henry, applying for a driver's license, took the test for it. He got one of the answers wrong. The question was "When is it legal to enter an intersection and drive straight through it, when a steady red light is shown, in the absence of a police officer's signal?" The correct answer, according to the authorities, was "never." What was Henry's argument as he disputed the answer?

Clues: 206 Answer: 370

Taking Turns

Left-Turn Lisa and Right-Turn Ronnie were both at home, talking to each other on the telephone. "I think left turns are easy," said Lisa. "The right turns are the ones that give me trouble." "It's the other way around with me," replied Ronnie. "Right turns are not a problem. Left turns can be a real bother, though." Why did they disagree?

Clues: 227 Answer: 376

Driving the Wrong Car

Hermie the Hermit had a car, which needed repair but was still drivable. He had another car that worked. He drove the first car to a repair shop. To avoid asking someone else to drive him home, he fastened his two cars together and towed one with the other. He therefore arrived at the repair shop with two cars instead of one and could easily drive away with the working car. But why did he tow the working car with the broken one, and not the other way around?

Clues: 184 Answer: 354

The Unused Jacket

A man and a woman walked arm in arm along a street. The man removed his jacket. "Do you want to borrow this jacket? It's a cold night," asked the man. "No, I have a perfectly good coat," the woman replied. "You must be freezing in only your shirt." The man carried his jacket without wearing it, even though the temperature was in the 50's and there was a wind that made him uncomfortably cold. Why?

Clues: 251 Answer: 386

Walked On The Other Street

Jeff the Genius lived on First Street. He worked about 30 blocks away, also on First Street. Every day, he walked to and from work. He made no intermediate stops in either direction. When he walked home after work, he walked along First Street. But when he walked to work, he did so by walking to Second Street, walking 30 blocks along it, and then walking back to First Street again. His trip to work, therefore, was two blocks longer than from work. He was not bothered by sun in his eyes or interested in a more pretty walk; he merely wanted to save time. Why did he walk to work on Second Street?

Clues: 272 Answer: 319

He Wasn't Parking

Why did Vick shut off the engine of his car while driving it on an unobstructed highway at sixty-five miles per hour, without even slowing down first?

Clues: 288 Answer: 347

Safe Smashup

A car slowly started to move forward. Then it picked up speed. Faster and faster it went, until it crashed through a guardrail and went over a cliff. It fell over a hundred feet and was badly damaged. No one was killed or injured. In fact, no one was even afraid of being killed or injured. Why not?

Clues: 297 Answer: 330

A Token Wait in a Token Line

Smart Stephanie worked in a city and took the subway to work every morning during rush hour. In the evening, also during rush hour, she took the subway home again. To use the subway, she had to put a subway token into a turnstile as she entered the station from the street. Although she was one of numerous commuters at those hours and had to stand in crowded subway cars, she never had to wait in a long line to buy tokens. Why not?

Clues: 184 Answer: 381

Contagious Carsickness?

Stan and Jan were driving along a highway. Fran, a small child strapped into the back seat, said "I feel sick." "It's probably carsickness," replied Jan. "We'll be stopping the car soon," said Stan. "Then you can get out for some fresh air." Less than ten minutes later, Stan shut off the engine and they all got out of the car. But within half an hour, Jan complained: "Fran has motion sickness, and I do, too." Jan did not normally get carsick. What was happening?

Clues: 251 Answer: 339

What Drained the Battery?

Walter forgot to allow for the slowness of traffic in the rain and was late for work. He hurriedly drove into the parking lot, parked, turned off the windshield wipers, jumped out of his car, slammed the door, and ran for the main entrance. That evening, he could not get the car started. The battery was nearly dead. He got a jump-start from a co-worker, drove home, and used his battery charger to put a good charge on the battery. But despite careful testing, he never figured out why the battery went dead. Can you?

Clues: 206 Answer: 310

She Arrived On Time

Daryl and Carol had arranged to meet at a coffee house. But something came up. Daryl looked in the telephone book, learned Carol's home telephone number, and called her. "We were supposed to meet in the coffee house two hours from now, but my boss called and I have to reschedule. Two hours from now, I'm due at the office." "That's too bad," replied Carol, "but I can meet you at the coffee house in two minutes if you'd like." Daryl agreed and, because he lived right across the street from it, was there in two minutes. He was content to wait, but Carol was waiting for him. "You live clear across town," noted Daryl. "How could you get here so fast?"

Clues: 289 Answer: 357

by Edward J. Harshman

Easy Repair

Walter drove to the airport to catch a late-night airplane flight. A week later, when he returned to his car, the headlight switch was on and none of the lights worked. But Walter easily started his car, without receiving help from anyone, and drove away. How?

Clues: 273 Answer: 347

Seasonal Mileage

Claude gets noticeably better mileage while driving the last mile to or from work than he does during any other part of the trip in summer. But not in winter. Why not?

Clues: 227 Answer: 364

The Late Train

Amanda got onto a train. After traveling about one thousand miles, she got off. She arrived at her destination forty-five minutes late. There had been no delays, and the train had picked her up on time. Why was it late?

Clues: 252 Answer: 370

Odd Offices

Stubborn Steve

Steve went to an office supply store and got a ream (500 sheets) of standard sized paper. "We have a special today," a sales clerk helpfully told Steve as he carried the ream to the checkout counter. "We offer better paper than what you're carrying; and it's cheaper, too." Steve investigated; and he discovered that the paper on sale was the same size, the same color, and of a heavier weight than the paper he had in his hand. If used in certain printers or copiers, it would be less likely to jam than would the paper Steve had chosen. And sure enough, it was much less expensive. Why, therefore, did Steve decline the paper on sale and retain his original choice?

Clues: 207 Answer: 320

by Edward J. Harshman

Spaced-Out at the Computer

A secretary was working at her computer. She had a chart loaded into her word-processing program and had to rearrange it. The hard part of her job was removing extra spaces. The word-processing program had a "replace" command. She could replace any sequence of characters with any other sequence, or with nothing at all. So how could she replace many spaces in a row with only one space? Not the same as replacing all spaces with nothing, because then there wouldn't be the one space that she wanted.

Clues: 185 Answer: 310

Too Precise

Mary and Jerry were working in an office. Jerry was writing something, and Mary looked over his shoulder. "That's too precise," complained Mary. "We must make it more vague, harder to understand." "That's crazy!" replied Jerry. "The entire philosophy of the business we are in is based on that kind of reasoning, but I'm sure not going to tolerate it here!" "Precision is our great strength," admitted Mary, "and ordinarily I'd agree with you. But in this particular instance, no." Where were they?

Clues: 228 Answer: 348

The Hostile Voter

Charlie received a telephone call from the office of a local politician. A fast-talking campaign volunteer explained the benefits of the candidate, including a lecture on his platform. Charlie asked if the volunteer was calling at the request of the candidate, heard the volunteer's answer, and then announced firmly that he intended to vote for the candidate's opponent and hung up. Explain.

Clues: 273 Answer: 339

Exceptionally Vague

Mary accepted Jerry's explanation about what he was writing and easily agreed that it should be deliberately misleading. What was he writing?

Clues: 252 Answer: 376

Making the Grade

Nervous Nell, a college student with a straight-A average, walked into her professor's office. She told the receptionist that she was worried about her grade on the final paper for her course. "I want to be sure I pass this course," said Nell. "Is there some way I can be notified of my final grade as soon as possible?" The receptionist, sympathetic to her concern, replied, "If you hand in a self-addressed stamped postcard with your term paper, then the professor will write the grade for the term paper and for the course on it and mail it to you as soon as the paper is graded. That's much faster than waiting for a transcript." "Oh," said Nell, "but I don't think I can do that." Why not?

Clues: 272 Answer: 329

by Edward J. Harshman

Problems with Personnel

Raymond, a business executive in a large company, needed a department head. After placing a classified ad, he reviewed the responses sent on to him from the personnel department. One day, a colleague told him about a potentially suitable friend of hers who was looking for work. Raymond tracked down the friend, interviewed him, checked references, and hired him. Then he complained vigorously to the personnel department. Why?

Clues: 289 Answer: 320

More Problems with Personnel

It's true that all of his references checked out positively, and the interviewee was hired. But a few weeks later, the colleague who recommended him showed up—and the newly hired department head was fired on the spot. Explain.

Clues: 274 Answer: 310

Dismaying Dizziness

Raymond finally got an honest department head and had her office redecorated, installing new wallpaper, a refinished desk, and a bright ceiling lamp. He had received complaints that that office was dark and dirty, and he wanted to welcome his new employee. Unfortunately, she complained of dizziness in her office. He entered it to investigate, and he got dizzy too. Neither of them was dizzy anywhere else. What was the problem?

Clues: 187 Answer: 354

A Mystery Fax

When his private phone line rang and he answered it, the business executive heard an automated beeping noise. Why did he receive a fax call on his private line, which was known not to have a fax machine connected to it? (No, it was not a wrong or misdialed number.)

Clues: 228 Answer: 329

by Edward J. Harshman

Another Mystery Fax

One of the executive's subordinates sent a fax to a colleague. The subordinate would have preferred to have merely called the colleague in an ordinary way, but handwrote a note and faxed it instead. Why?

Clues: 207 Answer: 381

The Fast Elevator Trip

Bill was nearly late for an appointment in a tall office building. He ran into the building, reached the elevators that led to the correct range of floors, pressed the button, and waited. After a tense few minutes, an elevator arrived and opened its doors to receive passengers. Why didn't he get on?

Clues: 187 Answer: 364

The Nonstop Elevator Trip

Bill got to his appointment on time. "I was worried about those elevators for a minute," said Bill, "but I figured out a way to get here faster." Then he explained his reasoning. "Never thought of that," said Jill, who worked there and greeted him, "but if you just get in an elevator, it sure can take a long time. I have a way to beat the system, too." "What's your way?" he asked. "I just get in, and when the elevator first stops, I get out," she replied. He couldn't figure out how that strategy would save any time. Can you?

Clues: 207 Answer: 371

Asinine Actions

Giving Wayne the Boot

Wayne was asleep when a boot crashed through his bedroom window, waking him up. Loud music came from the house next door, further irritating him. He jumped up, shook his fist at his neighbor's house, and shouted some obscenities toward it. "It's three A.M.," he added truthfully. "If you don't turn that racket down *now*, I'm calling the cops!" The music persisted, and Wayne did as he threatened and called the police. When they arrived, they refused to prosecute for the noise even though it was obviously excessively loud. When the police explained the facts to Wayne, he was happy to forgive not only the noise but also the broken window. Explain.

Clues: 252 Answer: 348

by Edward J. Harshman

Racing the Drawbridge

Park Street included a drawbridge over a river. As its warning lights flashed, Clarence proceeded toward the bridge. The barriers were lowered, blocking the road. Clarence ignored them. The drawbridge itself opened, and Clarence gunned the motor and aimed right at it. But there was no collision. Why not?

Clues: 274 Answer: 339

Recycled Salt

Can salt be recycled? How?

Clues: 289 Answer: 376

115

Short-Lived Writing

Yolanda often passes a writing instrument across a surface for which it is intended and, within a few seconds, erases the result. What is she doing?

Clues: 208 Answer: 371

The Empty Wrapper

A woman was at the checkout lane of a supermarket. She removed several items from her pushcart and put them on the conveyor belt that led to the cashier. The cashier noted their prices and set them aside to be put in bags later. A perfectly ordinary process, except that one of the items was an empty wrapper. The cashier noted that the wrapper was empty, but charged for it. Why?

Clues: 253 Answer: 384

Secret Fuel

Marvin often sneaked into his neighbor's driveway in the middle of the night to play a prank. He would quietly unscrew the fuel cap from his neighbor's car and pour gasoline into its fuel tank. What was he up to?

Clues: 297 Answer: 364

Picture the Tourists

"I have a manual focus camera," said Sherman Shutterbug to his friend Sal as they sat next to each other on a tour bus. "Mine is autofocus," replied Sal. "It's much quicker, because the camera measures the distance to whatever I'm photographing and focuses automatically." "Then I think we'd better change places," said Sherman. Why?

Clues: 185 Answer: 320

Forgot to Stop?

Angus was driving along a road at about thirty miles per hour. Suddenly, he jumped out of his car. He had not applied the brakes, and the car was still moving. He was not a stunt man for a movie or otherwise involved in deliberately risky activity. What happened?

Clues: 228 Answer: 311

Haphazard Happenings

Magazine Subscriptions

Magazines often contain postcards meant for use by new subscribers. Some people consider them a nuisance and just throw them away. Some don't, even though they won't ever use them for their intended purpose. Why not throw them away?

Clues: 275 Answer: 329

Soliciting in Seattle

Two friends, who lived in different well-to-do neighborhoods in Seattle, were conversing. "Almost every week, I get a few people who knock on my door and ask for money for some charity or other," said one. "Odd. That rarely happens to me," replied the other. But there was a good explanation for the difference. What was it?

Clues: 187 Answer: 348

It's a Dog's Life

Fred and Jed saw a badly injured puppy. It had been hit by a car, and its left eye and part of its left front leg were missing. Fortunately, it had received competent treatment. A bandage covered what remained of its left front leg, and a patch was fastened over the left half of its face. Fred picked up the puppy and stroked it gently. It whimpered weakly as he put it down. "Poor thing," said Jed. "Look what it's been through." Fred nodded

118

his head grimly. "I know. But it will almost certainly be alive in a year. That healthy-looking dog over there won't," he added, pointing to a frisky dog that wagged its tail eagerly. What was Fred's reasoning?

Clues: 299 Answer: 356

Not From the USA

Belinda Blabbermouth told a riddle. "I am standing at a place from which I can travel north, south, east, or west and soon be in the USA. Where am I?" After everyone gave up, she answered, "The USA, of course!" After a few seconds, someone else spoke up: "Not necessarily. The country I come from, for example." Where was he from?

Clues: 253 Answer: 339

Dots on the I's|

"The teacher marked you wro-ong!" Jimmy sang out teasingly during recess. "You didn't put dots on all your I's!" "Is that so!" countered Timmy. "Betcha don't know how to draw a small I with a dot on it." Jimmy did so, and Timmy momentarily looked defeated. A minute later, Timmy retorted, "Well, now I have dots over my I's and *you* don't!" One glance at Timmy, and Jimmy burst out laughing. So did Timmy. Half the class did, too. Explain.

Clues: 290 Answer: 381

119

Power Failure

While Horace slept peacefully, a transformer on the street burned out and stopped all electrical power to his house. The power was restored two hours later, while Horace was still asleep. He awoke the next morning, and he noted with annoyance that all of his digital clocks had stopped and needed to be reset. "I hate power failures," he grumbled, as he carried his battery-powered watch to the living room clock, the microwave oven, and other devices that needed to be reset. But Horace never knew that the power had failed during the night. Explain.

Clues: 208 Answer: 311

Afraid of the Country

"The city is so hot and sticky during the summer," Willie said to his friend Nicolai. "I have a house in the country. Can you join me next weekend?" Nicolai smiled. "Ah, the country. Like a farm?" "Yes, you could say that," replied Willie. "I used to be on a farm a long time ago." "That's good," continued Nicolai. "When I was a boy in Russia, I lived on a farm. There were cows and pigs, and they were like my friends. It will be good to go away from this hot city and be on a farm again." "It's so peaceful there," said Willie, continuing. "Nice and quiet. No cars. Not even any animals." Nicolai sat rigidly and stared stiffly ahead, not even breathing, for several seconds. "No," he eventually whispered quietly, "I cannot go. You have made a lovely offer, and I would like to. But I cannot go." Why did Nicolai react as he did?

by Edward J. Harshman

Clues: 188 Answer: 320

They Had a Ball

Two men stood on a softball field and practiced throwing and catching just before a game. "Over here! Over here! A grounder!" shouted Ned, slapping his fist into his mitt. Ted threw a softball to him. "Good catch! Now throw me a grounder!" shouted Ted. Ned returned the ball by throwing it along the ground, as requested. "Now a high one! Right here! Right here!" Ned shouted. Ted threw the ball high in the air—and Ned ran about ten feet to his left, reached up, and caught the ball easily. "Good arm, but your aim is a little crooked," he announced. "No it isn't," replied Ted. "So what's wrong with throwing the high ball right where I was standing?" retorted Ned. What indeed?

Clues: 229 Answer: 330

Ballpark Befuddlement

Nine men stood together at the edge of a field. One of them watched a ball intently and swung at it. Missed! He took another swing. Whack! The ball sailed up and to the left. A third swing. Zoom! This ball soared up and directly forward, and the man was pleased. Why didn't anyone run to retrieve the third ball?

Clues: 253 Answer: 365

Kingfist

Kingfist Found Him

Horace, a chronic and boastful gambler, left town and refused to pay a large debt to Kingfist, a bookie with a reputation for vigorous debt-collection activity. Horace made no secret of his new location, an exclusive apartment complex with a tight-lipped staff that would not reveal his exact apartment. After about two months, a mail carrier rang Horace's doorbell and tried to deliver a letter, but failed to do so. A few days later, Kingfist surprised Horace in his apartment and forcibly collected the debt. Kingfist had used ordinary burglar's tools to break into Horace's apartment, but he had not first asked anyone exactly where Horace lived. He had not searched through garbage, traced Horace's car's license plate, or even come near the apartment complex before successfully identifying and breaking into his apartment. How did he locate Horace?

Clues: 229 Answer: 348

I've Got Your Number

Kingfist was pursuing Sam Skiptown, who owed him money and had a history of writing bad checks. From a distance, he spotted Sam and quietly followed him to his house. The house was well guarded, with a burglar alarm system and a climbable but inconvenient fence. Kingfist made plans. Within a week, he called Sam and warned him: "Pay now, or take the consequences." Sam was horrified. "How did you get my number?" he asked. "No questions," ordered Kingfist. "Let's just say

by Edward J. Harshman

I went to a lot of trouble to ask you nicely." Sam never figured out how Kingfist learned his telephone number, which was unpublished and known to only a few trusted friends. Can you?

Clues: 274 Answer: 339

Collecting Backwards

Kingfist "convinced" Sam Skiptown to write him a check. Then he took it to the bank to cash it. Why did he first deposit money in Sam's account?

Clues: 188 Answer: 356

Better Late Than Prompt

Kingfist was engaging in his usual habit of bullying a debtor into paying. "You don't have the cash? I'll tell you what I'm going to do," explained Kingfist. "Sign this contract, and I'll tear up the old one you signed earlier." The debtor reviewed the contracts and saw that the old one was his original loan and the new one was for the same amount, but for smaller payments that added up to the same total as the old one. The new one, overall, meant that the debtor didn't have to come up with money as fast and actually had a lower interest rate. And the new contract had no penalties for late payment, including harassment rights, that were not also in the old contract. The debtor was happy to sign. "Thanks!" replied Kingfist. "I'll be seeing you!" And that's exactly what happened. Kingfist was delighted, and the debtor soon realized he had blundered by signing the new contract. Explain.

Clues: 208 Answer: 311

The Debtor Paid

Kingfist had trouble with another debtor. "What can you do about it?" was the debtor's attitude. "The collection hassle is more than the bad debt is worth, and we both know it." But within two months, the customer paid the loan in full. Why?

Clues: 254 Answer: 371

Daffy Doctoring

She Was In The Hospital

Alan called the place where his wife worked. "I'm sorry," came the reply. "There was a bad accident on the highway a few minutes ago, and she's expected to be in the operating room for at least six hours." "That's too bad," he replied. "Can you ask her to call me when she gets out?" Sure enough, about six hours later, Alan heard from his wife. Why was she not upset that Alan didn't visit her personally?

Clues: 290 Answer: 321

Appendicitis

Zeke and his wife lived in a rural area. One evening, his wife felt ill. Zeke called the local physician. "Doc, I think my wife may have appendicitis," he explained. "Nonsense! I took out her appendix myself five years ago," replied the physician. But Zeke's wife proved to have appendicitis. Explain.

Clues: 276 Answer: 330

Crossed Vision

If your eyes are crossed, then you see worse than usual. But if your fingers are crossed, then you may be able to see better than usual. Explain.

Clues: 188 Answer: 376

Night Blindness Cure

What two questions can cure some cases of apparent night blindness, without formal eye examinations or blood tests?

Clues: 229 Answer: 365

A Sweet Problem

White, refined, sugar is frowned on as a dietary supplement and is especially to be avoided by diabetics (other than as an emergency treatment for insulin overdose or similar problems)—except for what?

Clues: 254 Answer: 381

Miracle Cures

Some resorts and shrines are known throughout the world for providing effective treatments for conditions believed to be incurable. One explanation is divine intervention, a literal miracle. Another is faith and belief in the cure, which can perhaps make the cure effective just because the patient believes in it. A third is an unknown but potentially discoverable scientific explanation, such as an unidentified ingredient in spring water. What is a fourth?

Clues: 209 Answer: 348

Disability

A man injured his leg in an accident and could no longer do his former work. He explained his situation to the local government disability office. Within a few months, he was receiving payments from the disability office, which were at least three times as high as the maximum amount a disabled person was allowed to receive. He did not commit fraud in any context. What had happened?

Clues: 299 Answer: 340

Not a Trusted Doctor

Cassandra and her boyfriend went to a lecture. At it, a doctor described a reputed cure for senility. "Nonsense!" said Cassandra. "He is no more a doctor than I am." "What do you mean?" asked her boyfriend. "He showed us his medical school diploma." What did she mean?

Clues: 276 Answer: 311

The Plumber's Pressure

A plumber received a checkup in the doctor's office. "You have high blood pressure," said the doctor, after measuring it with a cuff. "You'll have to watch the salt and take blood-pressure medicine." "That doesn't make sense, Doc," replied the plumber. "Didn't you tell me last visit that I had something else the matter with me?" "Yes, I did," replied the doctor, "and you still do." "But that's why I don't trust that pressure gauge of yours," continued the plumber. Why was he skeptical?

Clues: 300 Answer: 321

Rx Lead Poisoning

The doctor examined the patient and identified her ailment. Later, as they spoke, he filled in her medical records, including medical insurance coverage. Suddenly, the doctor said, "In that case, it may make sense to go to an old building and eat some lead paint chips from its walls." Why?

Clues: 302 Answer: 356

An Earful

The veterinarian said he would be happy to neuter the cat, but only if he could cut a notch in its ear too. Why?

Clues: 254 Answer: 384

The Curious Cardiologist

"I'd like to connect an electronic device and listen to your heart again," the cardiologist told his patient, who was in the hospital and recovering from a bad heart attack. "Oh dear, Doc. Not more tests!" the patient protested. "Nothing personal, but those medical bills worry me." "Oh no, sir. This one won't cost you anything. Actually, it's a personal favor to me." What was it?

Clues: 190 Answer: 330

A Headache of a Problem

The doctor got a headache and, because he did so, he diagnosed the patient. Explain.

Clues: 230 Answer: 371

Long Walk for the Disabled

A man had a serious accident and partially recovered from it. Previously, he was in good physical shape. After the accident, he was not disabled in a way that qualified him for handicapped parking rights. In fact, he often had to park farther from his destinations than he did before the accident. Explain.

Clues: 290 Answer: 386

Eccentric Electronics

Time for Repairs

Dilton got a new digital watch and put it on his wrist, confirming that it showed the correct time just before leaving for work and again ten minutes later. At work, he looked at the office clock and checked his watch. They showed the same time. Later that morning, he couldn't make sense of what his watch showed and decided to return to the store with it. Several times that morning, the watch showed the correct time; and several times, it did not. During his lunch break, he returned to the store. But the salesclerk to whom he showed the watch noted that it showed the correct time, and Dilton agreed that it did. Dilton was soon satisfied that he had a watch that worked perfectly. But the clerk neither opened it for repairs nor replaced it. Explain.

Clues: 230 Answer: 311

The TV Obeyed

Jake had some friends over to watch a movie on his brand new television set, with its state-of-the-art surround-sound speakers. As the credits ended and everyone started to the kitchen for some snacks, an obnoxious commercial came on. Jake turned to the set. "Oh, shut up!" he shouted angrily to the TV—and it did! Explain.

Clues: 256 Answer: 321

Strange Sounds

Modern movies, unlike those of half a century ago, are often made with the picture and the sound recorded at different times. Sound-effects technicians watch the picture and make the appropriate sounds, perhaps by walking in place on a hard floor to generate the sound of footsteps. How can this method of recording sound be detected in the final movies?

Clues: 276 Answer: 342

No Television Trouble

Stuart was driving a car along a highway. A small television set was on the dashboard, and Stuart could see its screen. The theme music from Stuart's favorite television show came on. At a police roadblock that was set up to try to catch drunk drivers, a state trooper observed Stuart and his television set, but did not warn or arrest him. Why not?

Clues: 189 Answer: 365

Happy with the TV Ad

A man went to a television station and bought one minute's worth of advertising time. He handed a CD recording of his one minute to the station manager and learned to the second exactly when his one-minute video would be on the station. Just before the scheduled time, the man turned on his TV set, turned it to the correct channel, and waited. At exactly the time for his ad, a test pattern came on. The sound, an intense pure tone, did not change for a full minute. The picture stayed the same, too. Then the man turned off his TV set. He was pleased. Explain.

Clues: 209 Answer: 349

Mad Money
Old Money But Good Money

What two changes affected U.S. currency in 1968 that, if considered together, scare certain conservatives?

Clues: 230 Answer: 330

Slow-Witted Customers

In northern Florida and some other parts of the USA, fast-food chains often have a pricing policy that works only because many customers do not think carefully. What is it?

Clues: 209 Answer: 357

Secret Business

Two men were on the telephone, discussing a multi-million-dollar business deal. They used electronic scramblers, so that no one could easily listen in on their conversation. They also each had much more sophisticated scramblers, which were harder to obtain and which encoded conversations more securely than the scramblers that they used. Why did they use the less secure scramblers?

Clues: 291 Answer: 377

Gas-Station Glitch

During a fuel shortage, George drove to a gas station and waited in line behind many other motorists. A man in the familiar gas-station uniform walked over and explained to him, "We have a ten-dollar limit. To save time, we are taking cash only and collecting payment in advance." George gave the man a ten-dollar bill. When he reached the front of the line and parked in front of a pump, he asked for his ten dollars' worth of gas. "The limit is five dollars," replied the attendant. What happened?

Clues: 231 Answer: 382

Marketing Muddle

What name of a car may, due to a preventable marketing tactic, provoke concerns about auto safety?

Clues: 255 Answer: 312

Too Much Money

An investor was reading the description of a proposed investment. It was a limited partnership, so that the investor would have no control over the management of the investment. But there were safeguards in place so that if the person who managed the investment made a profit, then the investor would too. Suddenly, the investor discovered something that made him decide not to invest. "Too much money," he announced, throwing the description onto his desk. Too little money invested in a company can be a bad sign, for it may go bankrupt. But why would the investor be afraid of too much money?

Clues: 277 Answer: 372

Goofy Gambling

Lottery Logic

Many states run lotteries as a way to raise money. For every dollar received from lottery-ticket sales, perhaps half a dollar is paid out to winners. Therefore, the weighted-average value of the expected winnings of a one-dollar ticket is perhaps half a dollar. Therefore, although a lottery ticket may be a fun expense because it carries a chance to get rich, it is never a good investment from a financial-planning perspective. Right?

Clues: 189 Answer: 321

Youthful Gamble

Some people gamble irrationally and are at risk of losing more money than they can afford to. Laws exist, therefore, to prohibit gambling except under special circumstances. It would seem especially important to keep young adults from gambling, for bad habits can be formed while young that cannot be easily corrected later. But certain young adults are allowed to gamble, in that they pay money and receive something of greater or lesser value, in exchange for that money, that is partially determined by chance. Explain.

Clues: 231 Answer: 340

Staged Roulette

Police officers, their spouses, and their families put together a talent show to raise money for their retirement fund. One of the events at the show was a skit about the evils of gambling. In one scene, a misguided man lost most of his money to a crooked roulette-wheel operator. It was learned too late that the audience could see the stage from above and would observe the number into which a roulette ball would drop. What did the producers do?

Clues: 255 Answer: 349

What is the Crisis?

Don't Bluff It

Your best chance of survival is to run toward the threat. But it is certain to kill you if it reaches you, and you know you cannot possibly bluff it. What is the crisis?

Clues: 210 Answer: 331

A Prayer for Escape

Whatever else happens, hold your palms firmly together. Doing so improves, though does not guarantee, your chance to escape. What is the crisis?

Clues: 291 Answer: 357

Down With Average

It occasionally happens to children. The ones most likely to survive with minimum adverse effects are the very smart ones and the very stupid ones. What is the crisis?

Clues: 231 Answer: 365

All Wet

Tie a shampoo bottle to a couple of towels. What is the crisis?

Clues: 277 Answer: 312

His Last Nap

Bruce knows he may be dead in three hours. He expects to be unconscious in three minutes. Oddly enough, being about to go unconscious doesn't worry him. What is the crisis?

Clues: 255 Answer: 343

Calisthenics for Neighbors

Close the doors, open the windows, jump up and down, wave your arms, and make lots of noise. What is the crisis?

Clues: 299 Answer: 377

Ouch!

Moan, scream, and cry out as if in great pain, even

though you're only in moderate pain. What is the crisis?

Clues: 300 Answer: 372

Positions, Everyone!

Assume a vertical position, with back, hips, and knees straight. Point your toes, hold your hands over your crotch, and clamp your buttocks together. At the correct instant, take a deep breath. These actions maximize your chance of survival. What is the crisis?

Clues: 189 Answer: 384

Telephones

No Forwarding

Jimmy had a nice house and a telephone with multiple options: caller-ID, call waiting, etc. But he didn't have call forwarding. If he had, he would have been put in prison. Why?

Clues: 232 Answer: 321

No Cell Phone

Jimmy got hold of a call diverter, which mimics call forwarding when connected across two different telephone lines, a second phone line, and a cell phone. He asked a discreet electronics expert to connect his monitoring receiver to the cell phone. The expert immediately refused. Explain.

Clues: 210 Answer: 340

by Edward J. Harshman

The Outside Line

The hospital receptionist answered the phone. "This is Dr. Jones. Gimme an outside line!" There was no Dr. Jones, and all patients had access to outside lines. Who was the caller, and why was such a call made?

Clues: 256 Answer: 349

A Phony Call

"What's the big idea, calling me at 3:00 AM?" "What are you talking about? It's *you* who called *me*!" The two people on the telephone angrily berated each other for the interruption and crossly hung up. What had happened?

Clues: 291 Answer: 382

A Devil of a Number

Janice was arranging for a telephone in her new house and was told of her new number. "I can't accept that. It ends in 666," she protested. What was wrong with such a number?

Clues: 277 Answer: 331

Even More Travel

Oo La La

Regina, a travel agent, was on holiday in Paris, France.

137

Hoping to get good pictures so her agency could make a travel brochure, she decided to set up her tripod at one end of the Champs-Elysées, famed boulevard, and took a picture of the entire street. To get as much detail as possible, she used a telephoto lens. Later, back at the agency, she eagerly brought in her developed film and prints, describing the picture she took. "Huh?" asked a colleague before seeing any of her pictures. "Thanks for trying, but I don't think we can use that one." Why not?

Clues: 232 Answer: 312

A Tiring Question

Four students were out partying the night before an examination, confident that they did not need to study for it. They overslept, missed the examination, lied to the instructor by saying their car developed a flat tire, and asked for a make-up exam. The instructor was smart and, not believing their story, hoped to catch them by asking, on the special exam that he gave them, "Which tire went flat?" But the students were smart, too. What happened?

Clues: 190 Answer: 357

Battery Badness

Leroy had a high-power sound system in his car. He sat in the car one night, playing his favorite music at top volume; and he enjoyed pressing the electronic-tuning buttons of the radio. Unfortunately, he left the headlights on, discharging the battery almost completely. So he jump-started the car, drove to a service station about three blocks away, and left instructions to get the battery charged. That evening, Leroy went to retrieve the car and was told that the battery was defective and had to be replaced. He paid for a new battery, got into the car, and started its engine easily. "Thanks for resetting the clock," he shouted happily to the surprised attendant. Less than ten seconds later, however, he stopped the car, jumped out, and demanded his money back. Why?

Clues: 257 Answer: 322

Sound Reasoning

Why did Leroy have the very good sound system removed from his car and a cheap feeble one installed instead?

Clues: 210 Answer: 365

Immovable Car

My car is exactly where I parked it last night. It is not out of fuel, its battery has a good charge, it ran perfectly when I parked it, and no one came near it since. No natural or man-made explosion or other disaster has damaged it. No one has parked so as to block it. There is no snow or other barrier of any kind in the driveway that separates it from the main road, and the main road itself is perfectly usable. The registration and insurance are intact and up to date. So why can't the car be used?

Clues: 232 Answer: 387

The Policeman's Signal

Sally drove her car toward an intersection. A

policeman raised his hand, signaling to her. Sally drove past the policeman, hardly slowing down. She was not driving an emergency vehicle. No law was broken, and he barely noticed her. What happened?

Clues: 191 Answer: 340

Airplane in Flight

Birds flap their wings up and down as they fly. Do airplanes?

Clues: 279 Answer: 372

Hats Off To You

"Quit leaning out the train window, or your hat will blow off!" a man ordered his young son, who wore a tweed hat, in the days when train windows opened and boys sometimes had tweed hats. Ignoring him, the son kept leaning out the window. Finally, the father had had enough. He snatched his son's hat and hid it under the seat. "There! I told you it would blow off. No hat for you!" The boy began to cry and apologized. "Look out there, and I'll whistle to bring your hat back," the man said. The boy looked out the window, and the man whistled and produced the hat. The boy eagerly took it and wore it. But they were soon very disappointed. Why?

Clues: 257 Answer: 331

Boat-Bashing

Brandon sold his motorboat. Although it was in good condition, the purchaser announced intent to have it destroyed. Brandon was curious and wanted to see it wrecked, paid some money to watch a video recording of its destruction, and was disappointed. But he did not ask for his money back and, had he done so, he would have had no legal recourse. Explain.

Clues: 292 Answer: 349

At Home Again

Screened Out

He was outside, working in the yard and doing general spring cleaning. Across the street, the old vacant house just had its For Rent sign removed; and people were working there too. They were taking the screens off the windows, which all had a conventional double-hung construction. Not satisfied with removing the screens and storm windows, they removed the aluminum frames into which they had been mounted. He could not figure out why the house, which was in good condition for its age, needed its screens and storm windows removed—until later, when further events made the answer obvious. Can you figure it out now?

Clues: 211 Answer: 312

The Wall-Mounted Sink

Why did the doctor prescribe a wall-mounted sink for his patient's bathroom, instead of one in a cabinet or on a pedestal? Three possibilities.

Clues: 233 Answer: 377

Bad Building Material

It is cheap, strong, natural, readily available, odorless, durable, nontoxic, and capable of being molded into any shape one wishes. But in most parts of the world, it would be laughed at as a potential building material. What is it?

Clues: 191 Answer: 323

Discarded Meat

The meat was unfit to eat, and Paul put it in a garbage bag and left on the curb in front of his house the night before the weekly garbage pickup. His neighbor was enraged at what Paul did and threatened legal action. Why?

Clues: 211 Answer: 358

The Marble

"Can I borrow a marble, sonny?" the electrician asked the little boy who was playing in the dining room and had a bag of them next to him. "You want to play?" he asked, handing him a marble. "No, I'm working in the kitchen," replied the electrician. Why did he need a marble?

Clues: 257 Answer: 142

Dreaded Doorbell

"Confound these kids!" the man shouted after answering the front door for perhaps the tenth time in two hours and finding no one there. "You should ask the school to do something about those ill-mannered pests." His wife, a school nurse, said "They are a nuisance, ringing the bell and running away like that. I have an idea of how to identify them, using that other neighborhood nuisance I mentioned." How did she identify the culprits?

Clues: 278 Answer: 340

Water in the Attic

"In the attic?" asked the salesman from the water-filter company. "But there's plenty of room for the tank that holds filtered water right under the kitchen sink." "There is, and I admit that putting a tank there won't cost us any usable cabinet space." "And it's right near the refrigerator, too, with its ice maker," persisted the salesman "So it is, sir. But the tank goes in the attic, just the same." Why?

Clues: 192 Answer: 382

Wrong-Way Elevator

Joe had an office on the third floor of an old twelve-story office building. Moe had an office on its tenth floor. They chatted at lunch. "When I summon the elevator, it usually seems to be going down," Joe said. "That's not my experience. When I wait for it, it's usually going up," Moe replied. Their conflicting observations have a good explanation. What is it?

143

Clues: 233 Answer: 331

Inefficient Elevators

Moe and Joe were discussing the elevator in the building where they worked. "Only one elevator for twelve floors. They really should install another," Moe said. "Yeah, two together, coordinated to work faster. But I've never seen two or more elevators properly coordinated. If I did, I'd know it just by looking at 'em," Joe said. "Just by looking at 'em? Not by riding them?" Moe challenged. "How?" Can you figure out how?

Clues: 257 Answer: 384

Mysterious Break-In

A shabbily dressed man, carrying no paperwork and not a government employee, had a gun sticking out of his pocket and a bolt cutter in his hands. He walked over to an abandoned house and broke the padlock that secured its door. Police officers, warned that the owner had just reported a break-in, picked him up and didn't believe his story. The first telephone call that they made at his request merely worsened his predicament. Then he had an idea that instantly cleared him. Oddly enough, there was no lying, deceit, or criminal intent by or of anyone involved. Why did the man behave as he did, and what did he do to acquit himself?

Clues: 192 Answer: 312

by Edward J. Harshman

An Appetite for Housing

When the shabbily dressed man entered the house, he made a surprising discovery. A friend jokingly suggested that he rent out the house to Overeaters Anonymous. Though the discovery was unpleasant, he thought the suggestion hilarious. Why?

Clues: 233 Answer: 322

Posted Property

He owned the abandoned boarded-up building downtown, awaiting a chance to sell it for a good price. There hadn't been much to do, just pay the taxes and keep the lawn mowed and tidy. But now the city demanded repairs, including rails for the front porch steps. The old steps to the front porch, built of solid concrete, had wooden posts for handrails that had broken off long ago. He wanted to pull the broken wood from the concrete, hammer new wood into the holes, and attach a new rail. But the wood was wedged firmly into the concrete steps and was broken off at the surface, and no tool could grip it and pull it out. What did he do?

Clues: 211 Answer: 349

Flour and Cement

Why mix equal amounts of flour and cement together?

Clues: 278 Answer: 358

Business Befuddlement

Forgiven

Mary photocopied a book that was under copyright. The publisher found out. Instead of taking legal action against Mary, the publisher thanked her. Why?

Clues: 258 Answer: 372

The Predictable Cold

He was very argumentative, so his boss told him that he was going to catch a cold. Sure enough, everyone watching him saw that he did. How did his boss know that?

Clues: 233 Answer: 365

Paper Profits

Marvin Moneybags attributes his wealth to careful stock-market speculation—helped by spies in the paper goods industry. Why there, if his investments are in all kinds of companies?

Clues: 292 Answer: 341

Cheap Advertising

"I hate this advertising expense," said a toy storeowner to a neighboring store manager at the new indoor shopping mall. "Even at its best, it's a loss until the Christmas season." The neighbor, who was opening a beauty salon, looked at the toy store's advertising invoice and winced. "Fortunately, I can get away without much advertising expense. I'll be spending only about a quarter." How could the beauty-shop owner get customers so cheaply?

Clues: 212 Answer: 331

The Ice Water

Richard was working in the kitchen and was handed some ice water. He was grateful for it, though he did not drink it or use it in food preparation. Why did he want it?

Clues: 300 Answer: 377

The Bad Letter

Sally and a friend were both out of work. Sally helped her friend by writing a letter to a possible source of earned income for her friend. She knew that potential employers are more favorably impressed by a letter and résumé that are well-written and have good grammar, but she deliberately wrote a poor letter with lots of misspellings and syntactical errors. Why?

Clues: 234 Answer: 387

Common Cents

When paying cash at a store, the amount due is usually an awkward number, not a round number. It's a nuisance for the customer. Is it a benefit for anyone?

Clues: 192 Answer: 313

Bought and Paid For

I bought something portable at a store and paid for it in full, with cash. It is not a prescription drug, explosive, firearm, or other regulated object; and there is no question about my legal right to own what I bought. Why am I not allowed to bring it home until the first of the following month?

Clues: 258 Answer: 323

Wooden Walls, Rubber Checks

Rick, a carpenter, buys his wood from a local lumberyard. He sometimes pays for it with checks, which bounce from time to time. This is not because he makes errors with his checkbook or intends to cheat the lumberyard. Despite his being scrupulously careful with his bank balance, why do the checks bounce?

Clues: 278 Answer: 382

Her Own Nasty Letter

Charlene, hurt by insider politics at her workplace, decided to get even. She wrote a letter to one objectionable boss, pretending that it was from another objectionable boss, carefully forging the signature, and knowing that its totally false and misleading contents, if seen at work, would cause great difficulty for her bosses. Then she put the letter in an envelope and mailed it to herself. Why to herself, if she already had it?

Clues: 302 Answer: 349

Children

Pierced Ears

Solomon, an Orthodox rabbi, was outraged that his teenage daughter wanted her ears pierced. "Older children have so many ways of asserting their independence," he told her. "But this way does exactly the opposite!" What was he thinking?

Clues: 234 Answer: 387

Dirty Conduct

Why did George's mother order him to wash his mouth out with soap, then compliment him for his selflessness and quick thinking?

Clues: 212 Answer: 358

Celebrity Discourtesy

Movie stars and other media celebrities sometimes do what pregnant women and their husbands sometimes consider intensely discourteous. What is it?

Clues: 193 Answer: 341

Dim-Wits

While students were taking an important test, the lights in the classroom kept getting turned off. But there was no power failure or breakdown in the school wiring. What was happening?

Clues: 258 Answer: 331

Canned

Adam was away at boarding school and was preparing to go home the next day for Christmas vacation. The housemaster of his dormitory had given strict orders that the rooms had to be clean and neat and that all trash, old newspapers, etc. had to be removed before students were to go home. Adam, an obedient student, cleaned and tidied his room, as instructed. So why did he go to the recycle bin in the basement and bring a bagful of empty soda cans to his room?

Clues: 292 Answer: 366

The Unwelcome Gift

Rudolph looked at two-year-old Fritz with dismay. "I know you brought me that as an act of love, but I wanted you to get rid of things like that, not bring them here." Why did Rudolph have such high standards for a two-year-old, and what was the gift?

Clues: 279 Answer: 313

Wild and Witty

Tied His Own Ankles

Ivan, a farmer, was working in his field and being disturbed by an evil person, who took pleasure in teasing and tormenting him. Why did Ivan take a piece of string and tie his own ankles securely together?

Clues: 193 Answer: 323

Plastered

Why did Fannie, the grumpy octogenarian, deliberately sit in a bucketful of wet plaster?

Clues: 234 Answer: 372

Artistic Appreciation

An artist worked long and hard to paint a portrait of a rich man, who was prominent in business. Unfortunately, the rich man decided not to buy it and gave the untrue excuse that it did not look like him. "As you wish," the artist said. "Write down a statement to that effect and sign it, and I'll be happy to refund the advance you gave me." The artist pocketed the statement and returned the advance in full. In a few days, the rich man was eager to buy the portrait for four times the artist's original asking price. Why?

Clues: 259 Answer: 378

Self-Portrait

The artist wanted to do a self-portrait, but did not want it to look like a mirror image of himself. What did he do?

Clues: 212 Answer: 385

Too Many Books

Adrian finally decided to move from his big elegant house to a smaller one that was easier to maintain. He had a large collection of books that he couldn't bring to his new house. How did he arrange for free storage for them, and in fact save money in the process?

Clues: 193 Answer: 349

Blouse Befuddlement

Christina picked up her custom-made blouse from her dressmaker and tried it on. "It looks great—fits wonderfully—but the buttons are a little difficult." The dressmaker replied, "They'll be all right, once you get used to them. I know your interest in saving money, and that's why I did them that way." Christina soon understood what the dressmaker did, and why. Do you?

Clues: 301 Answer: 358

Southern Insight

The eccentric old Southern gentleman had a flowing white mustache and a wide-brimmed hat. His clothing might have been current in 1840. His obvious pro-Confederacy sentiments made him a target for a group of young toughs, who threw him against a brick wall and shouted, "Who won the Civil War?" Bowing as much as he dared, the gentleman replied, "The Northern states won the Great Rebellion." "Should they have won it?" they persisted. The gentleman would rather die than betray his loyalty to the old South, but he preferred to live if possible. How did he pacify the toughs without lying?

Clues: 213 Answer: 341

A Cross Puzzle

Take a piece of wood. Drill three equally spaced rows of nine holes each, arranged in a grid such that there are also nine columns of three holes each. Extend the three centermost columns up by three holes and down by three holes each, so that they are nine holes high. Now, you have a Greek cross layout. Put a nail or golf tee in each hole except the center. A well-known puzzle is how to take a nail, move it past another nail which you remove, and put it in a vacant hole just beyond the removed nail. (Like jumping in checkers.) To solve it, you have to end with exactly one nail in the center hole. But with pencil and paper, it's easy to work out a solution. How?

Clues: 235 Answer: 313

Strange Science

Natural Crescents

Crescents on the ground. Thousands of crescents. A completely natural event. What is it?

Clues: 280 Answer: 332

Easy as Pi

The Greek letter Π (pi) is a useful memory aid when using tape to hang posters on walls. Explain.

Clues: 259 Answer: 366

Upside-Down Gravity

Judy held out a stone, offering it to Trudy. But Trudy was a little careless and dropped it. Why did it fall up, not down?

Clues: 293 Answer: 323

Water Under Pressure

Dip a soda straw into a glass of water, put your finger on the end, and lift the straw up. It will hold a small amount of water. Release your finger, and the water will fall out of the straw. A simple experiment in air pressure—or does this process have some practical value?

Clues: 235 Answer: 382

Mysterious Moon

The moon often looks bigger at the horizon than when it is directly overhead. But photographs and surveying instruments have demonstrated that there is no true difference in the size of the disk that we see. The theory that, when at the horizon, it seems bigger because of comparison with trees, buildings, etc. does not explain the persistence of the optical illusion at sea. The design of the human eye provides a different explanation. What is it?

Clues: 193 Answer: 373

Shot Down

A fighter pilot on a training mission was shot down. The incident was accidental, caused by friendly fire, with no involvement of enemy spies or terrorists. He was not shot at from the ground, and he was not flying in formation with other planes. What happened?

Clues: 259 Answer: 387

Peculiar Politics

Exiled

He was a prominent citizen, active in government, scrupulously honest, fair, altruistic, and beloved by all. Why, despite his admirable personal characteristics, was he ordered to move away from his home city?

Clues: 213 Answer: 350

Smash and Destroy

Activists in New York City have urged people to smash and destroy crockery, kitchen appliances, and furniture and tear up clothing. Why?

Clues: 301 Answer: 378

Work On This

The very rich and the very poor have traditionally had conflicting opinions about economics, including availability of jobs. What trend in the USA during the 20th century dramatically bolsters the attitude of the

155

very rich about jobs and employment?

Clues: 280 Answer: 313

Don't Bug Us

The insecticides are banned in the USA. Nevertheless, they are manufactured there and reach millions of people daily there, too. No laws are broken. Explain.

Clues: 303 Answer: 341

Underpopulation?

Some scientists use economic facts to challenge environmentalist beliefs that world overpopulation is dangerous. What are they?

Clues: 260 Answer: 333

Even More Crime

Trapped

"These spring-loaded bear traps are illegal and dangerous," the investigating officer said to Hiram while investigating the attempted burglary at his house. "But between you and me, no one but you had any business in your house. And that trap did leave us a great clue when it sprung, even though it didn't injure the burglar when he stepped on it." How did that happen?

Clues: 194 Answer: 359

Disappeared

Russell bought two of them at an auction. After a while, he had three, though he never bought the third. Still later, all three disappeared one night, never to be recovered. Because of that disappearance, his neighbor lost similar property, too. What were they?

Clues: 235 Answer: 323

Suitcase Stress

"It's all right, Sam. I forgive you," Pam said, after an intense quarrel reached a peaceful conclusion. "I packed your suitcase so you'll get to your meeting in time." Sam gratefully thanked her, picked up his suitcase, and went to the airport to catch a plane to a business meeting overseas. While waiting to check in, though, he recalled her vicious streak and her curious calm. He somehow knew he was being set up. No place to search his suitcase in the crowded airport. What did he do?

Clues: 293 Answer: 366

Not a Purse Snatcher

His clothing and build made him look out of place on the prosperous suburb's main street. Underweight, with the well-worn clothes of a derelict, he ran down the street with a new-looking lady's purse. A policeman was about to challenge him, when he suddenly did something to prove his intent completely honorable. What was it?

Clues: 260 Answer: 385

Give Me a Dollar

A native New Yorker wouldn't have been surprised to see him begging on the street, he was so decrepit-looking. And the owner of the new store in New York City looked uneasily at him from behind the counter. "Give me a dollar," the man told the owner, who gave several dollars happily, after a brief discussion. No begging or pressuring was involved. What happened?

Clues: 213 Answer: 387

Checks Cashed Here

Ronald worked as a cashier at a fancy downtown store. He would occasionally intercept checks given to him by customers in payment for merchandise and use his own cash to make good the money due the store. Though the customers in question were prestigious and aristocratic, he was not interested in collecting their signatures. What was he doing?

Clues: 236 Answer: 350

Silly Goose

According to an old Irish tale, a man goes to confessional and admits to the priest that he has stolen a goose. "May I give it to you, sir?" the man asks. "No, you may not. You must return it to its owner," the priest replies. "But the owner refused it," the man says. "Then you may keep the goose," the priest replies. What did the priest do wrong?

Clues: 194 Answer: 373

by Edward J. Harshman

Ragged Reasoning

Lights Out!

Why did the surgeon, in the middle of a complicated operation, tell the nurse to turn off all the lights?

Clues: 280 Answer: 314

The Devil and Idol Hands

What common habit at Christmas is reminiscent of pagan practices?

Clues: 301 Answer: 333

Ate His Words

"Greetings!" the vacuum-cleaner salesman shouted enthusiastically, throwing a handful of dirt through the front door and onto the living-room floor. "Lady, I guarantee that this vacuum cleaner will clean all this dirt—or I'll eat it all." Enraged at his interruption, the lady of the house brandished the knife she was already holding and ordered him to start eating the dirt, as he promised. He was convinced to give up his sales pitch without even trying to turn the vacuum cleaner on. How?

Clues: 260 Answer: 341

The Returned DVD's

"Honey, I left the rented DVD's on the kitchen counter. Can you drop them off for me?" he asked "Of course, dear," his wife replied, scooping them off the counter before driving away to go shopping. That evening, he looked in the living room for a DVD. "Are you sure you dropped off only the rented ones?" he asked. "Yes, dear. They all had stickers from the video store and were in the rental store's special hard plastic cases." Why did he become very upset?

Clues: 213 Answer: 323

Eager Surgeons

During the 19th century, serious injuries to arms and legs generally resulted in amputations. During the 20th century, improved surgical techniques allowed the salvage and reconstruction of damaged limbs, so that limbs that would have been amputated earlier could be saved. But very recently, the trend has reversed, toward amputation of limbs that would have been saved earlier. Why?

Clues: 236 Answer: 359

Costly Borrowing

Jim borrowed something from Tim, used it, and returned it. Though it was undamaged and Jim left it exactly where he found it, Tim was unhappy and put to great expense, greater than the cost of the item. No, it was not a cell phone. What was it?

Clues: 293 Answer: 378

by Edward J. Harshman

Yet Even More Travel

The Worrisome Guarantee

"This part of the car is guaranteed to last a lifetime!" bragged the eager used-car salesman to a wary customer. "Oh, dear," replied the customer. "I'd feel better if it was not." Why? And what was the part?

Clues: 214 Answer: 366

Cool Car and the Wire

Calvin, newly moved to New England from the South, drove into his neighborhood service station on a chilly autumn day. "I understand the winters here are worse than down south," Calvin told Hiram, the attendant. "Yep," replied Hiram. "Gotta use antifreeze and low-viscosity engine oil." Hiram lifted the hood and looked under it. "Let me unfasten that wire, too," said Hiram. "What for?" asked Calvin. "The device to which it leads works just fine now." "Sure does," agreed Hiram. "But it'll work almost perfectly in the spring if I disconnect the wire, or it'll burn out by December if we leave it." What part of the car were Calvin and Hiram discussing?

Clues: 260 Answer: 383

Cool Car Got Cooler

"As long as you're here," Hiram continued, "do you want me to fix the air conditioner?" "Of course not!" replied Calvin. "What do you think this is, Florida?" "But the air conditioner is needed in winter, too," Hiram started to explain. Why did Calvin let Hiram fix the air conditioner?

Clues: 236 Answer: 314

Cool Car, Dirty Windshield

Hiram, despite having put antifreeze in the radiator and having that one wire disconnected, forgot about the washer-fluid tank. The washer-fluid pump broke. After a heavy snowfall, Calvin drove his car on well-traveled roads and got muddy water splashed all over his windshield. When he could conveniently do so, he pulled over. What did he do, having left the car, that required no special materials and got his windshield clean?

Clues: 194 Answer: 350

Cool Car, Clean Windshield

Calvin told his friend Jenny about his system to clean the windshield. "You don't even have to get out of the car," said Jenny. "Use this," she said, handing him something cheap and readily available. What did she give him?

Clues: 281 Answer: 333

Toll Booth and Long Line

Conrad approached a toll booth. He got in the longest line of cars, even though there was a shorter one that did not require exact change and he did not have exact change himself. Why?

Clues: 302 Answer: 323

Toll Booth and Exact Change

Conrad, at a rest stop, learned that there was one more toll barrier, found out the amount of money due, and decided to use the exact-change lane. He drove to the toll barrier, threw the correct amount of money into the exact-change basket, and noted crossly that the gate in front of him did not rise. He blew his horn, and an attendant investigated. The attendant told Conrad not to pay the toll that way again, but thanked him for doing a personal favor and was very nice to him. Why?

Clues: 303 Answer: 341

Hub Cap Obsolescence

Glenda changed jobs and, to drive to and from work, was going to pass through a quarter-mile underground tunnel that had fluorescent lighting. Why did she replace her hub caps?

Clues: 237 Answer: 359

Unfare Increase

The New York City Transit Authority was short of money, and there was talk of increasing the bus and subway fare. Fewer people were using public transportation than previously, and a higher fare risked encouraging people to switch to cars and worsen the already bad traffic. What solution was proposed that would have permitted retaining the existing fare, discouraging cars, and bringing money into the Transit Authority budget without raising taxes or diverting money from other government activity?

Clues: 214 Answer: 373

No Littering Summons

Nancy parked her car on a highway. She took the floor mats out and threw them on the roadway. Then she opened the trunk and scattered its contents on the roadway also. Motorists shouted angrily because of her deliberate blocking of part of the highway, but a state trooper was pleased with her actions. Why?

Clues: 195 Answer: 385

Gunpoint

Kevin was ordered to pull over, for a minor traffic violation, by a policeman. The policeman asked Kevin for his license, registration, and insurance card. Although Kevin cooperated, the policeman drew his gun and pointed it at Kevin. Why?

Clues: 261 Answer: 314

Fast Broke

Crazy Kate drove a worn-out pickup truck along a limited-access highway. The speed limit was 55 MPH, but she drove at about 45 because the truck did not steer very well. Suddenly, she heard a rattling sound, which stopped after a few seconds, from under the hood. Why did she then speed up to 65 MPH?

Clues: 214 Answer: 366

Keys Locked In

Elmer parked the car, got out of it, and deliberately locked the keys in it. Why?

Clues: 281 Answer: 350

Failed Theft

The car window had been smashed. There was slight damage to the plastic sleeve around the ignition switch. A man sat in the driver's seat, holding a bright red steering-wheel lock and vigorously pulling the steering wheel. The man soon got out of the car without starting its engine. But he was happy. Why?

Clues: 237 Answer: 333

Not Phoning for Directions

Tony and Joni were about to get in the car and drive to one of Joni's relatives. "Your sister gives terrible directions," grumbled Tony. "They're worse than useless. I don't even think I'll bother taking them with us." "Don't forget, though, she just moved to our city," replied Joni, reaching for a telephone book and looking through it. "Hey, what are you doing that for?" demanded Tony, as Joni looked up not one but many listings in the telephone book. What was Joni up to?

Clues: 293 Answer: 324

License Unlost

William reported his driver's license lost and got a replacement for it. But he had not really lost his original license. What was happening?

Clues: 195 Answer: 378

License Lost

After William last used his old license, someone stole it. Nothing happened to William or his driving record, and no one framed him by using it to pass bad checks. But the stolen license was used often. What happened?

Clues: 215 Answer: 342

by Edward J. Harshman

Clues

Over the Wall

Q: Was his escape genuine and his fear of capture real (not an act, as for a movie?)

A: Yes.

Q: Was he in great danger from his pursuers?

A: Yes.

Q: Was the man a criminal?

A: No.

She Paid to be Seen

Q: Did she look attractive?

A: Yes.

Q: Did he have an unusual interest in looking at her?

A: Yes.

Q: Was this a professional visit?

A: Yes.

Truckin' Through the Intersection

Q: Did Chris expect the truck to get involved in an accident?

A: Yes.

Q: Did Chris plan on having long-lasting back pain after the accident?

A: Yes.

Q: Was the cooperation of people from his workplace important, even though they were not in the truck?

A: Yes.

Mess on the Rug

Q: Did Diana dislike the appearance of the rug after spilling the powder on it?

A: Yes.

Q: Did she immediately vacuum the powder?

A: Yes.

Q: Was the rug cleaner after the vacuuming than before the powder spill?

A: Yes.

Cheap Silver

Q: Had she had the silver for years?

A: Yes.

Q: Was she attached to it?

A: Yes.

Q: Was it relatively pure, like sterling silver?

A: No.

The Fifty-Pound Losses

Q: Was Andy happy about his loss, and were Bertie and Charlie displeased with theirs?

A: Yes.

Q: Were all three people rational in their reactions to their losses?

A: Yes.

Q: Were they all discussing the same kind of loss?

A: No.

by Edward J. Harshman

The Witnessed Break-In
Q: Was the officer honest?
A: Yes.
Q: Did the officer know the man?
A: Yes.
Q: Did the officer hope that the man would succeed in breaking in?
A: Yes.

Carried Away
Q: Was the woman happily married?
A: Yes.
Q: Did the husband call for the man to come and visit, aware of what he might do?
A: Yes.
Q: Had the man a special reason for his acts?
A: Yes.

Legal Conspiracy

Q: Were Mugsy and Butch working on plans to break into a bank?

A: Yes.

Q: Were the plans carefully designed to circumvent burglar alarms, even if elaborate activity was necessary?

A: Yes.

Q: Were the plans of a real bank?

A: No.

Beat the Water Shortage

Q: Did the woman have political influence or bribe the police?

A: No.

Q: Did she really wash her car with water, not just dust it off, during the water shortage?

A: Yes.

Q: Did she waste water that could have otherwise been saved for other use?

A: No.

Sweet Coffee

Q: Do you use "odd" to mean "unusual," and put 10 lumps into one cup and one lump into each of the other two?

A: No.

Q: Do you get a thirteenth lump, perhaps by carefully cutting one lump in two?

A: No.

Q: Do you put one cup or decant one cupful into another, so that one or more lumps can be counted twice?

A: No.

Don't Break the Scale

Q: Did she need coins, other known weights, or another scale?

A: No.

Q: Did she need the ruler?

A: Yes.

Q: Did she need anything other than the scale and the ruler?

A: No.

Wrong Answers are Plentiful

Q: Is the word common?

A: Yes.

Q: Is it an adjective?

A: Yes.

Q: Would it greatly help to know the length of the word?

A: Yes.

I Is Good At Grammar

Q: Was the mother using good grammar?

A: Yes.

Q: Did she understand the question and reply truthfully?

A: Yes.

Q: Did she refer to herself in her reply?

A: No.

Truckers Were Arrested

Q: Had they been traveling in opposite directions?

A: Yes.

Q: Is it significant that papers were dropped and that both men picked them up?

A: Yes.

Q: If either of them had tried to leave the turnpike at an exit different from the one that he actually used, then would he have been arrested?

A: No.

This Car Loves Hills

Q: Did the passenger have a reason not to have the car parked at that exact place that the driver was not to learn, for example because of an upcoming surprise?

A: No.

Q: Did the passenger own the car?

A: Yes.

Q: Was the passenger's request because of something unusual about the car?

A: Yes.

Hot Car

Q: Had she anything in the car that would have benefited from the additional heat, such as a frozen roast that she wanted to thaw?

A: No.

Q: Was she intending to be as hot as possible for other reasons, such as to sweat and lose weight?

A: No.

Q: Had she noticed something important by looking at the instrument panel?

A: Yes.

The Inferior Car Rental

Q: Had she expected someone else to borrow, use, or work on her car during the trip?

A: No.

Q: Was her car an antique, especially valuable, or otherwise such that she did not want to drive it very much?

A: No.

Q: Did she plan to drive directly to a distant destination and, from it, return straight home again?

A: No.

The Traffic Ticket

Q: Was there something unusual about his car?

A: Yes.

Q: Was the unusual characteristic of his car the reason that he was pulled over?

A: No.

Q: Would he have been driving legally if he had driven on ordinary roads, not on that particular highway?

A: Yes.

The Unpowered Outlet

Q: Did anyone help him?

A: No.

Q: Was any other outlet unpowered?

A: No.

Q: Could Alex correct the problem within a few seconds of learning its cause?

A: Yes.

Won't Stop Ringing

Q: Was the button part of a broken doorbell switch?

A: No.

Q: Did the bell ring because the button was pushed, and not start ringing at the same time merely because of a coincidence?

A: Yes.

Q: Was the front door open?

A: Yes.

Fix That Clothes Washer!

Q: Was there a design goof in the clothes washer or a pair of timer motors that just happened, by chance, to be defective?

A: No.

Q: Did the generator give power that differed significantly from 117 volts, even intermittently for a fraction of a second?

A: No.

Q: Could the problem with the timer motor nevertheless be traced to the generator?

A: Yes.

The Length of a Year

Q: Is it 365¼, the same as for a day as we ordinarily think of it?

A: No.

Q: Can it be calculated fairly easily from the information given and from the number of minutes in a day?

A: Yes.

Q: Is there another analysis that makes the calculation trivial?

A: Yes.

Brighter at Night

Q: Is the structure lit by artificial light, both by day and by night?

A: Yes.

Q: Is the difference in lighting caused by a timer, by a photoelectric device, or by the manual operation of a light switch by someone who works at or in the structure?

A: No.

Q: If those who used or benefited from the structure were fully informed of all safety factors, then would the structure be equally lit by day and by night?

A: Yes.

A Gift To Share

Q: Were two or more separately chosen items wrapped together?

A: No.

Q: Was it an ensemble of jewelry or such other set often broken up into two or more items of which each is generally considered useful alone?

A: No.

Q: Was half of the present completely useless to Laura?

A: Yes.

Half-Jaundiced

Q: Diagnosing the cause of jaundice in a particular patient requires special medical skill, but can this particular question be answered without it?

A: Yes.

Q: Could the answer be inferred by examining the patient's eyes?

A: Yes.

Q: When a bright light is shone on a normal person's eyes, the pupils constrict equally. Would this patient's pupils do so?

A: No.

Strong Enough Already

Q: Was Spike rational in not wanting to enter the program?

A: Yes.

Q: Was the program intended for athletes?

A: No.

Q: When Willie finished the program, was his arm stronger than it was six months before he started it?

A: No.

The Critical Student

Q: Was the medical student discouraged only because of the lecture?

A: Yes.

Q: Did the lecturer say anything that the student recognized as false or as poor medical practice?

A: No.

Q: Was the student upset because something was *not* said or inquired about?

A: Yes.

by Edward J. Harshman

Time in Reverse
Q: Was the clock to be used as a joke or a gag?
A: No.
Q: Was his occupation important?
A: Yes.
Q: Was his reason for wanting the counterclockwise clock related to a particular characteristic of where he worked?
A: Yes.

The Terrified Mother
Q: Did anyone display a weapon or otherwise threaten the mother?
A: No.
Q: Did the woman resemble anyone who had previously threatened the mother?
A: No.

Q: Had something very unpleasant happened to the mother and her baby?

Q: Yes.

Hot Jewelry

Q: Did she value her jewelry?

A: Yes.

Q: Was she trying to hide it from burglars?

A: No.

Q: Was she concerned about another hazard?

A: Yes.

Rainy Walk

Q: Did her parrots especially enjoy rain?

A: No.

Q: Were they restrained by a cage or leash when outside?

A: No.

Q: Could they fly?

A: Yes.

Catch The Dollar

Q: Do you distract him just before dropping the dollar?

A: No.

Q: Do you do something beforehand, perhaps get him to arm wrestle, to get his hand tired or tensed up?

A: No.

Q: Might he catch part, but not all, of the dollar?

A: Yes.

Still Hungry

Q: Were the man and the woman accompanied by anyone else?

A: No.

Q: Were they surprised at or disappointed by anything that happened in the restaurant?

A: No.

Q: Did they sit at a table in a room with other customers?

A: No.

Sprayed at the Lawn

Q: Had anyone tampered with the timer?

A: No.

Q: Did the incident happen on a Monday?

A: Yes.

Q: Could it happen again, for the same reason, within four months?

A: No.

Carpeted Laundry Room

Q: When a clothes washer breaks down, does a repair person often need access to the back of it?

A: Yes.

Q: Is there any other reason to expect the washer to be moved often?

A: No.

Q: Did Marjorie have special plans for the room behind the washer?

A: Yes.

Fix The Furnace

Q: Were the repairs completed properly?

A: Yes.

Q: Was the furnace out of fuel?

A: No.

Q: Did Chester test the system by adjusting its only thermostat?

A: No.

The Bumpy Street

Q: Was the objecting homeowner rational?

A: Yes.

Q: If the homeowner sold his house, then would its buyer probably object too?

A: Yes.

Q: Are motor vehicles driven similarly over a bumpy street and over a smooth street?

A: No.

Stolen License Plates

Q: Did the thief know that the plates, having been stolen, could never be legally used on a vehicle?

A: Yes.

Q: Were the stolen plates illegally used on a vehicle, for example to make a getaway car hard to trace?

A: No.

Q: If Steve had known where to look, could he have seen his license plates soon after collecting the two hundred dollars?

A: Yes.

Miracle Shopper

Q: Did Dolores's broken leg have a cast with a strong (walkable) heel on it?

A: No.

Q: Was the street to the store fairly level and well-maintained, with little traffic?

A: Yes.

Q: Did Dolores have to struggle to get up from where she was seated and into something else in order to go to the store?
A: No.

Not For Ransom
Q: Was the money genuine and not foreign?
A: Yes.
Q: Could it be easily used to pay a cabdriver to take her home?
A: No.
Q: Do most violent criminals give money to their victims while committing their crimes?
A: No.

Two Triangular Journeys
Q: Were they on earth, in a polar region?
A: Yes.
Q: Did either or both of them retrace his steps, in the same direction, while traveling?
A: Yes.
Q: Can their exact starting locations be inferred from the description (exactly two points exist that match the requirements)?
A: No.

Death of a Hunter
Q: Did a careless hunter, not one of the group and unfamiliar with the need to identify what is being shot at, fire the shot?
A: No.
Q: Was the shot fired deliberately?
A: Yes.

Q: Was the shot intended to scare or to hit any person?
A: No.

Rats!

Q: Although illegal, was Nat's action rational?
A: Yes.
Q: Could it lead to personal gain?
A: Yes.
Q: Did anyone live in the house?
A: No.

He Knew His Materials

Q: Can a left-handed adjustable wrench be distinguished from an ordinary adjustable wrench?
A: Yes.
Q: If you can dip a paintbrush into a can of paint and drag it along a wall so as to produce two strips of different colors, then do you have striped paint?
A: Yes.
Q: Can pipe thread be mounted on a spool?
A: Yes.

The Universal Solvent

Q: Is the solvent inactive unless two components are mixed together, so that its components can be stored separately?
A: No.
Q: Can the solvent be stored somehow in a special laboratory area or in a container?
A: No.
Q: Does the solvent have a conventional structure, of atoms and molecules?
A: No.

Dancing
Q: Did he need to watch the musicians, especially the drummer, to see the rhythm?

A: No.

Q: Did the music have a strong beat?

A: Yes.

Q: Was the rhythm noticeable in the bass?

A: Yes.

The Noble Lawyer
Q: In the days before formal welfare programs, was she in great danger of homelessness and starvation?

A: Yes.

Q: Could the miser afford to give her some money?

A: Yes.

Q: Is the lawyer's license to practice law relevant, not only his skill?

A: Yes.

He Called the Police
Q: Did he call a co-conspirator on the police force?

A: No.

Q: Before breaking in, had he intended to call the police?

A: No.

Q: Was he arrested?

A: Yes.

Response Team Right-of-Way
Q: Is it significant that, after only one incident, usable emergency vehicles became so few in number that outside help was required?

A: Yes.

Q: Did the ambulance dispatchers act to prevent further injury?

A: Yes.

Q: Was there something wrong with the new law?

A: Yes.

Driving the Wrong Car

Q: Did each car have a hitch and a compatible bumper, so that either car could tow the other for a short distance if they both worked?

A: Yes.

Q: Was the broken car smashed so that it could not be towed easily?

A: No.

Q: Was the only problem with the broken car related to its brakes, so that the other car could be towed with its brakes partially set?

A: No.

A Token Wait in a Token Line

Q: Did Smart Stephanie have someone else buy her tokens, or make a special trip to a subway station to buy tokens during off-peak hours, when the subway was little used?

A: No.

Q: Did she sneak under turnstiles, otherwise evade the fare, or have special permission to use the subway without paying (as can, for example, some police officers and subway employees)?

A: No.

Q: Did Smart Stephanie live in a strictly residential district and work in a strictly business district during ordinary business hours?
A: Yes.

Spaced-Out at the Computer

Q: Can it be done, in general, with only one "replace" command?
A: No.
Q: Can it be done by typing the same "replace" command over and over again?
A: Yes.
Q: Is there another way to solve the problem that involves typing three different commands, which always works regardless of the maximum number of spaces to collapse into one?
A: Yes.

Picture the Tourists

Q: Did Sherman want to change places so that he would get better pictures for himself?
A: No.
Q: Was Sherman originally sitting next to a window?
A: Yes.
Q: Was the window open?
A: No.

Table That Investment Plan

Q: Were the corporate executives motivated by charity or altruism and attempting to regulate a company that was causing pollution or other social ills?

A: No.

Q: Were the corporate executives trying to destroy a competitor and become a monopolistic supplier of furniture?

A: No.

Q: Did the corporation profit more in its other businesses, because of its management of the furniture company, than it lost in that company?

A: Yes.

The Fast Elevator Trip

Q: Was the elevator working properly and able to go to the floor where Bill had his appointment?

A: Yes.

Q: Was Bill prevented from getting on, as by a work crew loading a piece of heavy machinery?

A: No.

Q: Did Bill correctly reason that he would get to his appointment faster by not using that elevator?

A: Yes.

Dismaying Dizziness

Q: Was the dizziness caused by fumes from the office machinery or from any other source, or related to any toxic substance?

A: No.

Q: If the office had not had the listed changes, then would dizziness result from being in it?

A: No.

Q: Would the dizziness probably be worse after sunset than at midday?

A: Yes.

Soliciting in Seattle

Q: Did the two friends have similar age and ethnicity, live in similar single-family houses, and live in neighborhoods that, though not close to each other, have virtually identical demographic statistics?

A: Yes.

Q: Is the explanation related to an anti-canvassing ordinance that affects one neighborhood but not the other?

A: No.

Q: Could the difference be traced to the personal convenience of the canvassers?

A: Yes.

Afraid of the Country

Q: Is Nicolai's background significant?

A: Yes.

Q: Had be been subjected to abuse or torture on a farm in Russia?

A: No.

Q: Would he have enjoyed visiting an actual livestock farm?

A: Yes.

Collecting Backwards

Q: Was the check for more than the debt?

A: No.

Q: Was the deposit made in cash?

A: Yes.

Q: Would Kingfist have preferred not to have made the deposit?

A: Yes.

Crossed Vision

Q: Can you improve your vision by crossing your fingers behind your back?

A: No.

Q: Can everyone benefit from crossing the fingers?

A: No.

Q: Do you need to do something with your crossed fingers?

A: Yes.

No Television Trouble

Q: Is it legal for a television set to be operated so that the driver of a moving motor vehicle can see its screen?

A: No.

Q: Did Stuart know the state trooper, bribe him, or have any special influence?

A: No.

Q: Did Stuart hear the theme music in stereo, even though the portable television set had only one speaker?

A: Yes.

Lottery Logic

Q: Does this question have anything to do with the practice of paying lottery winners in monthly or semi-annual installments?

A: No.

Q: Can lottery tickets be a sensible investment, despite their payouts being biased against their purchasers?

A: Yes.

Q: Are they a good investment for everyone?

A: No.

Positions, Everyone!

Q: Are you held captive, perhaps by a deranged ballet critic?

A: No.

Q: Is the crisis always caused, directly or indirectly, by assailants?

A: No.

Q: After you take a breath, will you probably be unable to walk for at least a minute?

A: Yes.

The Curious Cardiologist

Q: Was what the doctor wanted to do part of a research study, or an experimental procedure?

A: No.

Q: Was it a test of any kind?

A: No.

Q: Was it dangerous?

A: No.

A Tiring Question

Q: Did the four students rehearse their story beforehand

so that they would agree on which tire they would say went flat?

A: No.

Q: Had their car really had a flat tire recently, so that they could recall the incident as a clue?

A: No.

Q: Nevertheless, did they outwit the instructor?

A: Yes.

The Policeman's Signal

Q: When the policeman raised his hand, was he signaling to motorists who were traveling in the same direction as Sally?

A: Yes.

Q: Was there a broken traffic light, an unusually congested intersection, a detour or accident, or another reason for a policeman to direct traffic?

A: No.

Q: Was the policeman standing when he gave his signal?

A: No.

Bad Building Material

Q: Have most people seen it, in other contexts?

A: Yes.

Q: If someone crushes it, stirs the resulting pieces into a glass of water, and drinks it, is he or she likely to get sick?

A: No.

Q: Though solid, if pure it generally cannot be walked on easily or safely. Is that why it is not used for flooring?

A: No.

Water in the Attic
Q: Is a kitchen cabinet usually a good place for a water filter apparatus?

A: Yes.

Q: Is the kitchen the only place someone might go to get a drink of water?

A: No.

Q: Is the water pressure of the filtered water the same as that of ordinary tap water?

A: No.

Mysterious Break-In
Q: Did he have a permit to carry the gun openly?

A: Yes.

Q: Was the report that sent the police to investigate completely accurate?

A: No.

Q: Did the person who called the police, nevertheless, believe everything that he said to them?

A: Yes.

Common Cents
Q: Is it helpful for the government, which collects sales tax?

A: No.

Q: Is it encouraged by banks, so that they can charge extra for rolls of small coins?

A: No.

Q: If the storeowner is at the cash register, would anyone at all benefit?

A: No.

Celebrity Discourtesy
Q: Does the discourtesy pertain to their lifestyle?
A: No.
Q: Do they have attention-getting habits and other characteristics, perhaps because of their agents?
A: Yes.
Q: By knowing a celebrity's name, and nothing else, can you tell if the discourteous thing is being or has been done?
A: Yes.

Tied His Own Ankles
Q: Was there a pattern in how the evil man teased him?
A: Yes.
Q: Did the evil one have a weapon?
A: No.
Q: Did Ivan have a weapon?
A: Yes.

Too Many Books
Q: Was there a relative or friend who wanted the books?
A: No.
Q: Did he mind if other people borrowed them?
A: No.
Q: Were they in good condition?
A: Yes.

Mysterious Moon
Q: Does the eye include a lens to focus light and a retina to receive an image and convert it to a nerve signal?
A: Yes.

Q: Is the eye completely rigid?

A: No.

Q: If an image is out of focus, is there more than one way to manipulate a lens to put it in focus?

A: Yes.

Trapped

Q: Did the burglar step on the bear trap, inducing its jaws to clamp shut on his leg?

A: Yes.

Q: Did the burglar escape uninjured, as the officer asserted?

A: Yes.

Q: Did the officer recover the burglar's shoe?

A: Yes.

Silly Goose

Q: Had the man really stolen a goose?

A: Yes.

Q: Had he, in fact, told the truth throughout his confession?

A: Yes.

Q: Nevertheless, was his motive that of a simple repentant sinner?

A: No.

Cool Car, Dirty Windshield

Q: Did Calvin have a rag, tissue, or anything else that he was willing to get dirty?

A: No.

Q: Did he have antifreeze washer fluid or other cleaner of any kind?

A: No.

Q: Did the windshield wipers themselves work?
A: Yes.

No Littering Summons
Q: Did she intend to cause a minor traffic jam?
A: No.
Q: Was her car parked off the road, for example on the shoulder?
A: No.
Q: Did her car break down?
A: Yes.

License Unlost
Q: Did William have a reason for having two identical driver's licenses?
A: Yes.
Q: Did he expect to have both identical licenses for a long time, even though they would not expire for over a year?
A: No.
Q: Did William plan to defraud anyone?
A: Yes.

His Plans for Her
Q: Would he have any interest in making a similar polite but anonymous call to her home?
A: No.
Q: If his voice was recognized, then could he be substantially worse off for having made the call even though he was not harassing anyone?
A: Yes.
Q: Was he happily married?
A: No.

The Teacher Hit Mary

Q: Did the teacher intend to hit Mary?

A: Yes.

Q: Did Mary resist standing in the corner or misbehave while there?

A: No.

Q: Was Mary standing next to an open window?

A: Yes.

He Crashed Deliberately

Q: Did he know the owner of the parked car?

A: No.

Q: Did he defraud an insurance company or withhold any facts from police?

A: No.

Q: Was the man driving a car with unsafe steering or otherwise at fault for the accident?

A: No.

Bewildering Bargain

Q: Was the woman intelligent and rational, not making an error or being confused by a price tag?

A: Yes.

Q: Had she any interest in the financial well-being of the store, other than that of an ordinary customer?

A: No.

Q: Could this incident have happened at the store where she usually bought toothpaste?

A: No.

Unequal Values

Q: Was Jack cheated, misled, or irrational?

A: No.

Q: Did Mack use what he purchased to rob or defraud anyone?

A: No.

Q: Did something bad happen to Mack that was not completely offset by the goods and services that he received?

A: Yes.

Arrested for Shopping

Q: Was the man previously known to the cashier as a wanted criminal?

A: No.

Q: Did the man cause a disturbance or threaten anyone?

A: No.

Q: Did the man commit or attempt a crime?

A: Yes.

The Four-Mile Conversation

Q: Did they use telephones, radios, or other communication aids?

A: No.

Q: Did they walk repeatedly around a round quarter-mile track, or similar track of different length, so that they could shout at each other?

A: No.

Q: Did they talk using sign language or other departure from ordinary spoken English?

A: No.

Heavy-Footed Harry
Q: Does Harry choose his shoes?
A: No.
Q: Do they reach up to his ankles?
A: No.
Q: Does Harry wear them to the racetrack, where he works?
A: Yes.

The Nine-Penny Ruler
Q: Was Lillian rational?
A: Yes.
Q: Did she really save money?
A: Yes.
Q: Is there any significance to the nine cents, not eight cents or a dime?
A: Yes.

They Love Each Other
Q: Did Pat really love Mary, as he said?
A: Yes.
Q: Did Mary love Pat?
A: Yes.
Q: Was Pat adopted, in that he was raised apart from his natural parents?
A: Yes.

Truckers and No Toll Money
Q: Did Hank intend to have money to pay the toll?
A: Yes.
Q: Did Hank pay the toll indirectly, even though he did not personally hand money to the attendant?
A: Yes.

Q: Did Frank, on the CB, say why he was not surprised that Hank had no money?

A: No.

His Car Was Identified

Q: Did Nick have a boat, fishing equipment, or anything similar on or in his recently purchased car?

A: No.

Q: Did Nick park in a prearranged spot in the parking lot or remain with the car while Dave looked for him?

A: No.

Q: Is their occupation important, given that special license plates or emergency lights, parking stickers, or type of vehicle driven are all not the answer?

A: Yes.

Saved by the Convertible

Q: Was this convertible exactly as crashworthy as a hard-top, except for the lack of a roof and the absence of shoulder straps?

A: Yes.

Q: Were the lack of a roof and the absence of shoulder straps irrelevant in a sideways collision that did not involve a car turning upside down?

A: Yes.

Q: Could Milton have been removed from a hard-top car and placed in an ambulance as quickly as from a convertible?

A: No.

Doesn't Need Hot Water

Q: Was the cup previously clean and unstained?

A: Yes.

Q: Was Dora trying to damage anything?

A: No.

Q: Was the cupful of water the only significant object in the oven?

A: No.

But the Patient Followed Orders

Q: Did the doctor prescribe medicine?

A: No.

Q: Was the patient's statement, to the doctor, accurate?

A: Yes.

Q: Did either the doctor or the patient expect that the patient would continue getting results at the same rate in the future?

A: No.

He's All Wet

Q: Were other people, who stood nearby or walked past him, wet?

A: No.

Q: Was it raining?

A: No.

Q: Had the umbrella been altered?

A: Yes.

Spoken By The Book

Q: Had the lecturer plagiarized something widely in print or otherwise well known to the entire audience?

A: No.

Q: Did the book contain material that the lecturer did not use?

A: Yes.

Q: Did the words of the lecture appear in the book in the same order that they were used in the lecture?

A: No.

Self-Destruction

Q: Has health care administration traditionally been a woman's job?

A: Yes.

Q: In an office setting, is an ambitious woman under pressure to dress elegantly?

A: Yes.

Q: Does the self-destructive behavior have to do with women's clothing?

A: Yes.

The Upside-Down Newspaper

Q: Was the upside-down newspaper a signal to anyone, perhaps a coded message from one spy to another or an attention-getting mannerism to provoke a friendly conversation from a stranger?

A: No.

Q: Did the man know that the newspaper was upside down?

A: No.

Q: He was reading, but was he reading the newspaper?

A: No.

Tied Up In Knots

Q: Do you use a particular kind of knot, such as a sheet bend, that is known to work if the rope sizes are not too different?

A: No.

Q: Do you unwind and attach strands of the ropes, or use glue, strong tape, or other fastening material?
A: No.
Q: Do you first make a knot in one rope?
A: Yes.

Eggs-Asperated

Q: Was Jill telling the truth about how to identify hard-boiled eggs?
A: Yes.
Q: Was a flat surface available on which to place an egg?
A: Yes.
Q: Could Bill or Jill have safely identified a hard-boiled egg, under the specific circumstances, by spinning it?
A: No.

I Brake for Snowdrifts

Q: Did Sandy have a good reason for putting on the parking brake?
A: Yes.
Q: Did Sandy put the brake on all the way?
A: No.
Q: Would it be left on after the car was freed?
A: No.

Wrong Again!

Q: Were the painters on the correct floor?
A: Yes.
Q: Had the foreman lost count?
A: No.

Q: Could this incident, with the same cause, have happened at a floor numbered ten or less?
A: No.

A Matter of Survival
Q: Had the three dead men really tried to rob him?
A: Yes.
Q: Is it significant that nearly a hundred shots had been fired but that the three dead men had revolvers, capable of only six shots before needing reloading?
A: Yes.
Q: Was Mort's report to the police completely accurate?
A: No.

She's Not Afraid
Q: Was Bertha's killing legal?
A: Yes.
Q: Was it in a boxing ring?
A: No.
Q: Was her victim six feet tall?
A: No.

Two In The Woods
Q: Was the person who was on the telephone telling the truth, not lying or describing an optical illusion or hallucinating?
A: Yes.
Q: Were the two people who entered the woods related?
A: Yes.
Q: Did both people who left the woods walk out of it?
A: No.

Tea-ed Off

Q: Had something happened to the stored tea bags that had affected their flavor?

A: No.

Q: Had the secretary removed all the coffee grounds from the coffee maker, so that no taste of coffee could remain?

A: Yes.

Q: Did the secretary intend to heat water for tea?

A: No.

Money and Laundering

Q: Is the list complete?

A: No.

Q: Is the incompleteness of the list related to environmental damage, perhaps due to the burning of gas in a dryer or the release of chemicals from detergent?

A: No.

Q: Is the missing item on the list likely to result in a small expense, or increase in a previously existing expense, at least once per month?

A: No.

Smashed Taillights

Q: Did the owner give Bob permission to smash the taillights?

A: No.

Q: Had the car been stolen?

A: No.

Q: After the taillights were smashed, was something important revealed behind them?

A: Yes.

Mowing the Pool

Q: Was the son trying to lengthen the time spent doing the job, perhaps because he was paid by the hour?

A: No.

Q: Was the mower's engine running while he pushed the mower around the pool?

A: Yes.

Q: Are the trees significant?

A: Yes.

The Test Question
Q: Was the apparently correct answer truly correct?

A: No.

Q: Did Henry, until he got a job, expect to drive always as if the answer given by the authorities was literally correct?

A: Yes.

Q: After he got a job, would he sometimes drive differently?

A: Yes.

No Ransom Demand
Q: Was the man rational, even though his actions seem inexplicable?

A: Yes.

Q: Is it significant that he was able to bring a firearm past a metal detector?

A: Yes.

Q: Did anyone help him, perhaps to allow him to sneak a gun into the building?

A: No.

What Drained the Battery?
Q: When Walter returned to the car, was anything switched on or any door open?

A: No.

Q: Had anyone been in the parking lot since Walter parked his car and ran inside?

A: Yes.

Q: Did Walter lock his car?

A: No.

Stubborn Steve

Q: Did Steve choose paper that was multiple-part, tractor-feed, or otherwise special or unusual?

A: No.

Q: Was the sales clerk completely honest and accurate?

A: Yes.

Q: Was the paper intended for an exotic use that was not reasonably expected by its manufacturer, such as papier-mâché or examination under a microscope?

A: No.

The Nonstop Elevator Trip

Q: Were they on a high floor in an office building?

A: Yes.

Q: Did the building have separate groups of elevators to serve separate ranges of floors?

A: Yes.

Q: Could anyone get into a crowded elevator on the ground floor and reasonably expect to get directly to the floor where Bill was, without having the elevator stop at other floors first?

A: No.

Another Mystery Fax

Q: Was the fax a real one, intended to be received and read just like an ordinary fax, with no codes or secret messages involved?

A: Yes.

Q: Did the colleague prefer or insist on a fax in preference to an ordinary telephone call, perhaps because of deafness?

A: No.

Q: Did the content of the fax include any tables or other lengthy material that is more easily explained in writing than by speaking?
A: No.

Short-Lived Writing

Q: Are computers or any other electronic devices involved?
A: No.
Q: By what she is doing, does she intend to communicate to anyone?
A: No.
Q: Although it is immediately erased, does her output from the writing instrument in turn help erase something else?
A: Yes.

Power Failure

Q: Did Horace sleep away from his house and return to it to find the clocks all stopped?
A: No.
Q: Was he of sound mind and with good vision?
A: Yes.
Q: Did he own an electric clock that had an hour hand and a minute hand?
A: No.

Better Late Than Prompt

Q: If the debtor would have honored the original contract, then would Kingfist have offered the new one?
A: No.

Q: Did Kingfist collect more readily under the new contract than under the old one?

A: Yes.

Q: Did Kingfist collect completely legally?

A: Yes.

Miracle Cures

Q: Is the additional explanation known to those to whom it applies?

A: Yes.

Q: When that explanation applies to someone, does it always work?

A: Yes.

Q: After it works, can it ever be identified, even with exhaustive medical tests and scientific scrutiny?

A: No.

Happy with the TV Ad

Q: Had an accomplice damaged the television station, its transmitter, or anything related to it?

A: No.

Q: Did the man hope to sell diagnostic television repair services or TV sets?

A: No.

Q: Would he have been pleased if the test pattern had appeared at a different time or on another channel?

A: No.

Slow-Witted Customers

Q: Is it based on deception or misleading advertising, or otherwise actually or potentially illegal?

A: No.

Q: Are coupons, other marketing devices, acquired outside of the restaurants required to qualify for special savings?

A: No.

Q: Is it, by its nature, impossible to use other than by a fast-food restaurant?

A: Yes.

Don't Bluff It

Q: Would a revolver do you any good?

A: No.

Q: Can you hide from the threat?

A: No.

Q: If it killed you, would your death be accidental?

A: Yes.

No Cell Phone

Q: Was the expert unwilling to help Jimmy or in fear of arrest himself?

A: No.

Q: Had he the skill to make connections to cell phones?

A: Yes.

Q: Nevertheless, was the task just plain impossible?

A: Yes.

Sound Reasoning

Q: Had he previously paid for the good sound system, in full?

A: Yes.

Q: Was he going to sell his car?

A: No.

Q: Was he worried about his hearing?

A: No.

Screened Out

Q: Did the house need repairs of any kind, perhaps correction of subtle rotting of the windowsills or new paint?

A: No.

Q: Were the screens and storm windows in good condition and appropriate for that climate?

A: Yes.

Q: Would they later be put back exactly as they were before?

A: Yes.

Discarded Meat

Q: Had Paul followed guidelines from the city trash collectors, putting garbage in properly secured bags?

A: Yes.

Q: Was there already a legal dispute already between Paul and his neighbor?

A: Yes.

Q: Did Paul deliberately make the meat unfit to eat?

A: Yes.

Posted Property

Q: Could he drill a hole in the old wooden posts, then hook them with a nail or other tool?

A: No.

Q: Did he break the concrete?

A: No.

Q: Were any tools needed, other than ordinary items one might find at home?

A: No.

Cheap Advertising

Q: Was there a cooperative venture with another store, perhaps sharing the advertising expense in a lopsided way?

A: No.

Q: Did the beauty shop make dishonest promises?

A: No.

Q: Nevertheless, was something unethical going on?

A: Yes.

Dirty Conduct

Q: Was speaking involved, perhaps including profane words?

A: No.

Q: Was the mother rational?

A: Yes.

Q: Did the mother fear danger if George didn't wash his mouth?

A: Yes.

Self-Portrait

Q: Did he look at a photograph of himself, or use a video camera apparatus?

A: No.

Q: Did he get help from another artist?

A: No.

Q: Did he look in a mirror not only at himself, but also at the painting in progress?

A: No.

Southern Insight

Q: Had he openly declared sympathy to the Confederacy, would they probably have injured or killed him?

A: Yes.

Q: Was his reply vague or ambivalent?

A: No.

Q: Did the man oppose slavery?

A: Yes.

Exiled

Q: Was he, or someone he loved, framed for or falsely accused of a crime?

A: No.

Q: Did gangsters or other evil people want to oust him to take advantage of his absence?

A: No.

Q: Would he ever be allowed to return?

A: Yes.

Give Me a Dollar

Q: Was there shoplifting or any ill intent?

A: No.

Q: Was the man alone, unaccompanied by actual or potential accomplices?

A: Yes.

Q: Did he do any work for the store owner?

A: No.

The Returned DVD's

Q: Did she return the rented DVD's, as she promised, so as to avoid any late fees or damage expense?

A: Yes.

Q: Did she follow his instructions exactly?
A: No.
Q: Did he now have a problem with the video store?
A: Yes.

The Worrisome Guarantee
Q: Was the customer rational?
A: Yes.
Q: Was the part used whenever the car was driven?
A: No.
Q: Would the customer have preferred a guarantee that was worded differently?
A: Yes.

Unfare Increase
Q: Would the proposal have made on-street parking easy to find for many people who otherwise would have to search extensively for a parking space?
A: Yes.
Q: Would traffic decrease?
A: Yes.
Q: Would a very rich person, if willing to pay for it, get a benefit from the proposal that is not otherwise available at any price?
A: Yes.

Fast Broke
Q: Was there much traffic on the highway?
A: No.
Q: Did Crazy Kate know what caused the rattling sound and infer that something broke that remained broken when the rattling stopped?
A: Yes.

Q: After the rattling stopped, did she know from looking at the dashboard that she had only a certain amount of time before her truck would stall?

A: Yes.

License Lost

Q: Did anyone copy anything from the stolen license when the thief tried to use it?

A: No.

Q: Did the thief use it while driving?

A: No.

Q: Was William less than 25 years old?

A: Yes.

She Didn't Like His Picture

Q: Is it a common practice to exchange photographs with overseas pen pals?

A: Yes.

Q: Knowing that photographs are usually exchanged, was he nevertheless surprised at her request for a particular kind of photograph?

A: Yes.

Q: Could this incident have occurred if the Asian woman knew English, including idioms, perfectly?

A: No.

The One-Penny Contribution

Q: Was the charity sarcastic?

A: No.

Q: Was the rich man a miser?

A: No.

Q: Is it significant that the rich man did not reach into his pocket to remove a penny?

A: Yes.

Forgiven Break-In
Q: Were the police officers bribed to permit crime, or otherwise dishonest?
A: No.
Q: Did the man commit a crime by breaking in?
A: No.
Q: Were the owners upset by the man's actions?
A: No.

He Didn't Mean to Kill
Q: Was the prosecutor or any other official bribed or under pressure to be lenient?
A: No.
Q: Did the passenger's family want to hide his identity or not press charges for some other reason?
A: No.
Q: Was there something about the passenger that made it impossible to prosecute the drunk driver for his death?
A: Yes.

He Made a Killing
Q: Was it legal for Scott to invest as he did?
A: Yes.
Q: Did Nancy turn pale only because of the conversation as described, not because of a medical condition or a special connection with Scott's business associates?
A: Yes.
Q: Does the explanation have to do with the commodities in which Scott invested?

A: Yes.

Another Bad Check

Q: Could Sam have written other, good, checks from the same account, even if larger than that which Sam gave his creditor?

A: Yes.

Q: Did Sam write the check, under the angry eyes of his creditor, with the ordinary pen that the creditor told him to use, not secretly switching it for another pen or putting special ink in it?

A: Yes.

Q: Aware of an upcoming visit from his creditor, had Sam done something to the check before writing on it?

A: Yes.

Just Like Prison

Q: Does the visitor have a common lifestyle?

A: Yes.

Q: Can the visitor reduce his exposure to his lifestyle simply by behaving politely and scrupulously obeying rules, as a prisoner can sometimes do to get time off for good behavior?

A: No.

Q: Is the visitor's lifestyle expected to last a total of more than five years?

A: Yes.

The Unwelcome Strike

Q: Did the new contract permit the member to walk off the job at any time without reason?

A: No.

Q: Did the union member intend to cause difficulty, perhaps because of a personal grudge against the manager?

A: No.

Q: Did work resume within a minute or two after the union member called the strike?

A: Yes.

She Hated Leftovers

Q: Was there any leftover meat?

A: No.

Q: Did Sally serve each hamburger and each hot dog in exactly one roll?

A: Yes.

Q: Were there any leftover rolls?

A: No.

Was Her Job At Risk?

Q: Did Benny want to replace Jenny?

A: No.

Q: Did Jenny want the advertisement to be run?

A: Yes.

Q: Would Jenny have eventually lost her job if the advertisement had not been run, but otherwise probably been able to keep it?

A: Yes.

Weird Words

Q: Do they have six nonrepeating letters in a particular order?

A: Yes.

Q: Are the letters in alphabetical order?

A: Yes.

Q: Are they the only two English-language words that consist of six letters in alphabetical order?

A: Almost.

Full Speed Ahead

Q: Did he remember an appointment or other reason to hurry, or receive a message on a beeper, cellular telephone, or CB?

A: No.

Q: Was something wrong with the car that forced him to speed up or gave him a reason to do so?

A: No.

Q: Could this incident, for the same reason, have happened during broad daylight?

A: No.

Snow on the Windshield

Q: Was Melanie's car completely covered with snow, including the windshield, before she moved it?

A: Yes.

Q: Was Melanie's car, though parked on a street, very close to her landlady's driveway?

A: Yes.

Q: Was Melanie's windshield covered with snow after she parked her car in the driveway?

A: Yes.

The Cold Fire

Q: Did they open a door or window, turn off a heater, or do anything to change the indoor temperature other than build the fire?

A: No.

Q: Was the fire an ordinary heat-producing fire, produced by firewood, and safely contained in the fireplace (not burning down the house or any part of it)?

A: Yes.

Q: Was there a design goof in the house that involved an electric or electronic device?

A: Yes.

Rope on its End

Q: If a piece of rope could be made rigid, then could it be stood on end, perhaps leaning against something?

A: Yes.

Q: Does the rope have a hollow interior, like some sash cords, so that a rigid rod can be threaded into it?

A: No.

Q: Is the solution most easily demonstrated with special equipment or during a particular season?

A: Yes.

Approximately Seven Days per Week

Q: Is the probability either approximately or exactly 1/7th?

A: Yes.

Q: Can it be proved either exactly 1/7th for all dates or not exactly 1/7th for all dates?

A: Yes.

Q: Is it exactly 1/7th?

A: No.

by Edward J. Harshman

The Mail is In!

Q: Had Oscar put the order form into the outgoing mail slot next to the mailboxes the previous day, after that day's mail had been delivered?

A: Yes.

Q: Did the mailboxes have big pods nearby, so that a mail carrier could put a parcel in one of them and the key to that pod in that resident's mailbox?

A: Yes.

Q: Did Oscar pay particular attention to the pods?

A: Yes.

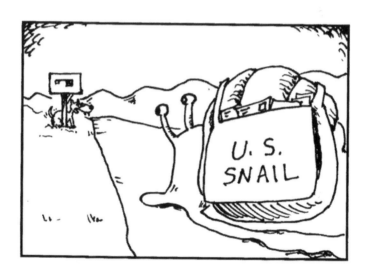

Ski Through The Tree

Q: Was the tree tall and rigid, not a knee-high sapling that could be skied over?

A: Yes.

Q: Were there ski-pole prints or footprints near the tree, showing that the skier removed one ski, or any lightening of a ski track there?

A: No.

Q: Were both tracks made by one expert skier?

A: Yes.

She Cheated

Q: Other than noting that Sherry and Mary had sat next to each other, had the teacher noted anything suspicious as they took the test?

A: No.

Q: Had the teacher graded other essay tests from those same students?

A: Yes.

Q: Did Sherry have a perfect mastery of English grammar?

A: No.

Zelda Was Cured

Q: Did Zelda, like many new mothers, often pick up and hold her baby?

A: Yes.

Q: Was her husband taller than her?

A: Yes.

Q: Did her husband also like to pick up and hold the baby?

A: Yes.

Belligerent Bus Driver

Q: Could a motor vehicle legally drive past the school bus while it was receiving children?

A: No.

Q: Did Cal damage or disable the school bus or threaten anyone in it?

A: No.

Q: Can a bicycle, wheelbarrow, or other wheeled device that is moved by human energy legally pass a school bus, if no one is hurt or endangered in the process?

A: Yes.

Mystery Gate

Q: Is the residential street in a bad part of town, an area from which the hotel management feels compelled to take special security precautions?

A: No.

Q: Is the gate there to protect hotel customers from some danger on that part of the hotel grounds?

A: No.

Q: Do hotel customers, in general, expected to use the gated entrance to the hotel?

A: No.

Lost Again

Q: Did any of them have a compass or see familiar landmarks?

A: No.

Q: Did the son infer the direction by the slope of a hill or the flow of a stream or river?

No.

Q: Is it important that there was enough light to see, even at night?

A: Yes.

Silent Murder

Q: Were the neighbors deaf?

A: No.

Q: Was there a silencer on the shotgun at the time of the murder?

A: No.

Q: Could anyone have heard the shotgun's being fired at the time of the murder?

A: No.

Defying Gravity

Q: Was he working on a stage or movie set that depicted damage from a bomb or natural disaster?

A: No.

Q: Was he working on a house that had really been similarly damaged?

A: No.

Q: Was he using a brush that was of a size and shape normally used for painting houses?

A: No.

Nothing Done

Q: Did the contractor intend to cheat her?

A: No.

Q: Did the workers count the floors very carefully, as promised?

A: Yes.

Q: Did Marjorie's future upstairs neighbor have any immediate plans for finishing or remodeling his apartment?

A: No.

The Microscope

Q: Is the microscope used regularly and used in the ordinary way, looking very closely at things?

A: Yes.

Q: Was anything other than astronomy studied in the laboratory?

A: No.

Q: When special photographs are taken, do astronomers like to study them in detail?

A: Yes.

Brian Braggart's Fish Story

Q: Is it possible to breathe through a tube and swim deep underwater?

A: Yes.

Q: Can nitrogen intoxication (the "bends") be induced by swimming underwater at a depth of 30 feet?

A: No.

Q: Nevertheless, would Brian have been killed by swimming as he described, even if the big fish was harmless?

A: Yes.

Not A Worthless Check

Q: Was the check good?

A: Yes.

Q: Was the check not cashed because it was originally intended to pay a debt that was later canceled or otherwise settled (example: merchandise originally paid for with the check was returned)?

A: No.

Q: Did the man expect to get more money by not cashing the check than by cashing it?

A: Yes.

Supposed to Kill?

Q: Did the intended victim run or call for help?

A: No.

Q: Having learned that the gun was not loaded, did anyone try to grab it or otherwise forcibly intervene?

A: No.

Q: The incident did not result in death or serious injury. Did anyone want it to?

A: No.

Hearing them Quickly
Q: Was the father telling the truth?
A: Yes.
Q: Did he intend to keep Dana from hearing the concert?
A: No.
Q: Is it significant that the father was reading the television listings at the time?
A: Yes.

Taking Turns
Q: Were they telling the truth about their personal driving experiences?
A: Yes.
Q: Were they referring to ordinary traffic on ordinary two-way streets?
A: Yes.
Q: Was this a typical social telephone call between young women, one for which there is a nominal or no per-call charge because of residential and personal use?
A: No.

Seasonal Mileage
Q: Does the answer have to do with snow on the ground or snow tires on the car?
A: No.
Q: Does Claude drive along exactly the same roads in summer as in winter, and in the same car?
A: Yes.

Q: Are the windows open in summer, so that there is significantly increased wind resistance, until Claude closes them near the end of a trip?

A: No.

Too Precise

Q: Did Jerry and Mary correctly believe that vagueness was generally believed important to their business?

A: Yes.

Q: Did they intend to bring profit to their boss?

A: No.

Q: Were they paid for their work?

A: No.

A Mystery Fax

Q: If the executive had anticipated the call and connected a fax machine to his telephone line, then would the fax call have resulted in his receiving a useful fax transmission?

A: No.

Q: Did the executive know who or what originated the fax call?

A: Yes.

Q: Did he fear being overheard while using the telephone?

A: Yes.

Forgot to Stop?

Q: One minute before Angus jumped out of the car, did he expect to do so?

A: No.

Q: After he jumped out of the car, did he expect to get into it again?

A: No.

Q: Did more than two minutes pass between when Angus jumped out of the car and when he reached the ground?

A: Yes.

They Had a Ball

Q: Did Ted intend to give Ned practice at running to catch a high ball?

A: No.

Q: Could Ted have aimed the ball directly at Ned if he had wanted to?

A: Yes.

Q: Is their location significant?

A: Yes.

Kingfist Found Him

Q: Was the letter part of Kingfist's plan?

A: Yes.

Q: Did Kingfist hope that the letter would get delivered?

A: No.

Q: Would Kingfist have been happy if the letter had been thrown away after the mail carrier tried to deliver it?

A: No.

Night Blindness Cure

Q: Is medical knowledge necessary to ask the questions or interpret the answers?

A: No.

Q: Are drugs or nutritional supplements needed?

A: No.

Q: Is the setting in which night blindness exists an important clue?
A: Yes.

A Headache of a Problem
Q: Was the patient repulsive?
A: No.
Q: Did the patient come to his office?
A: No.
Q: Was the patient in the hospital?
A: No.

Time for Repairs
Q: Did the watch work properly, even though at first Dilton didn't think it did?
A: Yes.
Q: Earlier, had Dilton properly set it to the correct time?
A: Yes.
Q: When Dilton believed that the watch didn't work properly, did he see an incorrect time and infer that the watch was too fast or too slow?
A: No.

Old Money But Good Money
Q: Were the changes deliberately made simultaneously and with the same intent?
A: No.
Q: Did exactly one of them affect the ideology of why money is considered valuable?
A: Yes.
Q: Was the other considered desirable by some conservatives and ironic by others?

A: Yes.

Gas-Station Glitch
Q: Was the attendant who announced the five-dollar limit telling the truth?
A: Yes.
Q: Did George, after receiving fuel, receive five dollars in change from the attendant?
A: No.
Q: Was George likely to be one of several very angry customers at the gas station?
A: Yes.

Youthful Gamble
Q: Is the gambling sometimes managed or controlled by a state government or one of its agencies?
A: Yes.
Q: Are certain young adults not only allowed but also required to gamble?
A: Yes.
Q: Can the gambling be repeated by putting one's winnings at financial risk?
A: No.

Down With Average
Q: Can it happen to adults, too?
A: Yes.
Q: When it happens, is it usually accidental?
A: Yes.
Q: Does it involve weapons or other dangerous objects?
A: No.

No Forwarding

Q: Was there a billing dispute with the phone company?

A: No.

Q: Did he drive?

A: No.

Q: Had he ever been arrested?

A: Yes.

Oo La La

Q: Did the colleague know of anything unsightly on the Champs-Elysées which, if shown, would make the picture unattractive?

A: No.

Q: Was there a technical problem, such as improper exposure, rain or fog, passers-by who interfered, or any other obstacle to a clear sharp picture?

A: No.

Q: The travel agency could not use the picture, but might some other kind of organization?

A: Yes.

Immovable Car

Q: Are the keys lost?

A: No.

Q: Were any legal papers served or processed, such as a subpoena for evidence or a transfer of title to a new owner?

A: No.

Q: If I do nothing, then can I reasonably expect to be able to use the car a few hours from now?

A: Yes.

The Wall-Mounted Sink
Q: Can wall-mounted sinks be more convenient for some people?
A: Yes.
Q: Can they indirectly reduce problems from allergies?
A: Yes.
Q: Is there an important option in their installation that is not available for the other two kinds of sinks?
A: Yes.

Wrong-Way Elevator
Q: Are their observations strictly accurate, and not related to remembering delays when they were rushed, for example?
A: Yes.
Q: Was there only one elevator?
A: Yes.
Q: Did the elevator change direction only at the top and the bottom of its shaft?
A: Yes.

An Appetite for Housing
Q: Did he walk into every room in the house?
A: No.
Q: Was there a person or a locked or boarded-up door that stopped him from doing so?
A: No.
Q: Was he in danger?
A: Yes.

The Predictable Cold
Q: Was there a medical explanation, perhaps that his boss exposed him to cold viruses without his

knowledge?

A: No.

Q: Did his boss know with absolute certainty what would happen?

A: Yes.

Q: If he stopped his frivolous arguing, would he recover, otherwise not?

A: Yes.

The Bad Letter

Q: Was her friend happy that Sally did so?

A: Yes.

Q: Did the recipient of the letter already know Sally or her friend?

A: No.

Q: Were Sally and her friend competing for the same kind of work?

A: No.

Pierced Ears

Q: Was he angry about his daughter's declaring allegiance to a peer group?

A: No.

Q: Was his religious background significant?

A: Yes.

Q: Was his objection, his assertion that pierced ears deny independence, literally correct?

A: Yes.

Plastered

Q: Was a bet or dare involved?

A: No.

Q: Was she treating a medical condition?

A: No.

Q: Nevertheless, after doing so, could she eventually expect to sit more comfortably?

A: Yes.

A Cross Puzzle

Q: Do you write the moves as you make them?

A: Yes.

Q: Is there more than one correct solution?

A: Yes.

Q: Do you know the first correct move before you are halfway finished?

A: No.

Water Under Pressure

Q: Would it likely have value if the fluid were not water?

A: No.

Q: Is water available where the process is useful?

A: Yes.

Q: Is the intent to tease or annoy anyone?

A: No.

Disappeared

Q: Did Russell or his neighbor commit a crime or receive stolen property?

A: No.

Q: Was Russell's third one a gift or inheritance?

A: No.

Q: Can they be owned today, generally?

A: No.

Checks Cashed Here

Q: Was he honest?

A: No.

Q: Was he working alone?

A: No.

Q: Though the action described did not cost the store anything, was the store the victim of fraud?

A: Yes.

Eager Surgeons

Q: Is the trend motivated by saving money, as for medical insurers?

A: No.

Q: Are patients happy with the trend?

A: Yes.

Q: When badly damaged limbs are saved, do they always function as well as before the injury?

A: No.

Cool Car Got Cooler

Q: Did Calvin have any interest in selling the car or otherwise want the air conditioner to work except for ordinary winter use in New England?

A: No.

Q: Could Calvin's car, when the air conditioner worked, have both the heater and the air conditioner on at the same time?

A: Yes.

Q: Does the air conditioner do anything to the air other than cool it?

A: Yes.

Hub Cap Obsolescence
Q: Did Glenda do so only because of the tunnel?
A: Yes.
Q: Was her decision concerned only with safety?
A: Yes.
Q: If the tunnel had incandescent lighting, then would Glenda have replaced her hub caps?
A: No.

Failed Theft
Q: Was the steering column unlocked so that the steering wheel could turn, even though the engine was not running?
A: Yes.
Q: If an honest police officer had watched him, then would he have been arrested?
A: No.
Q: Was he trying to steal the car?
A: No.

Her Unromantic Reply
Q: Did they describe their feelings accurately?
A: Yes.
Q: Did she intend to offend?
A: No.
Q: Were they in a romantic setting?
A: Yes.

Burning Down the House Again
Q: Was the man paid for the fire, as by a film crew making a movie?
A: No.

Q: Did the man burn down the house to conceal evidence of a previously committed crime?

A: No.

Q: Other than creating a dangerous condition, for which the man carefully avoided prosecution by bribing the fire marshal, did he arguably do something wrong by burning down the house?

A: Yes.

The Car Won't Run

Q: Did Keith prefer owning a disabled car to owning a working car?

A: No.

Q: Did Keith expect to repair the wires?

A: Yes.

Q: Had Keith a financial incentive to cut wires if he knew he would have to repair them?

A: Yes.

He Voted

Q: Did Ellery have a special interest, such as being a friend or relative of Ramona, having bribed her, or otherwise expecting her to give him a tangible or intangible personal benefit?

A: No.

Q: Was Ellery's reasoning rational?

A: Yes.

Q: Was the election a general election?

A: No.

by Edward J. Harshman

Money in the Mailbox
Q: Did he want to give or send the money to anyone?
A: No.
Q: Is it important that he did not put all of his money into the mailbox?
A: Yes.
Q: Did he hope to get the money back later?
A: Yes.

He Overpaid
Q: Did Rick make a mistake, perhaps misreading the bill?
A: No.
Q: Had Rick a special reason to put money out of reach of his bank, where only the credit card company could easily get it?
A: Yes.

Q: Was Rick acting illegally or conspiring to defraud anyone, given that the check was good?

A: No.

The Victim was Arrested

Q: Was the owner framed by the three men?

A: No.

Q: Were the three men previously known to the police?

A: Yes.

Q: Did the three men spend the money that they took, or set it aside so that they could spend it years later?

A: No.

Shoplifting Backwards

Q: Is the smuggling done with intent to defraud the store?

A: Yes.

Q: Is the smuggling done with intent to return merchandise, whether defective or not, for a refund?

A: No.

Q: Is the merchandise that is smuggled in identical in brand, size, and product type to merchandise already offered for sale?

A: Yes.

There's a Fly in my Soup!

Q: Did the man suspect that the waiter would just remove the fly and not supply a new serving of soup?

A: Yes.

Q: Did the man see what the waiter did in the kitchen?

A: No.

Q: Did the man do something with the soup when he was served a second time?

A: Yes.

Mysterious Captions

Q: Was there a closed-caption decoder that was part of or connected to any device that fed its signal to the television set?

A: No.

Q: Was the movie previously recorded, legally, on a video tape?

A: Yes.

Q: Could the movie have been instead been recorded on a laser disk or a commercially sold DVD?

A: No.

Does This Bulb Work?

Q: Did his bulbs fit in an ordinary socket?

A: Yes.

Q: Did he hold the bulb to a strong light so that he can look through it and see the filament?

A: No.

Q: Did he use the soft-white bulbs of which the interior coating is easily scratched by a broken filament, thus easily identifying the bulb as burned-out?

A: No.

He Followed Instructions

Q: Could the student have obtained the folder without following the instructions on the cabinet?

A: Yes.

Q: Did the student expect to be scolded for making noise?

A: Yes.

Q: Had other students served their detention time by working in the same office?

A: Yes.

Vowels in Order

Q: Other than the word "unquestionably," was any word spoken that included all the vowels?

A: No.

Q: Was the mischievous student's attitude part of the answer, not just pointless behavior?

A: Yes.

Q: Did the last student actually give a good answer by openly refusing to give a decisive answer?

A: Yes.

The Crooked Headlight

Q: Did he intend to shine his headlights into the eyes of oncoming drivers or cause other unpleasantness or danger?

A: No.

Q: Could he have driven safely without misaiming the headlight?

A: No.

Q: Is there a reason why he pulled over, instead of misaiming the headlight before starting to drive?

A: Yes.

The Bicycle Bolt

Q: Was the color, strength rating, or metallic content of the bolt incorrect?

A: No.

Q: Did her son make a mistake, not getting a bolt that matched Edith's stated criteria?

A: No.

Q: Might an experienced bicycle store clerk have suspected a problem with Edith's specifications?

A: Yes.

The Happy Cabdriver

Q: Did the cab driver take the speculator to the center of town (not to a nearby bus stop, for example) without making him share the ride with another passenger?

A: Yes.

Q: Did the speculator give the cab driver useful information that would help while driving subsequent customers?

A: Yes.

Q: Would that useful information have any importance after the city was no longer brand new?

A: No.

Find Bingo!

Q: Was Jimmy's request reasonable?

A: Yes.

Q: Could a hamster have reached the window?

A: No.

Q: Was Bingo a hamster?

A: No.

Steamed Up

Q: Did she wear cooler clothing or otherwise adjust to the annoying temperature and/or humidity?

A: No.

Q: Did she use a dehumidifier, which would have definitely made her comfortable if the air conditioner was on too?

A: No.

Q: Did she use another electrical appliance?

A: Yes.

Perfectly Efficient

Q: Is special technology needed, such as superfluids or other components that are not commonly available?

A: No.

Q: Is the device intended to produce mechanical energy?

A: No.

Q: Can mechanical devices not achieve 100% efficiency because of the unwanted conversion of energy to heat?

A: Yes.

She Easily Went Home

Q: Did the physician correctly identify a serious heart attack?

A: Yes.

Q: Was there a miracle treatment for the heart attack?

A: No.

Q: Did the woman expect to be walking easily right after the physician called the ambulance?

A: Yes.

One Way to Liberty

Q: Is the direction of travel on the staircase reversed every five minutes or so?

A: No.

Q: Is there a hidden elevator or staircase that is behind a wall and that is regularly used?
No.
Q: While climbing the spiral staircase, can you see stairs that are intended for downward travel?
A: Yes.

Safe Landing

Q: Did he land on ordinary hard ground, not in water or on a trampoline or other cushioning object?
A: Yes.
Q: Did his mother fear for his safety?
A: No.
Q: When he jumped from the top of the tree, did he fall less than a hundred feet?
A: Yes.

The Will

Q: Were Pat, Leslie, and Terry all law-abiding?
A: Yes.
Q: Did Evelyn's son have any siblings or cousins?
A: No.
Q: Was Leslie paid for getting the women pregnant?
A: Yes.

Wet in the Winter

Q: Is she reacting to the high price of electricity during the summer or to having an income that varies with the season?
A: No.
Q: Does she live where the winters are very cold, often below freezing?
A: Yes.

Q: During the winter, does she dry her laundry indoors, on racks, at home?

A: Yes.

Old-Time Digital

Q: Are all digital sound-playing devices powered by electricity?

A: No.

Q: Was the woman thinking of a digital sound device that was common soon after the turn of the century (1900)?

A: Yes.

Q: Could the device play music from a full orchestra?

A: No.

Safe from the Fire

Q: Did the house have any ladders or fire escapes?

A: No.

Q: Was the house split-level or otherwise built into a hill, so that the upper floor could be left without using the stairway?

A: No.

Q: Was the stairway used?

A: No.

Bad Directions

Q: Was there anything confusing or contradictory in Ethan's directions or the notes that he later made?

A: No.

Q: Did Ethan expect to be with his relatives until after nightfall?

A: Yes.

Q: Did Ethan live on Main Street?

A: Yes.

There Goes The Sun
Q: Does the sun ever really rise in the west or set in the east, as seen by a stationary observer on earth?
A: No.
Q: Was Edgar on an iceberg that had turned around during the night?
A: No.
Q: Could this incident happen only during a particular time of year?
A: Yes.

Trials of the Uninvited
Q: Was anyone upset with the kids' actions?
A: No.
Q: Did the kids complain?
A: No.
Q: Did they usually eat grass?
A: Yes.

Legally Castrated
Q: Is the surgery common?
A: Yes.
Q: Did a person other than the patient request and authorize the surgery for that particular patient?
A: Yes.
Q: Did the doctor have an MD or DO degree?
A: No.

Poker Assault
Q: When a dealer picks up face-up cards carefully and shuffles stiffly, is there reason to suspect cheating?

A: Yes.

Q: Is it important that more than one deck of cards was used?

A: Yes.

Q: Were the two decks identical?

A: No.

Too Heavy

Q: Did he under-report its weight?

A: No.

Q: Did he repack it?

A: Yes.

Q: If the machinery was reweighed when it reached its destination, then would it appear to be heavier than when shipped?

A: Yes.

She Kept Her Cool

Q: Were both Alexis and the sales person knowledgeable and truthful?

A: Yes.

Q: Did Alexis want two air conditioners only in case one broke?

A: No.

Q: When the weather is uncomfortably hot or humid, can the temperature and humidity be assumed to be similar to what they were when the weather was previously hot or humid?

A: No.

by Edward J. Harshman

He Won't Hear From Her

Q: Was he married, aware of something about to happen, planning to move away, or otherwise expecting to become unusually inaccessible or deliberately hard to reach?

A: No.

Q: Would he have liked to hear from Bertha?

A: Yes.

Q: He was not literally a "blind" date, in that he could see well; but did he have a perceptual difficulty?

A: Yes.

Brian Braggart and the Equator

Q: Is there a high mountain in Kenya crossed by the equator?

A: Yes.

Q: Can the sun pass directly overhead on the equator?

A: Yes.

Q: Does the sun pass directly overhead every day on the equator?

A: No.

The Debt Was Paid

Q: Could the debt have been paid when it first became due?

A: No.

Q: Was there a rational reason that the store owner did not pay the debt as soon as he had enough cash to do so?

A: Yes.

Q: Was the wholesaler the only creditor who had debt-collection trouble?

A: No.

Welcome, Slasher

Q: Were the boy and the policeman what they appeared to be and not, for example, actors for a movie?

A: Yes.

Q: Was the policeman honest?

A: Yes.

Q: Did the boy act in retaliation, perhaps to deter a criminal who could not be prosecuted by normal methods?

A: No.

Slippery Sidney Slipped Up

_Q:_ Had Sidney tried to sell the rented car by forging a title to it?

_A:_ No.

_Q:_ Did Sidney return the car intact and drivable, with no collision damage and no replacement of good major parts with inferior ones?

_A:_ Yes.

_Q:_ Was the fraud obvious to the rental-car company, but only after at least a month had passed?

_A:_ Yes.

Happy that She Cursed Him

_Q:_ Was he a masochist, who generally liked being unpleasantly treated?

_A:_ No.

_Q:_ Did the woman love him?

_A:_ Yes.

_Q:_ Did he believe that her words of anger were really directed at him?

_A:_ No.

The Unused Jacket

_Q:_ Were they both dressed in formal clothing?

_A:_ Yes.

_Q:_ Were they of European descent?

_A:_ No.

_Q:_ Was there a sidewalk on the street?

_A:_ No.

Contagious Carsickness?

_Q:_ Was there something wrong with the car?

_A:_ No.

Q: When Jan felt sick, were they all breathing fresh air?
A: Yes.
Q: Were they then outside of the car?
A: Yes.

The Late Train

Q: Does the lateness have anything to do with the train's having crossed from one time zone to another?

A: No.

Q: At the time Amanda got onto the train, did its crew expect it to become late before she got off it?

A: Yes.

Q: Could this incident, for this reason, happen only at a particular time of year?

A: Yes.

Exceptionally Vague

Q: Did Mary want part of the candidate's political platform to be obscured for any reason?

A: No.

Q: Was it part of a press release or an internal memorandum?

A: No.

Q: Did it consist of ten or fewer words?

A: Yes.

Giving Wayne the Boot

Q: Were the police officers honest and Wayne's neighbor not politically influential?

A: Yes.

A: Was it the same person who turned on the loud music and threw the boot through Wayne's window?

Q: Was the neighbor happy when the police arrived?

A: Yes.

The Empty Wrapper

Q: Was the incident an attempt to cheat the customer, or related to fraud in any context?

A: No.

Q: Did the woman who removed the wrapper from the cart know that the wrapper was empty?

A: Yes.

Q: Was the woman accompanied while she shopped?

A: Yes.

Not From the USA

Q: He was not from the USA, but would he necessarily speak English with a recognizably foreign accent?

A: No.

Q: Was he referring to dry non-USA land that was not an island?

A: Yes.

Q: Could the USA be reached by traveling less than 150 miles north, east, south, or west from one point in his home country?

A: Yes.

Ballpark Befuddlement

Q: Was the man unhappy with the results of the first two swings?

A: Yes.

Q: Did the final ball go over a fence?

A: No.

Q: Did the man run anywhere right after the third swing?

A: No.

The Debtor Paid

Q: Was Kingfist the actual creditor, not a collection agent for someone else?

A: Yes.

Q: Can a creditor use collection methods that a collection agent cannot?

A: Yes.

Q: Did Kingfist receive any of the money that was collected?

A: No.

A Sweet Problem

Q: Is the sugar swallowed?

A: No.

Q: Can any other common substance substitute for the sugar?

A: No.

Q: Under specified conditions, can the sugar be similarly used by people who are not diabetic?

A: Yes.

An Earful

Q: Did the veterinarian love animals and do all his treatment gently and humanely?

A: Yes.

Q: Did the cat have an injury or infection on its ear?

A: No.

Q: Was the cat someone's pet?

A: No.

Marketing Muddle
Q: Is the car a known model in the USA?
A: Yes.
Q: Would the name provoke concern if it were displayed, in advertising, only with ordinary letters (no stylistic changes)?
A: No.
Q: Is knowledge of a foreign alphabet important?
A: Yes.

Staged Roulette
Q: Could the skit be rewritten so that the roulette bet was concealed from the view of the audience, or removed entirely?
A: No.
Q: Could the roulette wheel be partially hidden?
A: No.
Q: Was gambling a significant problem in that town?
A: Yes.

His Last Nap
Q: If he dies within three hours, will he regain consciousness first?
A: No.
Q: Is he thinking rationally?
A: Yes.
Q: Does anyone nearby want him dead?
A: No.

The TV Obeyed

Q: Did Jake shout to operate a sound-sensitive switch or, while shouting, manually operate a remote-control device or an ordinary switch?

A: No.

Q: Did Jake see the television screen just before he shouted?

A: Yes.

Q: Prerecorded DVD's usually have their durations printed on their boxes. Is that fact significant?

A: Yes.

The Outside Line

Q: Did the call originate from within the hospital?

A: No.

Q: Was the call made by someone named Jones?

A: No.

Q: The caller was deceitful by asking for an outside line under false pretenses, true; but was there other evidence of a dishonorable lifestyle?

A: Yes.

Battery Badness
Q: Did Leroy, or anyone else in his presence, raise the hood at any time?
A: No.
Q: Would the bill that he paid have been reasonable if a new battery had in fact been installed?
A: Yes.
Q: Is it important that he had a modern sound system?
A: Yes.

Hats Off To You
Q: Was the boy genuinely sorry about having leaned out the window?
A: Yes.
Q: Did he disobey his father after he got his hat back?
A: No.
Q: Nevertheless, was his behavior disconcerting?
A: Yes.

The Marble
Q: Did the electrician usually use a marble at work?
A: No.
Q: Had he forgotten something?
A: Yes.
Q: Did he need it for the glass, which does not conduct electricity?
A: No.

Inefficient Elevators
Q: Is Joe thinking of elevators that really exist, other than perhaps as rare curiosities?

A: No.

Q: Could they be built now?

A: Yes.

Q: When people get on an elevator, do they usually know where they intend to get off it?

A: Yes.

Forgiven

Q: Was the photocopying for research in an academic setting, part of a court case under government control, or otherwise explicitly protected by law?

A: No.

Q: Due to Mary's action, were thousands of copies printed and distributed?

A: Yes.

Q: Was the book a popular bestseller when she photocopied the book?

A: No.

Bought and Paid For

Q: Must I await alterations or some other part of the manufacturing process, or prepare my home for it?

A: No.

Q: Do I owe the store money for a previous purchase, or in any context whatever?

A: No.

Q: Is the time of year important?

A: Yes.

Dim-Wits

Q: Did a mischievous person keep turning them off?

A: No.

Q: Did lights in other classrooms, not used for the

important test, go off too?

A: No.

Q: Was there a design goof?

A: Yes.

Artistic Appreciation

Q: Was the artist famous, critically renowned, or dead when the rich man bought the painting?

A: No.

Q: When the rich man changed his mind about the painting, was he happy?

A: No.

Q: Was the statement that the signed important?

A: Yes.

Easy as Pi

Q: Is the number 3.14159 relevant?

A: No.

Q: If posters are taped onto walls, do they fall down from time to time?

A: Yes.

Q: If tape gives way at one corner but not the others, can a poster rip?

A: Yes.

Shot Down

Q: Was he shot down from the air?

A: Yes.

Q: Did he fly very fast?

A: Yes.

Q: Did he pay close attention to his flight path?

A: No.

Underpopulation?

Q: Are they readily available, if you look them up?

A: Yes.

Q: Are they commonly taught in schools nowadays?

A: No.

Q: Do they show a steady or decreasing population?

A: No.

Not a Purse Snatcher

Q: Did he open the purse?

A: No.

Q: Would he mind encountering its owner?

A: No.

Q: Did the policeman remember him, perhaps from a prior arrest?

A: No.

Ate His Words

Q: Is it significant that she was already in the living room and holding a knife when he arrived?

A: Yes.

Q: If she had not threatened him with the knife, might he have shown that the vacuum cleaner worked?

A: No.

Q: Is this incident more likely at noon than, for example, at 8:00 PM?

A: Yes.

Cool Car and the Wire

Q: Was Hiram acting in good faith?

A: Yes.

Q: Did Hiram expect a lot of snow in that part of the country?

A: Yes.

Q: Would the snow risk damaging part of the car unless that particular wire was cut?

A: Yes.

Gunpoint

Q: Was Kevin, or someone who looked like him or who drove a similar car, wanted for a previous crime?

A: No.

Q: Did Kevin intend to resist the policeman?

A: No.

Q: Did the policeman act rationally and without intent to harass?

A: Yes.

He Wanted the Copy

Q: Was the original videotape easily available?

A: No.

Q: Did the man need special equipment to copy the videotape?

A: Yes.

Q: Would the man have been able to sell the videotape at one of the video stores?

A: No.

One Bad Check

Q: Was Sam's account closed, impounded, or otherwise restricted from normal check-paying activity?

A: No.

Q: Had the particular check that Sam wrote, or the checkbook from which he took it, been previously reported lost or stolen?

A: No.

Q: Did Sam do anything unusual when he wrote the check?

A: Yes.

Burning Down the House

Q: Was he being paid for the fire, for example by a film crew making a movie?

A: No.

Q: Was he interested in clearing the site so that it could be used for a new building or other structure?

A: No.

Q: Did the house contain a living or dead person or any evidence of a crime that the man wanted to destroy?

A: No.

Do Away with Diamonds

Q: Was the second store another jewelry store?

A: No.

Q: Did the stores compete against each other?

A: No.

Q: Is the phrase "sound recommendation," instead of "good advice," a hint?

A: Yes.

The Trained Athlete Loses

Q: Did George's weak heart keep him from running fast?

A: Yes.

Q: Was Frank exceptionally good at clearing hurdles?

A: Yes.

Q: Did George expect to beat Frank?

A: Yes.

Strange Bedroom

Q: Did he drive, or did someone else drive him, back to his home?

A: No.

Q: Did Bill have a second home with a bedroom identical to his first home?

A: No.

Q: Was there something distinctive about his home?

A: Yes.

The Stubborn Door

Q: Did the boy first knock on the door, ring a bell, or otherwise request help from someone on the other side of the door?

A: No.

Q: Other than the lock to which the boy had a key and the latch that was operated by the door knob, did anything prevent the door from opening?

A: No.

Q: Did everything on or attached to the door work properly?

A: Yes.

He Hated Bad Attitudes

Q: Was the government form a false report or one that was intended to allow a tax evader or other criminal to be easily identified or prosecuted?

A: No.

Q: Did Percy forge anything, write a document in the name of someone else, or break any law?

A: No.

Q: Was Percy rich?

A: Yes.

Give Them a Hand

Q: Was Bill in any apparent or real danger from the tall figure?

A: No.

Q: Did Charlie understand what Bill was asking for (no, it wasn't applause)?

A: Yes.

Q: Did Charlie give Bill what he asked for, literally?

A: Yes.

She Paid Easily

Q: Was it more convenient for Cecily to pay the toll?

A: Yes.

Q: Was there anything wrong with any door or window of the car, such as a jammed window next to Cooper?

A: No.

Q: Were Cooper and Cecily both in the front seat of the car?

A: Yes.

The Roundabout Taxi Route

Q: Was she waiting for a second person to join her in the taxi?

A: No.

Q: Were taxis very scarce then, for example during a change of shift or a bad rainstorm?

A: Yes.

Q: Did a specific event prevent her from entering the taxi and having the driver take her directly to her destination?

A: Yes.

Another Cold Fire

Q: Was the fire safely contained in the fireplace, as before?

A: Yes.

Q: Was the air in the house approximately the same temperature as that of outside air earlier in the day?

A: Yes.

Q: Did the fire burn vigorously and induce a strong draft up the chimney?

A: Yes.

No Place for Women

Q: Does it have to do with the attitudes of the sales staff or a fault in the store's floor plan (cramped dressing rooms, etc.)?

A: No.

Q: Does it have to do with any particular article of clothing?

A: No.

Q: Is the placement of the merchandise needlessly inconvenient?

A: Yes.

The Mail Must Go Through

Q: Were the stake, chain, and collar able to restrain the dog and properly installed and fastened for that purpose?

A: Yes.

Q: Was anyone or anything else present, such as another, unrestrained, dog?

A: No.

Q: Could the dog get to the front door?

A: Yes.

Short Swing
Q: Can Ned's bat box hold at least a dozen bats?
A: Yes.
Q: Does it have a lid that opens and closes?
A: No.
Q: Is it designed to be moved from place to place?
A: No.

He Held His Liquor
Q: Did Andy drink from his bottle, not pour beer on the floor or into a hidden container?
A: Yes.
Q: Did Andy have an unusual tolerance for alcohol?
A: No.
Q: When Andy ordered from the bartender, did he order two beers?
A: No.

Tiresome Questions
Q: Did Marla ask for any information about the truck or its tire size?
A: No.
Q: Was the new truck ever driven on an unpaved surface?
A: Yes.
Q: Was Carla's driveway paved?
A: No.

No Sale

Q: Was there something with the telephone, any telephone wiring, or the number that the solicitor dialed?

A: No.

Q: Was the solution to the problem known to the person whose number was dialed?

A: Yes.

Q: Could the person whose number was dialed have only one telephone number in the household or office?

A: No.

Sprayed at the Lawn Again

Q: Had anyone reset the timer?

A: No.

Q: Did Henry return from work early?

A: No.

Q: If Henry looked around carefully inside his house, then could he have figured out what went wrong?

A: Yes.

Can't Turn It Off!

Q: Was the lamp completely ordinary, with a simple on-off switch (not a dimmer switch), and not battery-powered?

A: Yes.

Q: Was light coming from the bulb of the lamp?

A: Yes.

Q: Was the light the same as it usually was, equally bright?

A: No.

You Have To Stop

Q: Is the sign in the path of motor vehicles and not, for example, on the center island of a divided highway?

A: Yes.

Q: After stopping at the sign and proceeding, would a driver always expect to encounter an intersection?

A: No.

Q: Is the sign on a well-traveled road, one that carries at least one car per hour during the day?

A: No.

Unsolved Robbery

Q: Did the police have any information about the robbery that could lead to an arrest?

A: No.

Q: Did the second man have information that the police did not?

A: Yes.

Q: Is the location of the conversation important?

A: Yes.

Unexplained Theft

Q: Did the burglar steal the small objects?

A: Yes.

Q: After tripping the alarm and running away, did the burglar return to steal anything?

A: No.

Q: Would a careful examination of the house reveal what had happened?

A: Yes.

Unusual Office Buildings

Q: Does it have anything to do with not having a traffic light on each corner, unlike most New York City intersections that have traffic lights?

A: No.

Q: Do tall and prestigious buildings have elevators?

A: Yes.

Q: Are the elevators equipped with safety bumpers in case, due to mechanical problems, they descend dangerously fast?

A: Yes.

Brian Braggart's Space Story

Q: Could sufficiently intelligent beings study English from radio and television transmissions?

A: Yes.

Q: Could the moonmen have access to their metabolic equivalents of food, water, and oxygen?

A: Yes.

Q: On the distant moon, with its limited gravity, can people or other beings talk to each other and rely on ordinary sound waves through an atmosphere?

A: No.

The Investment Scam

Q: Was the fund manager a Ponzi scam artist, who deliberately defrauded the investors?

A: Yes.

Q: Did anyone help him?

A: Yes.

Q: Did anyone look for him?

A: No.

Honest Ivan

Q: Had Ivan wanted to use the car for at least two months, including driving back to Florida for a vacation with his family?

A: Yes.

Q: Did Ivan cause the collision that damaged the car or contribute to it in any way?

A: No.

Q: Had Ivan creatively reacted to the difference between auto insurance rates in Florida and those in Washington, D.C., where he lived?

A: Yes.

Making the Grade

Q: Did Nell want a good grade on the course, so that she was planning to have her paper properly written and handed in on or before the deadline?

A: Yes.

Q: Did she have any reason to doubt the receptionist?

A: No.

Q: Is her straight-A average, which suggests good study habits, significant?

A: Yes.

A Crying Problem

Q: Did Sandra or her parents-in-law mention any painful subjects or otherwise depart from casual or encouraging conversation?

A: No.

Q: When her husband's parents said that they were happy for the telephone call, were they telling the truth?

A: Yes.

Q: Did Sandra explain her motive for making the call?

A: No.

Walked On The Other Street

Q: Were there any construction sites, fenced-in parks, early morning store deliveries, or other variations from ordinary straight city blocks that can be walked uneventfully?

A: No.

Q: Did every intersection have a traffic light?

A: Yes.

Q: Were the two streets both two-way streets?

A: No.

Easy Repair
Q: Did he push his car to the top of a ramp, jump in, and start the car by shifting into gear and removing his foot from the clutch?
A: No.
Q: Before arriving at his car, did he expect none of the lights to work?
A: Yes.
Q: Was the battery dead?
A: No.

The Hostile Voter
Q: Had Charlie decided whom to vote for before receiving the call?
A: No.

Q: Did he think that the volunteer told the truth?
A: Yes.
Q: Did he notice an inconsistency in what the volunteer said that alerted him to a problem?
A: Yes.

More Problems with Personnel
Q: Did the colleague and the new person conspire to defraud Raymond's company?
A: No.
Q: Was the colleague thoroughly honest?
A: Yes.
Q: Although the reference-checking turned up no evidence of a problem, was the newly hired person honest?
A: No.

Racing the Drawbridge
Q: Was Clarence sensible?
A: Yes.
Q: Did he turn away or stop?
A: No.
Q: If the drawbridge had been closed, then would Clarence have approached the bridge?
A: No.

I've Got Your Number
Q: Did Kingfist obtain the telephone number by asking confederates at the telephone company or from Sam's friends?
A: No.
Q: Did he enter the house?
A: No.

Q: Is the fact that the fence around the house was climbable significant?

A: Yes.

Magazine Subscriptions

Q: Could the need anticipated by those who save them be satisfied by blank paper of similar size and shape?

A: No.

Q: Are they used to cause troublesome paperwork by writing someone else's name on them and then mailing them?

A: No.

Q: Is their reply-paid status very important, more so than for an ordinary post card?

A: Yes.

Appendicitis

Q: Does removing the appendix make appendicitis permanently impossible?

A: Yes.

Q: Did the physician confuse Zeke with someone else or otherwise remember incorrectly?

A: No.

Q: When the physician responded to the call and saw Bill's wife, did he instantly consider appendicitis even before examining her?

A: Yes.

Not a Trusted Doctor

Q: Are apparent cures for senility likely to be fraudulent?

A: Yes.

Q: Did Cassandra have any reason to believe the diploma to be counterfeit, borrowed, or stolen?

A: No.

Q: Did the boyfriend know very much about Cassandra's past?

A: No.

Strange Sounds

Q: Are the sounds and pictures out of sync, as when dubbed words on a foreign-language movie don't match the lips of those who speak?

A: No.

Q: Can mistimed sounds—too early or too late—give it away?

A: No.

Q: Are some sounds inappropriately absent?

A: Yes.

Too Much Money

Q: Had the investor any reason to suspect shady financing, a conflict of interest, fraud, or anything even remotely dishonest?

A: No.

Q: Would the investor, who would be a limited partner, give up control of the investment if someone else invested a bigger amount of money than he did?

A: No.

Q: The investor was deterred by some money. Was that money already invested in the company or intended to be invested in it later?

A: No.

All Wet

Q: Is your life in immediate danger?

A: No.

Q: From where you are, can you see anyone?

A: No.

Q: If you had a hair dryer, could you use it instead of the shampoo bottle?

A: Yes.

A Devil of a Number

Q: Did she have any religious objections or fear crank calls from devil-worshipers or other people with a special interest in 666?

A: No.

Q: Did she recognize the phone number as formerly belonging to a particular person or organization?

A: No.

Q: Did she want to avoid nuisance calls in general?

A: Yes.

Dreaded Doorbell
Q: Is her occupation significant?
A: Yes.
Q: Was anyone other than the unwelcome children likely to ring their doorbell?
A: No.
Q: Was there any violence?
A: No.

Flour and Cement
Q: Is the intent to make a building material?
A: No.
Q: Does the mixture taste good?
A: No.
Q: Nevertheless, might it be eaten?
A: Yes.

Wooden Walls, Rubber Checks
Q: When the checks bounce, does he immediately make good the loss with cash, including bank charges?
A: Yes.
Q: When he pays for lumber with a check, does he sometimes pay additional with cash, too?
A: Yes.
Q: Though he won't cheat the lumberyard, is he totally honest?
A: No.

by Edward J. Harshman

Airplane in Flight

Q: Do airplanes move their wings up and down as a way to apply forward and upward force?

A: No.

Q: Does the answer have anything directly to do with storms or rough weather?

A: No.

Q: Can you sometimes see the wings go up and down if you are a passenger in a large airplane?

A: Yes.

The Unwelcome Gift

Q: Was Rudolph totally rational?

A: Yes.

Q: Was Fritz his son?
A: No.
Q: Is child labor involved?
A: No.

Natural Crescents

Q: Is it common?
A: No.
Q: Are the crescents all oriented the same way, and not having their points in random directions?
A: Yes.
Q: Is direct sunlight needed?
A: Yes.

Work On This

Q: Does it involve unions and labor laws?
A: No.
Q: Does it involve extortion, corruption, or active government involvement?
A: No.
Q: If you consider an ordinary well-to-do USA household of 1900 and compare it to one of 2000, will the trend be obvious?
A: Yes.

Lights Out!

Q: Was darkness normally necessary for this particular operation?
A: No.
Q: Was there an equipment malfunction, such as sparks in a lamp or a leak of flammable anesthetic?
A: No.
Q: Nevertheless, did the surgeon perceive an

unexpected threat to the patient and act rationally to correct it?

A: Yes.

Cool Car, Clean Windshield

Q: Was it a device commonly found in auto supply stores?

A: No.

Q: Was it intended for other uses?

A: Yes.

Q: Could Jenny, who did not have a driver's license, be expected to be more familiar with the device than are most drivers?

A: Yes.

Keys Locked In

Q: After he did so, were the keys visible through the car window?

A: No.

Q: Did Elmer have alternative transportation available?

A: Yes.

Q: Did Elmer own the car?

A: No.

Burning Down the Building

Q: Did anyone bribe the landlord?

A: No.

Q: Did the fire destroy evidence of a crime?

A: No.

Q: Did a tenant set the fire, perhaps out of anger?

A: No.

It's Not a Gamble, Son!

Q: Was the casino dishonest or involved in any scheme as a participant or as a victim?

A: No.

Q: Did the son become rich through his actions at the casino?

A: Yes.

Q: Was something illegal going on?

A: Yes.

Shoot That Eagle!

Q: Were the men looking for eagles?

A: Yes.

Q: Did they hope to shoot one?

A: Yes.

Q: Did the eagle live after being shot?

A: Yes.

Two Copies, Not One

Q: Did she get two copies, not counting the original?

A: Yes.

Q: Were the copies the same size as the original, without reduction?

A: Yes.

Q: Were the copies identical to the original?

A: No.

The Clock was Right

Q: Is their occupation important?

A: Yes.

Q: Did the clock have a conventional face, with an hour hand and a minute hand?

A: No.

Q: Were they heavily concentrating on binary-number (machine-language) programming?

A: Yes.

Child Driver

Q: Did the child hold the real steering wheel, not that of a toy?

A: Yes.

Q: Did the mother have access to a second set of controls, like those of driver's-education cars?

A: No.

Q: Was the car's engine running?

A: No.

Loves Being Stranded

Q: Did Herbert know why the car stalled and make a correct inference?

A: Yes.

Q: Was the car in heavy traffic, moving rapidly on a highway, or otherwise capable of causing an accident because it stalled?

A: No.

Q: Did Herbert expect to start the car easily and drive away?

A: Yes.

Dangerous Safety Glass

Q: Is the glass accessible to people?

A: Yes.

Q: Is the chemical composition other than that pertaining to its shatterability important, for example as a refractive prism or an ultraviolet-permitting lens?

A: No.

Q: Is the ease of shattering the glass important?

A: Yes.

Afraid of the Bar

Q: Was she wanted for a crime she had previously committed?

A: No.

Q: Would she be committing a crime, but less likely to be arrested for it, if she was 64 years old instead of only 24?

A: Yes.

Q: If she wanted to, could she have gone to her car, returned, and then entered the bar with Bill legally?

A: Yes.

Where's the Sunshine?

Q: Are there places in which the sun is due south at noon standard time?

A: Yes.

Q: Is the sun always due south, slightly west of due south, or slightly east of due south at noon standard time (continental USA)?

A: Yes.

Q: If you moved an accurate sundial east or west, keeping it in the same latitude and the same time zone and carefully not rotating it, would it become inaccurate?

A: Yes.

The Switch of Mastery

Q: Was the mother telling the truth?

A: Yes.

Q: Were there other buildings within a half-mile or so?

A: No.

Q: Was the approximate time of day important?

A: Yes.

Picking Good Apples

Q: Did they shake or climb the tree?

A: No.

Q: Did they prop a fallen branch against a branch of the tree and shake the branch?

A: No.

Q: Would ripe apples fall from the tree after only a minor disturbance?

A: Yes.

Pleased With Pork

Q: Would an observant Jew eat pork?

A: No.

Q: Did the restaurant represent itself as kosher?

A: No.

Q: When the man entered the restaurant, did he expect to eat there?

A: No.

Hazard In The Code

Q: Can the second hazard be prevented without violating the code?

A: Yes.

Q: Is the hazard commonly observed in residential areas?

A: Yes.

Q: Is it a hazard to able-bodied adults?

A: No.

No Help

Q: Could the other man walk normally, in that he had no leg injury?

A: Yes.

Q: Were his mental status and his sense of direction impaired in any way?

A: No.

Q: If he had walked away and sought help, by trying to follow a well-marked trail for two miles, then would he have been likely to find it?

A: No.

Death in the Pool

Q: Was the pool properly filled with water?

A: Yes.

Q: Did the swimmer tie a weight to himself or otherwise try to commit suicide?

A: No.

Q: Other than water, was the pool empty?

A: No.

Her Good Message

Q: Did she act in his best interest?

A: Yes.

Q: Did he forget something important?

A: Yes.

Q: Could the client have realistically expected the boss to have been in the office?

A: No.

Destructive But Useful

Q: Is the scientist well-meaning and rational, not intending to threaten or to destroy?

A: Yes.

Q: Can it, if properly handled, perhaps eventually reduce or postpone a threat to the earth?

A: Yes.

Q: Is the threat one that the scientific world, and informed lay people, can foresee now?

A: Yes.

Brian Braggart and the Ant

Q: Are there two different reasons why an ant cannot be as large as a person?

A: Yes.

Q: Do ants breathe air into lungs, like people?

A: No.

Q: If an ant were enlarged to the size of a person, then would its strength/weight change adversely?

A: Yes.

The Counterfeit Money

Q: Was the man angry with the clerk?

A: Yes.

Q: Did the man attempt to buy anything with his counterfeit bills, exchange them, or give them away?

A: No.

Q: Did the man originally possess the counterfeit bills that the clerk tried to pass?

A: Yes.

Robbing the Bank

Q: Was the tip-off about the paychecks correct?

A: Yes.

Q: Did the bank have more cash on hand then than usual?

A: Yes.

Q: Did the robbers obtain any cash?

A: No.

He Wasn't Parking

Q: Was Vick a stunt man or other actor for a movie?

A: No.

Q: Did Vick intend to get out of his car while it was still moving?

A: No.

Q: Was something wrong with the car?

A: Yes.

She Arrived On Time

Q: Could Carol have driven from home to the coffee house, in two minutes, at less than a hundred miles per hour?

A: No.

Q: Did she use special or exotic transportation, such as a helicopter?

A: No.

Q: Did Daryl dial her home telephone number correctly and reach her by doing so?

A: Yes.

Problems with Personnel

Q: Had the friend seen the advertisement?

A: Yes.

Q: Had the friend followed its instructions and applied for the position?

A: Yes.

Q: Did the personnel department exactly follow the instructions that Raymond had given?

A: Yes.

Recycled Salt

Q: Are we talking about ordinary table salt, sodium chloride, that is used in food (not an industrial application, for example)?

A: Yes.

Q: Is the salt eaten?

A: Yes.

Q: Is the same salt eaten twice?

A: Yes.

Dots on the I's
Q: Is a small I with a dot over it commonly seen?
A: No.
Q: If Timmy had written his second statement, instead of spoken it, then would that part of the puzzle be easy?
A: Yes.
Q: Was Timmy talking about the same thing that Jimmy mentioned earlier?
A: No.

She Was In The Hospital
Q: Did Alan and his wife genuinely love each other?
A: Yes.
Q: Nevertheless, was Alan pleased with the news?
A: Yes.
Q: Would his wife have been happy if Alan had tried to visit her when she left the operating room?
A: No.

Long Walk for the Disabled
Q: Did he park farther so that he could walk more, for the exercise?
A: No.
Q: Did he park farther because he needed to drive another kind of vehicle, perhaps giving up an easily parked bicycle or motorcycle and driving a car instead?
A: No.
Q: Did he have a car and have to alter it because of his injury?
A: Yes.

Secret Business

Q: Did they use scramblers because they suspected that their telephones were tapped?

A: Yes.

Q: In this particular context, would the secure scramblers, which were compatible with each other, have been as useful as the ones that they actually used?

A: No.

Q: Did the men discuss all of their plans on the telephone?

A: No.

A Prayer for Escape

Q: Does the answer involve prayer or divine intervention?

A: No.

Q: If you cannot escape, are you certain to die because of the crisis?

A: No.

Q: Is at least one other person present?

A: Yes.

A Phony Call

Q: Had they dialed carelessly?

A: Yes.

Q: Was the telephone company at fault?

A: No.

Q: Were they the only people who were bothered by misdialed calls?

A: No.

Boat-Bashing

Q: Did the purchaser plan to destroy more than one boat?

A: Yes.

Q: When Brandon sold his motorboat, was it an ordinary sale at a fair value with no conditions, special relations between buyer and seller, coercion, etc.?

A: Yes.

Q: Did Brandon pay more than twenty dollars to watch his boat get wrecked?

A: No.

Paper Profits

Q: Is his reasoning rational?

A: Yes.

Q: Does he buy recyclable paper and look for documents that have not been shredded?

A: No.

Q: Do the spies supply secret information about many different kinds of companies?

A: Yes.

Canned

Q: Was he going to take the cans home?

A: No.

Q: Did he intend to disobey the housemaster?

A: No.

Q: Would he return the cans to the recycle bin before going home?

A: Yes.

Upside-Down Gravity

Q: Does the answer have anything to do with astronauts, space travel, or moving faster than the speed of gravity?

A: No.

Q: Was the stone perfectly natural and genuine?

A: Yes.

Q: When the incident occurred, could Judy and Trudy converse by speaking normally?

A: No.

Suitcase Stress

Q: Did he correctly believe Pam had done something harmful as she packed his suitcase?

A: Yes.

Q: Did he fear the absence of business papers or necessary supplies?

A: No.

Q: Did he arrive at the airport with time to spare?

A: Yes.

Costly Borrowing

Q: Could it be carried with one hand?

A: Yes.

Q: Did Tim let Jim borrow it?

A: No.

Q: Could it be bought at a store?

A: No.

Not Phoning for Directions

Q: Did she look up her sister's address and/or telephone number?

A: No.

Q: Did she make any telephone calls?

A: No.

Q: Did she know how to drive to every place that she looked up?

A: Yes.

Hates to Break Windows

Q: Was Tina acting sensibly?

A: Yes.

Q: Could she have picked up a chair and smashed the window?

A: Yes.

Q: Was Tina at great risk of smoke inhalation because of the smoke in the room?

A: Yes.

The Five-State Golf Drive

Q: Is a specific part of the country required, like that of the four-state solution?

A: No.

Q: Is a specific generic place, as opposed to a particular nameable or unique place, required?

A: Yes.

Q: Is a particular time or event needed?

A: Yes.

No Side Effects

Q: Do most physicians recommend them?

A: No.

Q: Can they be swallowed easily?

A: No.

Q: Are they available over the counter (no prescription needed) and legal?

A: Yes.

Truckers Went Separate Ways

Q: Did the highway have restrooms, places to eat, and fuel stations, so that Hank and Frank could stop together for ordinary needs?

A: Yes.

Q: Did Hank, but not Frank, expect to proceed directly along the highway to their final destination?

A: Yes.

Q: When Frank decided not to proceed directly on the highway, did he and Hank learn why not at the same time?

A: Yes.

The Brighter Bulb

Q: Does the remaining 100-watt bulb glow exactly as brightly as before?

A: No.

Q: Does the current through the 100-watt bulb exactly equal the current through the 25-watt bulb?

A: Yes.

Q: Is the voltage difference between the two wires that supply power to the 25-watt bulb less than the voltage difference between the wires that supply power to the 100-watt bulb?

A: No.

Hold Still!

Q: Was the flash bright for only a very short time, perhaps a hundredth of a second?

A: Yes.
Q: Did it illuminate the background?
A: No.
Q: Was the background very dimly lit?
A: Yes.

A Shocking Problem

Q: Did Louie or Lucy, while making connections with the ends of the wire, accidentally connect the two conductors together, perhaps by overlooking a loose strand or two?
A: No.
Q: Did Louie put a polarized plug on the wire, so that the plug could fit into an outlet in only one way?
A: No.
Q: Did Louie omit something important when he instructed Lucy?
A: Yes.

Towing the Car

Q: Is it because the car, though legally parked, was crashed into and pushed into traffic?
A: No.
Q: Is it because the car is parked on a street and the street suddenly needs emergency repairs?
A: No.
Q: Does the owner give permission for the car to be towed?
A: Yes.

Brian Braggart in Japan

Q: Were the slides, including the factory one, taken in Japan?

A: Yes.

Q: Did Brian give himself away with any false statements?

A: No.

Q: Did any slide show recognizable readable signs or writing in our 26-letter alphabet?

A: No.

Caught in the Act

Q: Was he really a pickpocket?

A: Yes.

Q: Did he want to be arrested?

A: No.

Q: Did he act rationally?

A: Yes.

Safe Smashup

Q: Was the car controlled by a radio-operated device, as for a movie?

A: No.

Q: Was the car deliberately damaged?

A: No.

Q: Did the car catch fire after its fuel line burst?

A: No.

Secret Fuel

Q: Was the gasoline adulterated, the wrong octane rating, or otherwise intended to make the car run poorly?

A: No.

Q: Did the neighbor know of Marvin's activities?

A: No.

Q: Was the car covered by a warranty?

A: Yes.

Hurried Funeral?

Q: Was he transported eastward across the International Date Line or westward more rapidly than one time zone per hour?

A: No.

Q: Two days before his death, did he expect to die when he did?

A: No.

Q: Was he buried in a cemetery?

A: No.

This Burglar Got In

Q: Did the man open the front door from inside and let the burglar in willingly, perhaps because the burglar was a friend?

A: No.

Q: Were there valuable objects in the house?

A: Yes.

Q: Did the burglar intend to steal the valuable objects and remove them from the house?

A: No.

She Never Fixed Him Up

Q: Was Mitch genuinely interested in a blind date?

A: Yes.

Q: Did he trust Anna's judgment?

A: Yes.

Q: Was Mitch transferred or reassigned to a kind of work in which a social life would be unconventional or impossible?

A: No.

It's a Dog's Life

Q: Was the healthy-looking dog less than five years old and truly healthy and uninjured?

A: Yes.

Q: Did both dogs have the same owner?

A: Yes.

Q: If not for its serious injuries, would the puppy be expected to live for more than one month?

A: No.

Disability

Q: Had anyone else, perhaps in the disability office, committed fraud on his behalf?

A: No.

Q: Was the disability office, or any branch of any government, at fault, so that the man was receiving payment for injury liability and not just for being disabled?

A: No.

Q: Though he could not do his former work, could he work in some other way?

A: Yes.

Calisthenics for Neighbors

Q: Is there any direct threat to life, or of major injury?

A: No.

Q: Is it a medical emergency, such as a seizure or a psychotic incident?

A: No.

Q: Would a badminton racquet be both useful and, incidentally, funny?

A: Yes.

The Misleading Telephone Message

Q: Did the message sound exactly like a telephone-company number-change message except that both numbers on it were the same?

A: Yes.

Q: Did the store owner expect that message to be delivered to possible customers?

A: No.

Q: Was the message intended to confuse and frustrate?

A: Yes.

The Plumber's Pressure

Q: Was his occupation relevant?

A: Yes.

Q: Was his reasoning correct?

A: Yes.

Q: Did he have another common ailment?

A: Yes.

Ouch!

Q: Is your life in danger?

A: Yes.

Q: Would withstanding the pain in silence worsen the situation?

A: Yes.

Q: Is the pain deliberately inflicted?

A: Yes.

The Ice Water

Q: Was he suffering from heatstroke or a similar condition?

A: No.

Q: Was his need for ice water recognized and predictable for anyone doing what Richard did?
A: Yes.
Q: Was the ice water in a glass or pitcher?
A: No.

Blouse Befuddlement

Q: Was Christina rich, but unwilling to waste money?
A: Yes.
Q: Did she buy clothes intending them to last a long time?
A: Yes.
Q: Did her blouse have lace frills or other obviously feminine characteristics?
A: No.

Smash and Destroy

Q: Could the instructions of the activists be followed completely legally?
A: Yes.
Q: Was the intent to recruit martyrs or otherwise make a political statement?
A: No.
Q: Other than the people directly involved with the incident, would there be any obvious consequences?
A: No.

The Devil and Idol Hands

Q: Is it mentioned in the Bible?
A: No.
Q: Does it endanger people or cause a disturbance?
A: No.
Q: Does it upset people for exactly one reason?

A: No.

Toll Booth and Long Line

Q: Was Conrad interested in delaying his arrival at his destination, perhaps because he was going to a family gathering and disliked the people there?

A: No.

Q: Did Conrad see the shorter line and know he could have entered it, but deliberately choose the longer line?

A: Yes.

Q: Did Conrad choose the longer line because it was long, and not because it was nearest an exit that was directly beyond the toll booths?

A: Yes.

Rx Lead Poisoning

Q: Would lead poisoning, the only foreseen consequence of eating lead-based paint, have helped treat the ailment?

A: No.

Q: If not for the fact that the patient was covered by medical insurance, would there be any reason for the doctor's strange suggestion?

A: No.

Q: Did the doctor intend to treat the lead poisoning?

A: Yes.

Her Own Nasty Letter

Q: Did she mail it to herself at work?

A: No.

Q: Did she expect a spouse or other roommate to see it and comment on it?

A: No.

Q: Would she do something further with it when she received it in the mail?

A: Yes.

Don't Bug Us

Q: Is there any use of fraudulent documents, smuggling, political favoritism, etc.?

A: No.

Q: Do the insecticides drift in on trade winds or other air currents from Mexico or Canada?

A: No.

Q: Does the answer involve a special exemption for at-home production, like that for ethyl alcohol?

A: No.

Toll Booth and Exact Change

Q: Did Conrad pay the toll by throwing the exact amount, in coins other than pennies, into the exact-change basket?

A: Yes.

Q: Were any coins bent, foreign, or counterfeit?

A: No.

Q: Was Conrad driving a truck or towing a trailer, in which case he would not have been allowed to use the exact-change lane?

A: No.

Solutions

The Teacher Hit Mary
The teacher did not intend to punish Mary by hitting her; standing in the corner was the only intended penalty. But a hornet had flown into the classroom and landed on Mary's arm; the teacher wanted to swat it and did so. Everyone agreed that the teacher's blow hurt less than a hornet's sting would have hurt.

Money in the Mailbox
The man was being approached by probable muggers, and he turned a corner so that they could not see him briefly. He put most of his money into a mailbox hoping that the muggers would have the satisfaction of taking all of his remaining money and be content. He then planned to ask the postmaster for his money back from the mailbox, where he considered it safer than on his person. He may have also known that, if the muggers broke into the mailbox, then they would be committing a federal crime and may not have wished to do so.

The Witnessed Break-In
The man and the officer were husband and wife, and they accidentally locked themselves out of their own house.

Shoot That Eagle!
The men carried rifles because of wildcats in the area, but they also carried cameras with tripods and telephoto lenses. Seeking a good local photograph of a bald eagle, which would be used by a political movement opposing their killing by wind turbines, they were happy to get one.

by Edward J. Harshman

No Side Effects

Prominent house numbers. Not only can an ambulance driver find your house more quickly, in case of a heart attack, but also a fire engine driver can find and rescue you quickly in case of fire.

The Nine-Penny Ruler

Nine pennies weigh about an ounce. Lillian put a pencil under the midpoint of a ruler and noted that an envelope on one end of the ruler was not heavy enough to hold it steady as she put the nine pennies on the other end of the ruler. Therefore the envelope weighed less than an ounce, and only one standard first-class postage stamp was necessary.

I Is Good At Grammar

She said, "I is a vowel." "I is the ninth letter of the alphabet" or a similar reference to the letter I is also a correct answer.

Full Speed Ahead

The man, driving at night, saw the glow of the yellow lights pointing toward the intersecting road and knew that the red light pointed toward him would change in a few seconds. The yellow showed clearly on the sunshields around the green-light lenses. He was sufficiently far from the intersection that he could accelerate and still not reach it before the light turned green for him.

Snow on the Windshield

Melanie removed the snow from the rear window of her car and backed it into the driveway, a short distance away. She would have otherwise had to turn her car around and clean not only the rear window but also the windshield.

Safe Landing

The tree had been recently uprooted by a tornado and lay sideways on the ground. The top was only about ten feet from the ground, and Vick hung from it before jumping.

Perfectly Efficient
A heater.

Dangerous Safety Glass
The glass covers emergency switches or equipment, such as a fire extinguisher, and is intended to be broken easily when necessary.

The Length of a Year
The answer is 366¼. A 24-hour day measures the position of the earth relative to the sun: 24 hours are needed from noon (the sun is highest in the sky) to noon the next day. This time interval is a solar day. A sidereal day, 23 hours 56 minutes, is how long it takes for the earth to rotate completely as viewed from a point outside the solar system. It is not the same as a solar day, because the earth moves slightly around the sun during a day. Our ordinary calendar shows that, to a good approximation (which, here, is considered exact), a year is 365¼ solar days. There are 60 x 24 = 1440 minutes per solar day. A year, therefore, contains 365¼ x 1440 =

525,960 minutes. Dividing 525,960 minutes per year by 1436, the number of minutes in a sidereal day, proves that there are 525,960 / 1436, or approximately 366¼, sidereal days per year. Alternatively, put a dime and a quarter on a table. Move the dime in one circle around the quarter, without rotating the dime. From your viewpoint, the dime will not rotate. From the viewpoint of the quarter, the dime will rotate once: the nearest point on the dime will vary so as to form a complete circle around the dime. (If you still do not understand, then ask a friend to walk around you in a circle while facing a certain wall continuously. Then have the friend walk in the same circle while you do not stand inside it.) The number of rotations as viewed from inside the circle (solar) and from outside the circle (sidereal) will differ by exactly one. Because the rotation of the earth is in the same direction as its travel around the sun, the sidereal day is shorter and there is one more sidereal day per year than the number of solar days per year.

Strong Enough Already
Willie had had a stroke, which temporarily paralyzed his arm. Rehabilitative exercises and neurologic recovery helped him regain some, but not all, of his arm strength.

Hot Jewelry
She had a dependable burglar alarm, but lived in a wooden house and feared fire. She knew that the insulation of a self-cleaning oven, designed for keeping heat in, can also keep heat out. The blanket also repelled heat.

Tiresome Questions
Marla could easily see tire tracks that the new truck had made. She hoped to find, and really did find, that a small pebble had got stuck in a tire tread. The pebble made a mark on the ground at intervals that matched the tire's circumference. Marla borrowed a tape measure, measured the distance between the pebble marks, learned the circumference of the truck tire, and divided it by 3.14 to calculate the boy's height.

Carpeted Laundry Room

The room behind the clothes washer and dryer, a bathroom, was to have a panel that unscrewed from the bathroom side. This panel could be easily removed to give access to the back of the laundry machinery, making repairs easier because the space would be better lit and less cramped than otherwise.

The Bumpy Street

The one homeowner lived on the bumpy street, but on the inside of a curve. His driveway met the street between two shade trees. He wanted drivers passing his driveway to go slowly, obeying the speed limit, so that he could see them in time to prevent accidents when exiting his driveway.

Two Triangular Journeys

At a certain latitude very near the South Pole, traveling east or west for one mile describes a complete circle; the endpoint is the same as the starting point. One of the explorers could have started from any point one mile north of this circle. Slightly south of that circle, there are other latitudes for which traveling east or west for a half mile, a third of a mile, a fourth of a mile, or another such fraction of a mile would describe a complete circle. Either or both of the explorers could have started from any point one mile north of any of these circles, subject only to the conditions that they start one mile north of two different circles and do not start at the same longitude.

Death in the Pool

He hit his head on an inflatable raft, breaking his neck and drowning.

Unexplained Theft

The burglar, aware of an alarm that monitored the doors, had broken in by prying open and crawling through a small window not wired to the alarm. After helping himself to ground-floor valuables, he heard movement upstairs and ran to escape the quickest way. The back door, though locked, opened easily from the inside.

by Edward J. Harshman

Unusual Office Buildings

Elevators require bumpers, which are tall, underneath their shafts. Because of the numerous railroad tracks that leave Grand Central Station to the north, some nearby Park Avenue office buildings have tracks under them, leaving no room for elevator bumpers. The bumpers must be at ground level instead. Therefore, many buildings on the west side of Park Avenue and immediately north of Grand Central Station have escalators to the floor immediately above ground level; and from that floor, elevators lead to all higher floors.

Brian Braggart and the Equator

The sun passes directly overhead on the equator only during the equinoxes, at the start of spring or the start of autumn. Brian's friend noted that winter had just begun; the time was therefore more than two months away from an equinox. The sun would have passed south of directly overhead if Brian's friend was in the northern hemisphere; it would have passed north of overhead of the friend was in the southern hemisphere.

The Debt Was Paid

The store owner had customers who were slow at paying their bills. Scared by the wholesaler's letters, he realized their potential effectiveness and sent retyped versions to his customers, collecting from them and gathering money to repay his own debt. He wanted to receive as many threatening letters as possible, so that he could collect as effectively as possible from his own customers.

Slippery Sidney Slipped Up

Sidney was arrested for turning back the odometer and understating the number of miles that he actually drove. While at a distant city, he received two parking tickets from two different officers and didn't pay them. The city charged the fines to the rental-car company, and the company inferred that Sidney had driven the car there. But Sidney had not put enough mileage on the car, according to the odometer, to have been able to do so. The evidence was strong enough to convict him.

Response Team Right-of-Way

The law required civilian motorists to yield to emergency vehicles, but did not require emergency vehicles to yield to each other. After a collision between a police car and a fire engine, which in turn was followed by ambulances' crashing into each other, the police dispatcher called to several neighboring lands. Only after one of the ambulance dispatchers insisted that the arriving ambulances have lights and sirens off, so that they would follow conventional traffic laws, were they sent.

What Drained the Battery?

Walter, in a rush, forgot to turn off the headlights and parking lights. No one else entered the parking lot until lunchtime, when managers customarily went out to eat. One of them turned off Walter's lights, although by then the battery no longer had enough power to start the engine.

Spaced-Out at the Computer

First solution: If you know the maximum number of spaces in a row, take the exponent of the next highest power of 2 and enter the command to replace two spaces with one space that number of times. (Example: seven spaces maximum. Next highest power of two is eight, which is 2x2x2, so use the command three times.)

Second solution: Choose two characters that are never adjacent in either order (in this example, &%). First command: replace each space with &%. Second command: replace each %& (reverse the order of the characters) with nothing (delete %&). Third command: replace each &% with space.

More Problems with Personnel

The applicant had had a roommate who was transferred overseas and who had impeccable credentials, but he himself was less scrupulous. He wrote to Raymond's colleague, pretending to be the roommate, and asked about work; they had never met although the colleague had met the roommate. Upon learning about the job vacancy working for Raymond, he applied for work and gave his former roommate's name, background, and references. When the colleague showed up one day and saw that her apparent friend was an impostor, she said so; and Raymond promptly fired him.

Forgot to Stop?
The car skidded off a bridge and fell into a lake, and Angus jumped out just as the car hit its surface.

Power Failure
Power failures occurred often. Horace, therefore, did not bother resetting clocks every time the power was restored. When the power failed during the night, the clocks had not been reset from the previous power failure and looked unchanged in the morning.

Better Late Than Prompt
Kingfist knew that the payments on the original contract were each higher than the limit at the small claims court. He restructured the loan so that he could sue in small claims court every time a payment was missed. A small filing fee would induce major inconvenience for the debtor, who would have to repay the filing fee also. By restructuring the loan, Kingfist avoided all collection expenses that he could not recover. The debtor knew that major credit problems would exist from multiple unpaid judgments and scrupulously repaid the debt.

Not a Trusted Doctor
Cassandra, unknown to her recently met boyfriend, had completed medical school and was a licensed physician. She carefully hid her income-earning ability from men that she did not know well because she did not want to be exploited. She was as much a doctor as was any other medical school graduate and was telling the truth. She considered the senility treatment worthless, and she said so.

Time for Repairs
When he first looked at his watch in the morning, it showed the time 8:08; ten minutes later, 8:18. Later that morning, it showed

9:06, 9:16, 10:01, and 11:11. During his lunch break, it showed 12:21. The rest of the morning, it did not show the correct time, for Dilton unknowingly wore the watch upside down.

Marketing Muddle

The Kia is marketed with the crossbar of the A missing: KIΛ. The Λ (lambda) is the Greek-alphabet equivalent of our letter L, which means that USA customers who know the Greek alphabet may read K-I-L and wonder about the auto's safety.

All Wet

Being accidentally trapped in a bathroom in an apartment building, as by a broken latch or loose doorknob. You are trying to lower something out the window that, when swung, will make a loud tapping sound on the bathroom window of the floor below so that your neighbor will investigate. A chain of towels, with a fairly heavy object at its end, will work. (If not, plug up a drain and run water so as to make a big spill on the floor; downstairs neighbors will complain urgently and you will be rescued.)

Oo La La

A telephoto lens acts to make what is far away look close. To do so, it seems to compress distance. The colleague knew that, by showing many cars in what looked like a short street, the picture would repel potential customers from its agency; for it would make Paris seem overrun with heavy traffic. Radical environmentalists, of course, would be pleased with the photo.

Screened Out

The house had been rented by a film crew. The screens and storm windows were removed for the filming and, when it was finished, were re-installed.

Mysterious Break-In

The man had a mortgage on the house and, after not getting paid, discovered that the owner (and mortgagor) had moved without leaving a forwarding address. Unknown to him, the owner lived next door. Right after foreclosing, the new owner took a bolt cutter and went to change the locks and look the house over. He also took a gun because the house was in a bad neighborhood. Because the previous owner had moved without a forwarding address and therefore did not get the notice of foreclosure, he thought he still owned the house and that a burglar really was breaking in. "Call the registry of deeds," the new owner pleaded. But they hadn't yet got around to recording the change of ownership and confirmed that the man who called the police was the owner. "Call my foreclosure lawyer!" he persisted - and easily went free.

Common Cents

Awkward amounts are intended to force the cashier to make change, which requires using the cash register and recording the sale. Otherwise, a dishonest cashier could easily pocket the exact amount due and steal from the store.

The Unwelcome Gift

Fritz, a playful cat, brought a mouse in from outside as a present to its owner.

A Cross Puzzle

Number the holes, or use another way to label them. Put exactly one nail in the center; no others. Pick up this nail, jump over a vacant hole, and put a nail in the hole just jumped. You have just done the opposite of the last move in solving the puzzle. Pick up either nail, jump over a vacant hole, and put a nail in the hole just jumped over. That's the reverse of the second-last move. Continue similarly until only the center hole does not have a nail. Write down the opposite of the moves you are making, in the opposite order, and you will have a solution to the puzzle.

Work On This

Live-in domestic servants were common in the USA in 1900, but they are scarce and expensive now. Many very rich people cannot reconcile apparent unavailability of jobs with their own inability to find competent domestic help.

Lights Out!

A fly had got loose in the operating room, which in turn had windows between it and the separately lit corridor. With no light except from the corridor, the fly could be expected to alight on a windowpane and get promptly swatted—thereby not alighting on the patient and spreading infection.

Cool Car Got Cooler

The air conditioner cools air and removes water from it. It is turned on when heater air is aimed at the windshield. Hot and dry air aimed at the windshield helps keep the windshield from fogging, which it would otherwise do if Calvin had all the windows closed on a very cold day. Hot and damp air is much less effective at defogging the windshield than hot and dry air.

Gunpoint

Kevin handed over his license, which was in his wallet. He had to open the glove compartment to remove the registration and insurance card. There was a gun in the glove compartment, which Kevin removed. The policeman did not know Kevin, saw him pick up the gun, and wanted to protect himself. As soon as Kevin put the gun on the dashboard and started to search the glove compartment, the policeman quietly put his own gun away.

She Paid to be Seen

The man was a dermatologist, who had previously diagnosed skin cancer in her and wanted to be sure that she had no recurrence. He also looked for yeast infections with a Woods light.

Burning Down the House

The man did not have clear title to the land; long-lost relatives fought him for the land and won. They nastily waited until the mortgage on the house was paid, and the man burned the house down out of spite because the relatives would not pay him a fair price for it.

by Edward J. Harshman

Bewildering Bargain

The woman was away from home, on a trip. She knew the cost per ounce of toothpaste at her usual store at home. She was at a more expensive store and correctly figured that she would pay her usual cost per ounce, plus some additional money. She wanted the additional money to be as little as possible and noted that, even though the additional money per ounce is more for small tubes, the total additional money is least for them. So she bought a small tube, knowing that it would be sufficient for the trip.

One Bad Check

Sam wrote the check with disappearing ink.

Shoplifting Backwards

The smuggled merchandise has a price or barcode sticker, perhaps from a previous sale or carefully peeled from a similar but less expensive item, that shows a substantially lower price than the real price. A dishonest shopper can show the lower price to a cashier and insist on paying the lower price for many other such items, saving far more than the cost of the smuggled-in item.

The Unwelcome Strike

The member of the baseball umpires' union, at a well-attended professional game, watched a batter refuse to swing at a fair pitch and correctly identified the pitch as a "Steee-rike!" to the annoyance of the batters' team manager.

The Stubborn Door

The boy learned that the door opened away from him, turned the knob, and *pushed* the door open.

Weird Words

The letters in the words are in alphabetical order. A third such word is known; take another look at that last hint.
A-L-M-O-S-T.

This Car Loves Hills
The car had manual transmission and a broken starter motor. It could be started while rolling gravity-powered down a hill, but not otherwise unless pushed.

His Car Was Identified
Dave found Nick's car backed into a parking space, instead of being parked head-in. While at work, they both had to back ambulances into their parking spaces; for there would be no time to turn them around if they received an emergency call. Their habit carried over into civilian life and, in the locale where they lived and worked, never applied to anyone else.

The Unpowered Outlet
The outlet was on the end of an extension cord, which Alex promptly plugged into the wall.

The Cold Fire
The thermostat, which controlled the temperature of the entire house by switching on and off the central heating, was very close to the fireplace. As the air near the fireplace, and the thermostat, warmed up, the thermostat switched off the central heating even though the rest of the house was cold.

Approximately Seven Days per Week
The calendar consists of a cycle of 3 365-day years and a 366-day (leap) year, repeated indefinitely, except that years that divide by 100 are not leap years unless they also divide by 400. In 4 consecutive years not at a turn of a century, the number of days is 365 x 4 + 1, or 1461. In 400 years, the number of days is 100 x 1461 - 3, or 146,097. The number of weeks in 400 years is 146,097 / 7. The division by 7 happens to leave no remainder; there are exactly 20,871 weeks in 400 years. Therefore, whatever associations between dates and weekdays exist in one 400-year period exist in all 400-year periods, i.e. forever. But 400 does not divide exactly by 7. Therefore, no 400-year period can have any date that has a 1/7th chance of falling on a particular weekday. Finally, whatever associations exist between dates and weekdays

in a 400-year period will repeat forever, so that no date can have a 1/7th chance of falling on a particular weekday.

Spoken By The Book
The book was an unabridged dictionary.

No Place for Women
Tall people, obviously including tall women, can easily reach upward to high racks or shelves that are out of reach of short people. Conversely, short women can reach shelves that are near the floor more easily than can tall women. Common sense would suggest putting tall sizes on high shelves and petite sizes on low shelves, but stores often do exactly the opposite. Such a practice may make a tall woman bend sharply forward, presenting a needlessly awkward display, and it may also force a short woman to request hands-on help when seeking clothing of her size that is out of her reach.

Picking Good Apples
The bad apples were not good to eat, but they were available and easily thrown. The ladies merely threw the bad apples at the clusters of good apples and knocked plenty of good apples to the ground.

Eggs-Asperated
They were in a moving train, which would make all eggs wobble similarly whether or not they were hard-boiled, additionally posing a risk that an egg would fall and break if tested.

Wrong Again!
The foreman had started counting with the ground floor as 1, up one flight as 2, and so on until reaching 15. He did not allow for the absence of a floor numbered thirteen, and he found painters on what was about to be called the sixteenth floor.

Stolen License Plates
The license plates, by coincidence, had the name of a new nightclub. The nightclub owner wanted to use them as wall decorations.

Two In The Woods
In the days before mobile phones became common, a married couple, the woman several months pregnant, entered the woods. She suddenly went into labor, gave birth, and collapsed of exhaustion. The man took the baby and quickly left the woods and went to a telephone to call for help.

Death of a Hunter
The hunter had climbed a tree in order to see farther. When he fired his shotgun, the recoil threw him off a limb. Off balance and tangled in the gun-sling, he could not break his fall or reorient himself for a better landing, so he was killed when he hit the ground.

Too Heavy
Since the machinery was made of sturdy metal and had an awkward shape, the shipping clerk tried removing some superfluous cushioning to make the package light enough. It didn't quite do the job, but he realized that the resultant air spaces might accommodate helium-filled balloons. Adding these did sufficiently reduce the weight of the package—although only for about a day until the helium leaked out.

Brian Braggart's Space Story
With sufficient intelligence and very fortuitous evolution, beings could exist that could learn English and communicate by the same radio frequency that Brian allegedly used. The moonman jumped off of the lunar surface, and Brian heard its speech although there was no atmosphere to carry sound waves. Therefore, it was speaking by using the radio frequency and Brian's radio worked. But it also heard the partner's statement about radio trouble, so that the partner was able to transmit properly. Brian did not receive his partner's signal even though he could receive and his partner could

transmit. He was not separated by a mountain or other large object, for he could see his partner. There is the contradiction: he did not receive a signal that he ought to have received.

Not A Worthless Check

In the days before the Internet and online ordering, the man had a judgment against a resistant debtor and was interested in locating the debtor's bank account. He wrote a fictitious ad for something that was an excellent bargain and very cheap and sent it to the debtor. The debtor filled out the fake order form and sent a check, easily identifying a bank account that could be impounded. If the man had cashed the check without delivering the (nonexistent) merchandise, then he would have been liable for mail fraud. Even if legal, cashing the check would have been redundant if he could seize all the money in the account.

Caught in the Act

In this true story, a neighborhood pickpocket was caught by a woman, the wife of nineteenth-century inventor Peter Cooper, who sewed fishhooks into her coat pocket. When he caught his hand on the hooks, she told him, "I am going to the police station, and you are coming with me." He cooperated to prevent serious injury to his hand.

A Crying Problem

After she and her husband had a particularly intense argument, he had stormed out. She suspected that, as he had done previously, he had returned to his parents. Therefore, she called them hoping that they would tell her where he was, as they had often done before. When, this time, they did not, she became very upset.

Walked On The Other Street

First and Second Streets were both one-way streets and ran in opposite directions. Traffic lights on them were set so that a car being driven on one of them at exactly the city speed limit would never have to wait for a red light more than once. Jeff knew from experience that if he walked to work on First Street, his pace made him wait at length for a red light at each of the 30 intersections. Walking on Second Street allowed him to travel nonstop by reaching every intersection while a green light showed. Saving 30 waits for red lights more than compensated for Jeff's walk to and from Second Street.

Stubborn Steve

Steve was going to use the paper in airmail letters to correspondents overseas. To save postage, he wanted paper as light as possible even if it was expensive and occasionally jammed his printer.

Problems with Personnel

Raymond, who was in charge of research, had requested and expected to hire someone with a master's degree. The applicant, who had a doctorate, was rejected by the personnel department because he didn't have a master's degree even though the doctorate was, in Raymond's opinion, preferable.

Picture the Tourists

Sal's camera focused by measuring the distance to the object in front of it, which would be the window of the bus. Sal's pictures of objects outside the bus would, therefore, be badly out of focus. But autofocus does not work when the distance is very small. Sherman wanted Sal to sit close to the window, so that the camera would ignore the window glass, focus for great distance, and take good pictures.

Afraid of the Country

This incident really happened. Nicolai was afraid of *silence*. While on a farm during World War II, he was exposed to the sounds of livestock. Under normal circumstances, farm animals move around and make noise from time to time. But when scared, they are still. They could hear German bomber airplanes when people could not—and became silent. Silence, to Nicolai, meant that an air raid was imminent and that he would have to hide in the basement. Despite many decades since the war, Nicolai never recovered from his fear.

by Edward J. Harshman

She Was In The Hospital
She was a recently hired trauma surgeon and was working in the operating room.

No Forwarding
He had been convicted for a nonviolent crime and was serving his sentence at home. He had to have an electronic device clamped to his leg and a receiver attached to his phone line. If he had call forwarding, then the authorities would know he could leave his house and, not trusting him to honor the house-arrest protocol, would imprison him.

The Plumber's Pressure
He had arteriosclerosis, which made his arteries more rigid than those of most people. Measuring blood pressure by compressing an artery and listening is unreliable if the artery is inflexible. The plumber recalled his use of pressure gauges while at work and the ineffectiveness of measuring water pressure in steel pipes by merely pinching them, and he very sensibly wondered if his blood pressure was really high.

Lottery Logic
Lottery tickets or other risky investments are very sensible when bankruptcy is imminent. Suppose, for example, you have $10,000 in assets and $20,000 in liabilities. If you merely pay your debts to the best of your ability, then you are certain to go broke. But if you buy as many lottery tickets as you can afford, then you have a chance of winning more than what you owe. Then you would be able to pay your debts and have some money left over. Although winning a large amount of money is unlikely, it is possible. That possibility converts certain bankruptcy into a chance to be rich.

The TV Obeyed
Eager to show off his elaborate new equipment, Jake had friends over. Not only did he set up his DVD player, but also he carefully reviewed the instructions for his television set, which included a timer that would turn it off a specified time later. He carefully set the shutoff timer to outlast the movie by a minute or two and, when

the ad came on, saw a warning on the screen that the television would turn itself off in a couple of seconds. He knew that it would be shutting off immediately anyway, so he shouted at the television set just for the fun of it.

Battery Badness

Leroy was pleased until he turned on the radio and discovered that it was on a strong station, and that when he absent-mindedly pressed one of the station-select buttons it tuned to another station, his favorite. Disconnecting power to the radio would have made it lose its memory of the pre-programmed stations. Because the radio still remembered his favorite stations, he knew that the original battery had never been removed from the car.

An Appetite for Housing

The house was in very bad condition. A severely leaking roof had allowed the floor to weaken so badly that he had fallen right through it onto the basement floor a few inches below. His friend mentioned Overeaters Anonymous as a joke, for falling through a floor is a strong incentive to lose weight.

Bad Building Material
Ice. Its only significant drawback as a building material, though obviously a severe one, is its vulnerability to heat.

Bought and Paid For
I bought a black cat at a pet store, in the rural Southeast, in October. To protect innocent black cats from voodoo practices and other grisly rituals on Halloween, the storeowner will not release black cats to me or to any other customers until November 1.

Tied His Own Ankles
Ivan was being mimicked by the evil man, who did not stop even when told to do so. Ivan was cutting wheat with his scythe, and the other man pretended to do so with a stick. So Ivan tied his own ankles together - and was mimicked - and cut himself free. The evil man could not do so and, therefore, was easily captured by Ivan.

Upside-Down Gravity
Judy and Trudy were diving underwater. The stone was pumice, which floats.

Disappeared
Slaves. The two had a baby, making three. Then they escaped, taking the neighbor's slaves with them.

The Returned DVD's
When he rented the DVD's, he also bought outright a previously rented DVD, paying a high price because it was out of print and rare. Unfortunately, his wife saw the rental sticker and familiar packaging and, not knowing his purchase, assumed it was a rental too and brought it back to the store.

Toll Booth and Long Line

Conrad had his wallet in his back pocket, and his seat belt was fastened. He knew that he needed time to fumble for his money and did not want to arrive at a toll booth without being able to pay the toll promptly. He chose a long line so that he would have time to retrieve his money and not slow down other drivers.

Not Phoning for Directions

She looked up the street addresses of various friends, acquaintances, and stores on her sister's street. She soon determined that it was between two familiar landmarks and, with that new information, knew that she could drive there quickly and easily.

Burning Down the House Again

The house was restrained from remodeling by having been declared a landmark. Furthermore, it was dilapidated and structurally unsound; and its owner was soon to receive a court order to repair it at great expense. Anticipating a major construction bill, which would have been more than the house was worth, the man burned down the house and avoided all landmark-related problems.

Child Driver

The car, having broken down, had been loaded onto a flatbed truck so that it could be taken to a repair shop. There was not enough room in the cab of the truck for all of the passengers and the truck driver, so two passengers stayed in the car. The child could not reach the pedals, and the steering wheel was locked. The car, therefore, was safe.

His Plans for Her

The man was getting a divorce and wanted very much to hide evidence that he was becoming interested in other women. He was interested in his wife's friend, but dared not show his interest too soon in case she told his wife about him while the wife could still interfere with the divorce. Also, he carefully prepared to contact her through her workplace, not her home, because he recalled that she also had been unhappily married and wanted to reach her without her husband's becoming suspicious.

Do Away with Diamonds
The second store was an electronics store, where in the old days its staff used to inspect diamond phonograph needles and recommend replacing them whenever they got sufficiently worn.

The Victim was Arrested
The three men were police officers, and they had a warrant for the seizure of the homeowner's counterfeit money.

The Trained Athlete Loses
They played checkers.

Hurried Funeral?
A coal miner was trapped by a cave-in and died of suffocation the next day.

Was Her Job At Risk?

Jenny was a foreigner with only a temporary work authorization. Ed, anxious to keep her, cooperated with Jenny's immigration lawyer. He ran an ad hoping to prove that no USA citizen could do Jenny's job and would be willing to do so. Such proof would have helped enable Jenny to get permanent work authorization and eventual USA citizenship.

Loves Being Stranded

Herbert tested the clutch of the car, which had manual transmission, by putting it in third gear and slowly releasing the clutch. If the car did not stall, then the clutch would have been badly worn. The car was stationary, perhaps at a red traffic light, when he did this.

The Roundabout Taxi Route

After the taxi pulled to the curb in response to Melinda's signal, a man jumped into it. Melinda, not expecting to be able to locate a second taxi quickly, told the driver that he was working for her because he pulled over on her signal. Then she gave the driver a twenty-dollar bill and told him to circle the block repreatedly, hoping that the man would resent the delay and get out of the taxi.

But the Patient Followed Orders

Obesity. The patient apparently dieted too strenuously and lost weight too fast. The patient lost weight at a known rate, and would have become lighter than air and literally hit the ceiling like a helium-filled balloon if the rate of weight loss did not later decrease.

Short Swing

Ned's parents, to control insects, had a box not for baseball bats but for flying mammals. A suitably designed box, open at the bottom and permanently mounted, encourages bats to move in.

No Sale

Irritated at receiving telephone solicitations, one recipient of them decided to retaliate. With a caller-ID device that identified the name and telephone number of incoming calls and a second telephone line, he looked at the name of each caller before answering the phone. If it was a magazine salesperson, then he did not answer the telephone. Instead, he quickly dialed the magazine's circulation department on the other telephone line and connected the two lines together. Neither the solicitor nor the circulation manager could easily figure out what happened, and the manager would receive the full effect of the nuisance calls.

Wet in the Winter

Winnie knows that heated air can be very dry. She fights wintertime low humidity by drying laundry at home, saving the nuisance of a humidifier and also saving a little money.

Nothing Done

The contractor and his staff were from Britain, and they started counting floors beginning above the ground-level floor. What they would have called the eighth floor was, by USA acceptation, the ninth floor. They remodeled the wrong apartment, and its owner was absent and did not notice the error.

Belligerent Bus Driver

Cal shut off his engine, got out of the truck, and pushed it past the school bus. Then he started the engine and drove away. He used the truck as a manually powered conveyance, which could legally pass the school bus. The driver, despite his belligerence, had no recourse; for the truck was not being operated as a motor vehicle for those few seconds.

You Have To Stop

The sign is on a chain across a private road, and the chain is padlocked between two posts to exclude trespassers. Because the chain is hard to see, especially at night, a stop sign suspended from it serves as a useful reminder to get out of the car and temporarily unfasten the chain.

Doesn't Need Hot Water

There was a loaf of bread in the oven with the cup of water. The loaf had just been removed from the freezer, and the microwave was used to thaw it.

This Burglar Got In

The man *was* the burglar. He had stolen the valuable objects and was preparing to defend himself against a police raid. He had used ordinary methods (a key, perhaps) to enter his own house before boarding it up.

Tea-ed Off

The secretary had been unhappy with the coffee from the coffee maker and had cleaned it out according to the directions that came with it. Diluted distilled white vinegar, poured into a coffee maker in place of water, helps remove mineral deposits. After such cleaning of the machine, water must be poured through it two or three times to fully rinse out the vinegar. The machine is then clean. The coffee maker was receiving a vinegar rinse when the

by Edward J. Harshman

boss, unaware of what the secretary was doing, used what looked like hot water to make his bad-tasting cup of tea.

He Won't Hear From Her
He was completely deaf, though a skilled lip-reader. Because of his affliction, he could not literally hear from anyone.

Smashed Taillights
Bob had been kidnapped and locked in a car trunk. Aware of police department recommendations, he fumbled for the tire wrench and, having loosened it from its storage brackets, broke the taillights and side markers from inside. Then, he was able to wave the wrench to passers-by and to call for help.

Happy that She Cursed Him
She was married to another man, and he suggested that she pretend that he was an obnoxious telephone solicitor if he called while her husband might overhear. His ruse apparently worked, and he was pleased.

Making the Grade
Nell could not hand in a postcard with her term paper because, although the paper was not due for another week, she had already handed it in. She was then free to write other term papers and study for exams in other courses.

A Mystery Fax
Quietly interested in changing jobs, the executive arranged for a cooperative recruiter to try to fax him a blank sheet of paper when trying to reach him. If he could talk, then he announced himself over the fax signal. If not, he called the recruiter later when he could discreetly do so.

Magazine Subscriptions
Postage for a first-class item with a reply-paid address must be paid by the recipient. City residents may hoard the cards in case of a garbage collectors' strike, perhaps believing that those who

contribute to the garbage problem should help solve it at their own expense.

They Had a Ball

The two men were not alone. Ted saw a teammate behind Ned and feared that if Ned missed the high ball, then the teammate might be hit by it. A gentler throw, a grounder, was different, for it would not hit anyone very hard if Ned missed it. Ted aimed his high throw so that if Ned missed the ball, it would not hit anyone.

Table That Investment Plan

The corporation was a health and disability insurance company. It encouraged its policyholders, especially its business clients for their workplaces, to use furniture that was designed to minimize back strain and other joint trauma. To do so, it needed a source of such furniture that was not too expensive. Therefore, it bought the furniture company and made it build orthopedically sensible furniture and sell it cheaply. It therefore ran at a loss, but it saved more than enough in reduced disability claims to offset that loss.

Safe Smashup

No one was in the car. It had been parked on a hill, and the driver who parked it left it in neutral and forgot to set the brakes. There was no spark or other flame source to set fire to the fuel.

Appendicitis

Since the earlier surgery, Zeke had remarried.

The Curious Cardiologist

The cardiologist wanted to attach a microphone and recording device to his stethoscope and record the patient's heart sounds. He was writing a CD-based study guide for heart examination and wanted to include the sound of the patient's rare murmur.

Old Money But Good Money

United States currency formerly included silver certificates, which stopped being redeemable for silver in 1968. Since then, there has been no formal precious metal backing to guarantee its value. 1968

by Edward J. Harshman

was also the first year that denominations higher than one dollar suggested fear of currency devaluations by carrying the words "In God We Trust." Religious zealots favored the wording; some conservative economists took warning.

Don't Bluff It

You are near one end of a one-track railroad bridge, over a deep ravine. A train is approaching from that end.

A Devil of a Number

On a telephone dial or keypad, the letter O corresponds to the digit 6. Janice, recalling a similar experience that a friend had, knew that people intending to call the number with the same first four digits as hers but ending in three zeros, probably a major company that receives hundreds of calls per day, would often mistakenly dial the letter O instead of the digit zero—and predictably disturb her.

Hats Off To You

The boy threw his hat out the window and said, "That was fun, Dad. Whistle for it again!"

Wrong-Way Elevator

At any instant, the elevator would be most likely above the third floor and most likely below the tenth floor. Therefore, if summoned at a random time, it would be more likely to travel down to reach the third floor and up to reach the tenth floor.

Cheap Advertising

By gluing a quarter to the floor in front of the beauty shop, its owner could assure a steady stream of disgruntled women customers with broken fingernails.

Dim-Wits

Motion sensors had been installed to turn the classroom lights off when there was little or no motion and the classroom was assumed to be empty. Whoever designed the school expected children to be rambunctious and did not allow for honors students as they took an advanced placement examination.

Still Hungry

The man and the woman were planning their wedding reception, which was to be at that restaurant. They selected the food to be served and paid a deposit.

Natural Crescents

In a moderately shady forest, or under a loose group of trees, sunlight is mostly blocked by the trees' leaves, but little points of direct sunlight shine through. Like a pinhole camera, these points project images of the sun, which normally results in circular blotches on the ground. They will be crescents, however, during a partial solar eclipse.

by Edward J. Harshman

Underpopulation?

First, modern agriculture technology has increased food yield per acre faster than world population growth, so that the number of acres needed to grow food to feed the world is decreasing despite population increase. Second, the inflation-adjusted cost per unit of energy is lower and the convenience of using it higher than a century ago. Third, the cost of unskilled labor is gradually rising, showing that any apparent surplus of people, relative to other economic resources, is disappearing and not worsening.

The Devil and Idol Hands

Placing gifts in front of a tree suggests tree worship. Protests against that practice usually originate from environmentalists who defend trees and oppose their being cut down for a temporary or frivolous use. But it violates the first two of the Ten Commandments, if they are interpreted very strictly.

Cool Car, Clean Windshield

Jenny, a child, handed Calvin a squirt gun, which could be pointed at the windshield through the driver's open window.

Failed Theft

The man was the rightful owner of the car and wanted to keep it from being stolen. Frightened by a recent failed attempt, he quickly bought a device that hooked the steering wheel to the brake pedal. While trying to install it, he noticed that the steering wheel was not in a good position. So he put the ignition key in the switch, turned it partway to unlock the wheel, and turned the wheel to a better position. He was happy because he succeeded at installing the device.

Over the Wall

The man was pursued by muggers and escaped them by entering the prison, sure that they would not follow.

Truckin' Through the Intersection

Chris received a back injury from a hit-run driver, and the medical expenses would have seriously impaired the small business at which he worked. Although insured, the business would have been badly hurt by higher employee health insurance premiums. The owner of the business suggested that Chris drive into an intersection exactly as its light turned green. He would sooner or later be hit by a vehicle, in front of witnesses from his workplace. The other vehicle would be legally at fault if it had entered the intersection just after the light turned red, hence the need for Chris to enter the intersection exactly when he legally could do so. The driver of the other vehicle would have to accept responsibility for Chris's back pain expense, relieving Chris's employer. Chris, unhappy about having no other recourse against the hit-run driver, cooperated and drove a pickup truck because it was heavier and safer than the average car.

The Car Won't Run

Keith was at an auto auction and planned to bid on the car. Because the car would no longer run, it would be sold cheaply. Only Keith knew exactly which wires were cut and how to repair them, so he was confident that his bid would be the highest for that particular car.

Unequal Values

An insurance policy. It may have been homeowner's insurance after which Mack lost personal property to burglars or fire, and it may have been medical insurance that paid for a long and expensive hospital stay for Mack.

Just Like Prison

The visitor is a student at a central-city school, one with metal detectors at its entrance to help intercept weapons.

Sweet Coffee

Crush one of the lumps and stir its sugar into the three cupfuls of coffee. Then add the other lumps as you wish (five to the first, three to the second, and three to the third is one of many possibilities). You have used up all the sugar while putting an odd number of lumps into each cup. You did not have to add all of the sugar in the form of lumps.

He Followed Instructions

Another student on detention, in a mischievous mood (that's why he was sent for detention), had earlier added his own sign to the instructions on the front of the file cabinet, saying BANG HERE FIVE TIMES TO OPEN.

Truckers Went Separate Ways

Another truck driver, on the other side of the highway and headed in the opposite direction, announced on his CB radio that there was an open truck-weight enforcement station ahead. Having passed it, this truck driver knew that Hank and Frank were going to encounter it. Hank was not overloaded, and he did not mind having his truck weighed. Frank did, however; for his truck was heavier than its official maximum safe weight. He took local roads to avoid the weight station. Because the station was off the highway itself and cars did not need to turn off of the highway to enter it, the sports-car driver did not notice it.

The Bicycle Bolt

The bolt had ordinary right-handed threading; the bicycle needed one with reversed (left-handed) threading so that it would not come unscrewed by the forces of riding. An experienced bicycle store clerk would have known to ask for the direction (left-hand or right-hand) of threading upon receiving a request for that particular kind of bolt.

Saved by the Convertible

Milton was badly hurt and needed emergency surgery as quickly as possible. He may also have needed on-the-spot treatment, such as starting an intravenous line or installing anti-shock clothing. He could not be treated or removed from the car after merely opening its door, not only because the door was smashed but also because he was physically very fragile. He had to be lifted upward. His car was enclosed by other wrecked vehicles. If he had been in a hard-top car, then the rescuers would have had to bring heavy tools over or around the other cars to break into Milton's roof. They could then remove Milton without further injury. But that step, especially if the other cars were on precarious wheels that might have suddenly collapsed, would have taken precious minutes. Because Milton was immediately accessible, rescuers could stabilize and remove him very quickly. That opportunity for prompt action may have saved his life.

The Brighter Bulb
The 25-watt bulb is brighter. Because the bulbs are connected in series, the current through them is exactly the same. All current flows through both bulbs. The 25-watt bulb, if connected directly to a 117 volt power source, would draw only 25 watts. The 100-watt bulb would draw 100 watts. The greater the power drawn, the less the resistance in the bulb to electric current flow. But because the bulbs are in series, the current through them is the same. The 25-watt bulb has higher resistance than the 100-watt bulb and therefore, with identical current through it, uses more energy than does the latter. It will therefore glow more brightly.

She Easily Went Home
The physician, not the woman with the sore throat, had the heart attack.

Hold Still!
The background was an open field, and the time was late night. The photographer knew that the field was full of animals at night that were not visible during the day, and he used a long exposure time to capture them. He used a flash to highlight his model in the foreground, knowing that light from the flash would not travel far enough to illuminate the field.

Self-Destruction
Some women tend to wear tight-fitting or high-heeled shoes, sometimes leading to hammertoes or bunions. Health administrators, many of whom rationally decide to wear visually

attractive shoes, notwithstanding the drawbacks, collectively resist having corrective foot surgery be declared an uninsurable expense, as this would put them at personal material risk.

Rainy Walk

Ima did not want her parrots to fly out of her reach, which parrots can do if full-flighted and taken outside. Heavy rain would wet her parrots' wings and make them incapable of flight, and Ima knew that they could be taken out safely under her umbrella. They would stay dry if they remained with her, but they would be forced to flutter to the ground if they left her.

Safe from the Fire

The bedrooms were on the ground floor, and the kitchen was on the upper floor. Leaving the house without using the stairway was quick and easy.

Fix The Furnace

The furnace was designed to circulate air, with its blower motor, if and only if the air in the furnace was hot. Chester had tested the furnace by adjusting the thermostat that controlled the burner. By turning it back and forth, he turned the burner on and off. But there was a second thermostat in the furnace. The second thermostat turned the blower on and off depending on the temperature in the furnace. The furnace needed a few minutes to heat up. The second thermostat meant that, when the burner first came on because the house was cold, Chester would be spared a frigid blast from the still-cold furnace.

I Brake for Snowdrifts

The differential is the part of a rear-wheel-drive car that divides the rotational force between its two rear wheels. On ordinary ground, there is very little slipperiness; and both wheels push against the ground and apply approximately equal forward-motion force. But if either wheel turns without resistance, then that wheel does so and the other wheel does not move. Sandy set the brake partway so that the spinning wheel would receive some resistance and the other rear wheel would receive some forward-moving force. It worked. The ordinary brake is far less useful in this context than the parking brake; for the former acts on all four wheels and the latter acts only on the rear ones.

Legally Castrated
The doctor was a veterinarian and neutered a cat.

Rats!
He wanted to buy the house, which was for sale, cheaply. By making it appear rat-infested, Nat hoped to discourage other potential buyers and get the house for a good price.

The Microscope
Light passed through a suitable prism is separated into its component wavelengths. Starlight can be passed through a prism and its component wavelengths studied in this way. For very precise work, the wavelengths can be photographed with high-resolution film and the film developed then scrutinized under a microscope.

Brian Braggart in Japan
Brian's slide show eventually showed a motor-vehicle factory where unfinished right-hand-drive cars (normally used where people drive on the left side of the road) were coming off the line and identified the cars as being built for export to the USA. In the background, on a service road, a truck was being driven away from the factory on the right side of the road—and a car was being driven toward it on the left side. The heckler inferred correctly that the slide was backwards, because USA cars are left-hand-drive. But because the slide was backwards it proved that the Japanese drive on the left side of the road, which the heckler had not previously known. Brian never noticed that the slides, many showing two-way traffic, were backwards. He could not possibly have missed that fact had he ever been to Japan.

Welcome, Slasher
A hurricane emergency had been declared, and poorly constructed buildings were at risk of major structural damage. Screens imposed

wind resistance, which might have stressed buildings enough to wreck them. Removing screens from screened porches was correctly announced as a safety measure, and the boy diverted his destructive tendencies to a good cause. The policeman knew that the frantic absent homeowners had requested the boy's help with this potential problem.

She Never Fixed Him Up

Mitch and Anna got married and lived happily ever after.

Contagious Carsickness?

Stan had, as he had planned, stopped the car on a ferryboat. Jan became seasick.

The Hostile Voter

Charlie heard an aggressive sales pitch about a candidate that supposedly believed in keeping government as unobtrusive as possible. The volunteer was engaged in a meddlesome act, that of telephoning voters at home. Because the candidate approved such intrusive actions, Charlie deduced that the candidate was not going to keep his word about an unobtrusive government and decided not to vote for him.

Racing the Drawbridge

Clarence was navigating a boat, and the drawbridge was opened to let it pass.

Not From the USA

Windsor, Canada, adjacent to Detroit, Michigan, is directly both south and east of parts of Michigan. It is north and west of some other USA states.

I've Got Your Number

Kingfist found the telephone wiring that led into Sam's house and connected a portable telephone, which had been equipped with alligator clips, to it. Then he called his own mobile phone, carefully noting the number that showed up as the calling number.

(If it showed up as Unavailable, then Kingfist would have called *82 then his own number.)

Disability

He was an orthopedic surgeon, and he broke his leg in a skiing accident. Standing for a long time was painful, and he could no longer work in the operating room. He therefore started working for the disability office doing physical examinations of other people who claimed to be disabled.

Youthful Gamble

College students, despite uniform room charges, are often assigned dormitory rooms of unequal sizes by lottery. Similarly, equal tuition payments do not necessarily result in equal education because lotteries are used to select which students get access to popular courses that have enrollment quotas.

No Cell Phone

There is a perceptible delay when a cell phone signal is transmitted and received. This can be demonstrated easily if two cell phones are calling each other from within the same room and a test sound is made at either mouthpiece. The expert knew that a monitoring device might receive a signal and have to respond instantly, within a few milliseconds. A half-second delay built into the cell phone carrier's circuitry would make such a rapid response impossible.

The Policeman's Signal

The policeman was off duty and driving an antique car, and he raised his hand to signal for a right turn. Sally, originally just behind him, passed him.

Dreaded Doorbell

After putting on some rubber gloves, she uprooted some poison ivy from the backyard, crushed their leaves, and rubbed them on the doorbell. When a child came to see her at school the next day with an itchy finger, she knew who the culprit was.

by Edward J. Harshman

Paper Profits
His spies give him information about the purchasing habits of the paper companies' clients. In particular, cardboard boxes for shipping. Changes in quantities of boxes ordered can precede formal announcements of sales figures, permitting profitable buying and selling of stocks.

Celebrity Discourtesy
They sometimes use a standard given name but alter its spelling so that, if pronounced according to its new spelling, it sounds the same. Or they use a name that is usually used by the opposite gender. Careful parents want to protect their children from the nuisance of repeatedly spelling out their given names, having them misspelled by others, or having any ambiguity of gender associated with their names, so they dislike the loss of the celebrities' given names as possibilities for their unborn children.

Southern Insight
He replied, "The side that should have won was the side whose commanding general was most strongly opposed to slavery." He carefully didn't add that Robert E. Lee was an outspoken opponent of slavery and that Ulysses S. Grant had owned four slaves.

Don't Bug Us
They are exported to Central and South America and applied to coffee there, and the coffee is imported to the USA.

Ate His Words
She had just moved into the house and was opening boxes with the knife. The electricity had not yet been turned on. Absence of electricity is obvious after sunset and, had he observed it, would probably have induced him to change his sales pitch.

Toll Booth and Exact Change
He paid the toll of $1.25 by throwing a quarter and an Eisenhower dollar into the basket. The toll-booth machinery did not recognize the obsolete Eisenhower dollar as a valid coin, but the attendant did and was happy to keep it for himself.

Strange Sounds

Some movies in the 1980's had scenes in which someone was typing, but the sounds of the keys were unrelated to the motion of the typist's fingers. Nowadays, scenes of typing conceal the hands to prevent that error. Reverberations remain a clue, as when a person walks from the outdoors into a narrow corridor and the footsteps do not reverberate indoors. Another clue is the absence of a companion sound, as when several people are walking and only one set of footsteps is heard. Or when a horse-drawn cart is shown and horses' hoofs are heard—but the cartwheels themselves are totally silent.

License Lost

A teenager, who looked as if he might be William's age, stole the license and pasted his picture on it. Then he glued clear plastic over the entire front of it. He now had what looked like a good proof of age so that he could enter bars and other adults-only places. Because the license was from another state and unfamiliar to bar employees, no one looking at it could easily see that it had been changed.

by Edward J. Harshman

She Didn't Like His Picture

The woman asked for a whole-body picture. She meant what is commonly called a full-length photograph, but the man sent her a photograph that showed his whole body (nude).

Burning Down the Building

The landlord set fire to his own building. It was occupied by tenants who paid a low rent that was restricted by law. If they moved out, then he would have vacant apartments that could be offered at a much higher rent than before. Incurring fire damage was a sensible investment, for it would remove the low-rent tenants and permit elegant remodeling into luxury apartments that could fetch a very high rent.

It's Not a Gamble, Son!

The couple smuggled a hundred thousand dollars' worth of chips from the casino. The son cashed those chips, evading gift, estate, and inheritance taxes.

Afraid of the Bar

Linda, much smaller than Bill and habitually afraid of date rape, carried a gun in her purse. Many states permit citizens to get concealed-gun permits, but do not allow even permit-holders to carry guns into places that are primarily intended to serve alcohol. This technicality helps prevent barroom brawls from becoming shootouts. Linda expected to have to open her purse, exposing the gun and risking arrest, if she was called on to produce proof that she was old enough to drink alcohol. By locking the gun in the trunk of her car, she would become free to enter the bar.

The Four-Mile Conversation

They were in a health club and walked on adjacent treadmills at slightly different speeds.

His Last Nap

After major trauma, Bruce is being wheeled to the operating room to get anesthesia and surgical repair.

Two Copies, Not One

The original had printing on only one side of each sheet of paper; the other side was blank. The copies had printing on both sides. Therefore, only fifty sheets of paper were needed to make each copy.

Vowels in Order

The mischievous student answered *facetiously*; and the last student, by not saying yes and not saying no (abstaining), answered *abstemiously*.

She Paid Easily

The car was right-hand-drive, rare in the USA but common in England. The tollbooth was on the left side of the car, right next to Cecily's window. Cooper, on the right (far) side of the car, would have had to reach past Cecily or get out of the car entirely to pay the toll himself.

The Happy Cabdriver

The speculator, familiar with the legal status of unsold property, told the cabdriver that driving across vacant lots was legal. The cab driver, not owning the cab, proceeded over curbstones and diagonally through vacant lots and delivered the speculator to his destination quickly and cheaply.

Fix That Clothes Washer!

The generator gave 117 volts DC (direct current). Zeke may have preferred DC because it can be used to charge batteries easily. That way, continuous power is available even while the generator is off; it comes on as needed to charge the batteries. If Zeke wanted power only for series-wound motors (as in power tools) and incandescent lamps, then DC would be adequate. Series-wound motors actually run better on DC than on AC. Unfortunately for Zeke, synchronous induction motors (as in timer motors), electronic devices, fluorescent lamps, and many other appliances require AC. Zeke, therefore, had to decide between advancing the washer cycle by hand and getting an AC generator or DC-to-AC voltage converter to supply power to the timer motor or even the entire clothes washer.

Brighter at Night

The structure is the interior of a long motor-vehicle tunnel. It is lit by only its lighting by day, but its lighting is supplemented by headlights at night. Drivers, if aware of the possibility of an accidental or deliberate shutoff of the tunnel lighting, would turn on their parking lights by day. Similarly, they would turn off their headlights by night to avoid needless rear-mirror glare for the drivers in front of them.

Rope on its End

Soak the rope in water so that it is thoroughly wet, then hang it outdoors in subfreezing weather or in a walk-in freezer. When the water freezes, the rope will be sufficiently rigid that a piece of it can stand on end. Soft-laid natural-fiber rope will work more effectively than hard-laid or synthetic-fiber rope.

She Cheated

The teacher recalled from Sherry's earlier essays, and from the current one, that she confused "its" with "it's." The question in dispute, with both answers identical, included a few misuses of "its" and "it's." Mary used those two words correctly in all her other work, so she must have copied Sherry's answer, errors and all.

Zelda Was Cured

Her husband lengthened the legs of the crib so that they could pick up their baby without bending down to do so. The incessant bending, especially when the back and pelvic ligaments have become loosened for childbirth, strains the back muscles. Increasing the height of the crib reduces the need for bending, a detail often ignored by many obstetricians.

She Kept Her Cool

Alexis knew that too much cooling power would make a room cool, but also uncomfortably humid. If they reduce the room temperatures of similar rooms by the same amount, a low-power air conditioner lowers humidity more effectively than does a high-power air conditioner. But against extreme heat, a high-power air conditioner is needed. Alexis wanted the flexibility available by being able to use a small air conditioner, a large air conditioner, or both. She would turn on both during a hot and dry spell, but only the small one during a humid day with a temperature just slightly too warm.

Lost Again
The son noted that the moon was almost, but not quite, full. If you stand facing south, the changes of phase of the moon move from right to left. A half-moon with its straight edge to the left has a luminous area at its right and is waxing. A half-moon with its straight edge to the right has a dark area at its right and is waning. Because the son saw the moon through the light cloud cover and remembered whether it was getting bigger or smaller, he easily located which way was south and inferred which way was north.

Not For Ransom
The men ran a prostitution ring; the woman had led a crusade to increase enforcement of anti-prostitution laws. The men gave her a five-hundred-dollar bill (very rare, but still legal). They noted that her being seen naked with five hundred dollars would appear to be a cheap publicity stunt, would perhaps gain little or no sympathy from the police, and would make her look ridiculous.

Her Good Message
The boss had a meeting scheduled with the client, at the client's office across town, only a few minutes later. The secretary inferred that the boss would be better off pleading a traffic jam than admitting that he had forgot about the meeting.

She's Not Afraid
The term "six-footer" can mean someone six feet tall, or, as Bertha used it, having six feet—like the cockroach that she had swatted.

by Edward J. Harshman

Money and Laundering
Laundry detergent, because it is strong enough to attack dirt, may weaken dye or fabric. Ignoring wear on clothing when selecting laundry detergents or other additives can accelerate wear and make clothing wear out faster than necessary. Money and clothes-shopping time can be saved by using a detergent that minimizes damage to clothing, even if the per-load cost of detergent seems high.

Honest Ivan
Noting the much lower per-day cost of renting a car in Florida than in Washington, Ivan rented the car in Florida. He had it shipped from central Florida to a town in northern Virginia, where he retrieved it. The shipping cost was less than the total savings from renting the car in Florida and returning it to where he got it. By proving that he had sent the car by train, he convinced investigators that the odometer reading was genuine.

He Wasn't Parking
Vick had just overtaken a truck as it drove slowly up a long steep hill. He had the accelerator pedal on the floor. At the top of the hill, he took his foot off of the pedal and discovered that it had jammed. He shut off the engine and was able to pull over safely as the car gradually slowed down. Merely shifting to neutral would have been dangerous, for he would have lost the benefit of engine drag and was at the top of another long steep hill.

Easy Repair
Walter knew that cars in long-term parking lots can be stolen fairly easily. After parking his car, he unfastened the battery cable and deliberately left the headlight switch on. He hoped that, if a thief broke in and tried to start the car, he would infer from the headlight switch that the battery was dead and would not bother further with the car. When Walter returned, he merely reconnected the battery and drove away.

Too Precise
In a politician's campaign office. They were volunteers for a candidate who believed in straightforward platforms instead of vague speeches.

Giving Wayne the Boot
Burglars had cut the neighbor's telephone wire and broken into his house. In self-defense, and without a mobile phone, he barricaded himself into an upstairs room and successfully provoked Wayne to call the police.

Soliciting in Seattle
In Seattle (as of 1997), one building housed the headquarters of several charity canvassing organizations. They sent workers out to collect money, and those workers usually walked from the building when they started canvassing and returned to it on foot when they were finished. Only one of the friends' two houses was within easy walking distance of that building.

Kingfist Found Him
The letter was sent by Kingfist, certified and with delivery restricted to the addressee, to a fictitious person care of Horace. Kingfist waited until the mail carriers on Horace's route got familiar with his apartment number, so that they could deliver a letter even if the apartment number was missing from it. Then he sent the certified letter and waited. The mail carrier tried to deliver the letter to the fictitious person, but Horace was not allowed to sign for it. Therefore, the letter was not delivered and was returned to the sender, Kingfist. By then, the carrier had written the apartment number on the front of the envelope. Kingfist merely read the apartment number from the envelope.

Miracle Cures
After pretending to have a serious back injury and collecting a large judgment, a malingering patient can go to a well-known source of miracle cures and pronounce himself recovered without leaving any evidence of fraud.

Happy with the TV Ad

The man was a political candidate running for a local office. Tipped off that his rival had bought a 30-minute infomercial time slot, he bought the minute just before it and broadcast a test pattern hoping to induce television viewers not to continue watching that particular channel.

Staged Roulette

The police chief had a crooked gambling joint raided and easily obtained a rigged roulette wheel for the show.

The Outside Line

The caller was a prisoner, who was allowed to call the hospital but not people in general. He was trying to bluff the receptionist into permitting an outside line so he could call whom he wished. (This scam was tried repeatedly at a hospital in Nantucket, Massachusetts, which was so small that the doctors and their voices were recognized. It failed, of course.)

Boat-Bashing

The purchaser was the production crew of a disaster movie in which Brandon's boat was to be used in a crash scene. Brandon paid to see the movie at a theater, but unfortunately that particular crash scene had been cut.

Posted Property

He sprayed the post stubs with lighter fluid and set them on fire. The ashes were easily removed with a spoon and a few damp rags.

Her Own Nasty Letter

After getting the letter in the mail, which she had addressed in pencil, she erased her address and typed a false address and a false return address on the envelope. Then she surreptitiously dropped it in the ladies' room at work, knowing that it would be discovered and opened and that vicious gossip would start.

Too Many Books

He donated them to the local library, getting a tax deduction and the right to borrow them again, during library hours, whenever he wished.

Exiled

In parts of ancient Greece, if disproportionate power was held by one man in the city, he was ordered out of the city for a year. There was no punitive intent, and he could expect a friendly welcome when he later returned. The exile was a protocol to protect against concentration and potential abuse of power, similar to term limits in our modern government.

Checks Cashed Here

The store was a jewelry store. By pocketing the checks given to him by prestigious customers and writing up sales to them as cash, he was obtaining checks at the cost of their face value. His accomplices, later, disguised as those same customers, used the genuine checks as part of their disguise and purchased same-priced items. Meanwhile, they shoplifted expensive jewelry. The store did not interfere because the customers' genuine purchases and goodwill were worth the shoplifting loss.

Cool Car, Dirty Windshield

Calvin made a snowball and rubbed it on his windshield. When it got dirty, he threw it away and used another snowball. Then he cleaned the wiper blades with yet another snowball, got in his car, and temporarily turned on the wipers. The windshield was clean.

Keys Locked In

The car was owned by Elmer's boss, who was away on business. The boss was expected to arrive at the airport, returning from the trip, at a late hour when taxis were scarce. Elmer and a co-worker, therefore, drove in two separate cars to the airport; and the co-worker drove Elmer from it. Elmer left the car keys in the trunk, as his boss had told him to do. The boss had a second set of keys.

by Edward J. Harshman

Forgiven Break-In
The house was on fire, and the fireman rescued a baby from a smoky room upstairs.

Hates to Break Windows
When she looked out the window, Tina saw dense clouds of smoke rising from the floor below. She knew that if she broke the window, she would have to breathe smokier air than she was already breathing.

The Fifty-Pound Losses
Andy was on a reducing diet and lost weight. Bertie lost fifty British pounds at a casino in London, but later won them back. Charlie lost his legs in an accident.

Legal Conspiracy
Mugsy and Butch were writing a mystery book, which proved to be very popular. Rocky's information on police procedures was useful to the authors, who happily paid him for it.

Strange Bedroom
David's home was a trailer, which was fastened to his car.

The Misleading Telephone Message
The message was recorded on the voicemail outgoing message of the store, by remote call-in, by a prankster who obtained the voice mail password of the store and who presumably had a gripe against the store and possibly the telephone company. It is possible to call several disconnected numbers on purpose, record the change-of-number messages, and edit the messages together to form a message that sounds exactly like the one described. Learning the remote call-in password on the store voice mail permits such a message to be planted as its outgoing message, frustrating and perhaps discouraging would-be customers.

Give Them a Hand
They were assembling mannequins for a clothing store display.

Hot Car

The engine temperature was higher than normal, and Lucy did not want to have the radiator boil over. To help cool the engine by removing excess heat, she turned on the heater. This act permitted her to finish her trip safely, if uncomfortably; she may have been stranded in a traffic jam if she had not done so.

Find Bingo!

Bingo was a parakeet.

Another Cold Fire

As the fire burned, hot air went up the chimney. Cold air from outside entered the house, cooling the house by more than it was warmed by the fire. John and Joan could have slightly opened a window near the fireplace and made sure to close all of the other windows; having the only open windows in one or more rooms far from the fireplace would have been the worst possible arrangement.

He Held His Liquor

Andy, after the first beer, ordered one beer and one serving of soda whenever he walked over to the bartender. He had become tired of being accused of unwillingness to drink heavily, and the bartender cooperated by pouring the soda into Andy's empty beer bottle.

Pleased With Pork

The man was a marketing expert, who had been hired by the restaurant's owners to increase its business. He was pleased to see that the restaurant already offered several pork dishes; for he knew of a planned advertising blitz by pork producers to promote their product and expected the restaurant, already with pork offerings, to make a profit from them.

Can't Turn It Off!

Her son, as a practical joke, had painted a burned-out bulb with phosphorescent paint, held it in strong light, and put it into her mother's bedroom lamp in place of its ordinary bulb.

by Edward J. Harshman

Half-Jaundiced
The patient had a glass eye.

A Matter of Survival
Mort, furious at being robbed almost weekly, had some friends with semi-automatic rifles help him stake out his store. Caught by surprise in a crossfire, a gang of three robbers could not retaliate or escape; and all three were killed. The police investigator looked at the weapons, the pattern of the bullet holes, and the known felons who lay dead and inferred what happened. Sympathetic, the investigator made a report that corroborated Mort's story and told him and the news media that no further inquiry would occur.

The Universal Solvent
In space. The so-called solvent is a black hole, which irreversibly absorbs everything that falls into it. Not all black holes are as massive as stars. The scientist has located a small one and plans to guide it into orbit by feeding it suitable masses from precisely calculated positions.

The Investment Scam
The fund manager took money from a few investors, got additional money from subsequent investors, and used that money to give the original investors a good return on their investment. These original investors, happy with their big returns, would recruit their friends and make additional large investments themselves. When the fund manager had enough money from investors, he disappeared. To keep investors from catching him, he had a confederate make telephone calls posing as an FBI agent and diverting attention away from his real hiding place in the USA and from the fact that no real investigation was already underway.

He's All Wet
The man had attached small rubber tubes to the umbrella ribs, pierced the tubes with a needle, and connected them to a water source. He was at a shopping mall and was deliberately keeping

353

himself wet because he was a charity volunteer seeking donations for flood victims.

Driving the Wrong Car

The battery on the broken car was dead, and Hermie knew that the electrical system was suspect. He wanted the car checked thoroughly. He jump-started it with the working car, after which it could be driven. The working car had a manual transmission and could be towed without transmission damage. But the jump-started car had an automatic transmission, which is affected by towing. Hermie, therefore, towed the car that had the manual transmission.

Dismaying Dizziness

The ceiling lamp was fluorescent, and the new wallpaper had closely spaced vertical stripes. Fluorescent bulbs do not glow steadily, but flash 120 times per second. When viewing vertical stripes in fluorescent light, the intermittent lighting can make the stripes seem to turn as you turn your head, when they really stay fastened to the wall. This inconsistency is disturbing and is what caused the dizziness. The simplest remedy is to use only daylight. A more practical solution is to replace the fluorescent lamp with one that does not flicker, or replace the wallpaper.

There Goes The Sun

Edgar was in a polar region, between the true north or south pole and its corresponding magnetic pole. If he were on a line connecting the true and magnetic poles, then the compass directions would be exactly backwards. On the vernal and autumnal equinoxes, the sun rises exactly in the east and sets exactly in the west. At no other time of year does the sun rise and set at exactly opposite points on the horizon. Therefore, Edgar was between a true pole and its magnetic pole during an equinox.

It's a Dog's Life

They were at an animal shelter, which had a surplus of unwanted pets and had to kill those that it could not give to willing owners. Fred knew that people were often more willing to adopt a disfigured pet than an intact one. The injured puppy was likely to be taken by a loving family, but the healthy dog had no special claim for compassion and was too old to bond to its owners as strongly as do young puppies. Therefore, Fred expected the older dog to be humanely killed.

Rx Lead Poisoning

Chelation with EDTA is the recommended treatment for lead poisoning, and most insurance companies pay for that treatment. It is also, according to many doctors, a useful treatment for atherosclerosis; but most insurance companies don't pay for it for that diagnosis. The doctor was unwilling to falsify an insurance claim or a laboratory test, but craftily noted that the patient could be maneuvered into receiving appropriate treatment that would be insured without making any false statements whatever.

No Ransom Demand

The man was a cancer patient and was getting weaker and weaker. He had no medical insurance and would soon need hospital care. Confined to a wheelchair, he sat on the gun as he entered the government building. He threatened people in a room next to the district attorney's office so that he would be apprehended as quickly as possible, and he happily went to prison. He knew that, while he was a prisoner, the government would pay his medical expenses and that life as a hospital patient is essentially identical with or without serving a prison sentence.

Collecting Backwards

Not enough money was in the debtor's account for the check to clear. Kingfist merely found out how much money he needed to deposit for the check to be good, then deposited it and quickly cashed the check. This procedure reduced, although it did not eliminate, the debt.

by Edward J. Harshman

She Arrived On Time
Carol was not at home. She had her telephone calls diverted to her mobile phone and happened to be in the coffee house when Daryl called her.

Slow-Witted Customers
The menus of the fast-food restaurants offer soft drinks in different-sized cups, labeled "Small," "Medium", and "Large," with correspondingly different prices. They also offer *unlimited free refills* on the same soft drinks!

A Prayer for Escape
Being tied up by kidnappers or other captors. You hope that the rope with which they will bind your wrists will be looped repeatedly around them while your palms are together and that your captors do not know that, when you later separate your palms, you may have enough slack in the rope to slip it off your hands.

A Tiring Question
Because of the engine weight, there is more weight on the front

wheels than the back wheels of a car. Additionally, because of steering around curves, front wheels travel farther than rear wheels. Because a paved road is slightly higher in the center than at its edges, for water drainage, broken glass and similar debris tend to migrate to its edge. Therefore, the students independently figured that the curbside front tire is most likely to go flat and, on the exam, identified that tire for the instructor.

Discarded Meat

The neighbor had an unrestrained vicious dog, who had attacked Paul's three-year-old daughter. Due to the Paul's lack of legal recourse against the neighbor in that particular southern city, he retaliated by smashing a bottle and putting the broken glass in a hamburger, which he then threw away. The dog, predictably, noticed the smell that night, ripped the meat from the bag, gobbled it down, and promptly died.

Flour and Cement

If the cement-flour mixture is placed near water, so the story goes, rats that are immune to rat poison will eat the mixture, drink the water, and die of indigestion. Bleah.

Dirty Conduct

Their cat had caught a violent respiratory infection and was wheezing, with fluid leaking from its nose. George sucked the fluid into his mouth and spat it out, several times, restoring its easy breathing but risking catching the infection himself. His mother, therefore, ordered George to wash his mouth hoping to reduce the chance that he would get sick.

Blouse Befuddlement

Christina was difficult to fit, so she got her blouse custom made. It was of a fabric that required dry cleaning. Because many dry cleaners charge more to clean a woman's blouse than a man's shirt of identical construction, the dressmaker put the buttons on the right and the buttonholes on the left, as on a man's shirt, so that Christina could call it a man's shirt and save substantial money over the life of the blouse.

by Edward J. Harshman

Trapped

It was a prosthetic leg that was caught in the trap. The burglar had to unfasten the artificial leg and hop away. Identifying him by the details of the artificial leg, by inquiring of local prosthetists, was easy.

Eager Surgeons

Prosthetics has improved greatly recently. Offered good-looking functional artificial hands and well-balanced artificial legs and feet, patients correctly realize that a mangled limb, even after the best possible surgical repair, would not work as well as its artificial replacement and prefer the latter. Good prostheses are very expensive.

Hub Cap Obsolescence

Her hub caps had a large stripe across them, which spun rapidly as she drove in daylight. Fluorescent lights do not glow continuously; they flicker very rapidly. Glenda knew that the stripe on her hub caps, in flickering light, would appear to move very slowly or in reverse. She did not want her car to appear to be stopped if it was moving, for she feared confusing other drivers.

Her Unromantic Reply

They were aboard a small ship, and she was seasick.

He Crashed Deliberately

A crazily driven car had swerved in front of him and was about to collide head-on. He wisely decided to hit a parked car instead of an oncoming car. The oncoming car, immediately afterward, crashed into a tree; and its driver was identified and held responsible for the accident.

He Overpaid

Rick's bank did not offer a debit card that would work outside the USA, and he was planning to take a trip overseas right after graduating. By making a large deliberate overpayment on his credit card, he compensated for the low credit limit that usually afflicts new and unemployed credit-card holders. By greatly increasing his available credit, Rick traveled without carrying significant cash or paying travelers' check service charges. He also got better exchange rates by making purchases with the card than he would have by exchanging dollars for local currency at his bank.

Arrested for Shopping

The man had switched the lid that was on the jar for another lid, the same size, that he had unscrewed from a smaller jar. The cashier noticed the inappropriate price and had the man arrested for attempted fraud.

Mysterious Captions

The movie had been previously received from a satellite or cable TV hookup and, while being broadcast, was recorded with a closed-caption decoder interposed between the satellite receiver or cable TV converter and the video cassette recorder. This apparatus was in another room, not connected to the television set that Susan was watching. Recording through the caption decoder put the captions on the tape so that any television set would show them. Taping such movies for personal use in the households that receive the signal is legal.

He Hated Bad Attitudes

Percy had substantial unearned income for which the income tax liability exceeded his earnings from his job. He merely filled out a W-4 form, instructing his employer to divert part of his earnings for income tax payments, that called for so much withholding that his paychecks were for only two cents. Percy had to send money to the Internal Revenue Service every three months to pay income tax on his unearned income, so he merely sent the IRS less to match the additional withholding. Sometimes he cashed his two-cent payroll checks immediately, sometimes he waited six months to cash them, and sometimes he threw them away entirely. Whatever Percy did with his paychecks, the payroll clerk had new difficulties.

by Edward J. Harshman

Truckers Were Arrested

They were on a turnpike, with a toll barrier at each entrance and each exit. On such a turnpike, a driver without an electronic toll-paying device takes a ticket from a booth when he drives onto it and gives it and the appropriate fee to the toll booth attendant when he drives off of it. When the papers were dropped, Hank and Frank accidentally swapped tickets. Then, when they tried to leave the turnpike at what looked like the same places they entered it, they were arrested for making illegal U turns.

The Traffic Ticket

Paul's car was an antique convertible. He put it in a rented small truck that just barely held it, carefully filled it with his other belongings, and drove the truck. He did not want to fasten a trailer to his antique car or subject it to highway stress. Paul's only mistake was driving on a highway that was restricted to cars and that did not permit trucks.

Steamed Up

She turned on the heater, leaving the air conditioner on. Her air conditioner circulated too little air to remove the uncomfortable humidity. By turning on the heater, she forced the air conditioner to take in and dehumidify more air.

Where's the Sunshine?

East-west position on the earth is measured in degrees east or west of a standard line that runs on the earth's surface between the north and south poles. A complete circle around the earth, at any constant latitude, measures 360 degrees. A time zone comprises a range of longitude that shares a common time, so that clocks need not be reset for travel entirely within the zone. The average width of these time zones is 15 degrees, so that moving from one time zone to another involves setting clocks backward or forward by one hour. A person standing on a 15-degree meridian would note that the sun is due south at high noon. Someone standing off of the meridian would note the sun off to one side, east or west, at noon. Most locations are not exactly on a meridian that is a multiple of 15 degrees.

The Will

Pat, Leslie, and Terry were women. Leslie worked in a fertility clinic and outraged local religious extremists. Terry married a male nurse. Evelyn, the only son, was not law-abiding and inherited nothing. The estate went 1/5 to each of Pat, Leslie, and Terry and 2/5 to Evelyn's son.

The Upside-Down Newspaper

The man was a recent immigrant and did not know English. He enjoyed sitting in the park, but he did not want to be recognized as knowing only a foreign language. He hid a native-language book behind the newspaper hoping that no one would notice that he was reading the book and not the newspaper.

Catch The Dollar

Drop not a paper dollar, but a stack of ten dimes. The question did not require the use of a dollar bill.

Hazard In The Code

Electrical outlets, if in walls, must be a minimum distance above the floor. This provision protects against electric shock when the floor is washed. Actually placing such outlets at that minimum legal height, however, makes them a hazard to young children, who may become entangled in the wires or "inspect" the outlet too closely. Too, such placement makes outlets inaccessible to adults without stooping or crawling. Tall, old, or handicapped people may need to ask others, even children, to plug and unplug electrical devices, because they themselves cannot reach the outlets.

Miracle Shopper

Dolores had been paraplegic and wheelchair-bound for years. She had broken her leg in a recent unrelated accident, but easily wheeled herself as usual to a local supermarket and back, carrying her groceries on her lap.

by Edward J. Harshman

He Knew His Materials

He went to a metalworks shop with an ordinary adjustable wrench and noted the right-hand thread of the adjusting screw and of the setscrew that held it in place. He had the metalworks shop make a wrench with left-hand thread for those two parts. Then he took an empty paint can and welded a vertical partition in it, so that the halves could be filled with different colors of paint. He fastened two small paint brushes together so that they could be handled as a unit, and he delivered the double brush with the two-sided can and explained that the brush should be dipped simultaneously into the two halves of the can and then dragged across a surface to paint stripes. Finally, he found a wooden spool and a short piece of threaded pipe such that the inner diameter of the pipe was slightly bigger than the diameter of the spool. He cut an end off the spool, put the piece of pipe on the spool, and glued the end back onto the spool. He now had pipe thread wrapped around the spool.

Brian Braggart's Fish Story

Thirty feet underwater, the pressure is greater than on land. Filling one's lungs with high-pressure air and then holding one's breath while ascending to the surface, which is at ordinary pressure, would make one's lungs burst. By gradually breathing out, one can ascend safely.

The Counterfeit Money

The man was angry with the clerk for a previous unrelated incident. He returned to the store and flashed his stack of counterfeit money. He aggressively demanded merchandise from the clerk, complained about it, and made the clerk show him more and more items. Finally, the man threw the counterfeit bills into a trashcan and stormed out in mock disgust. The clerk retrieved the counterfeit money and was promptly arrested when he tried to spend it.

Hearing them Quickly

The father had noticed the planned live concert and noticed that it was also to be on television. Microphones would be a few feet from the performers and would capture the sound for television transmission. The audience, potentially including Dana, would be farther from the performers than the microphones would be. Sound travels at about 800 feet per second. Television waves and the electric currents that create and respond to them travel over a million times faster than sound. The father correctly figured that the television audience would hear the performance sooner than the live audience, for there would be less delay while sound waves travel the short distance to the microphones and from TV speakers to viewers than while sound waves travel the full distance from performers to the live audience. The difference is only a fraction of a second, but the father was nevertheless telling the truth.

Seasonal Mileage
Claude uses the air conditioner during summer. Just before the end of a trip, he turns it off so as not to waste fuel. He does not want to pay to keep the car cool while he is not in it. He is sensitive to cold, however; and he keeps the heat on whenever he needs it including when just about to get out of his car.

The Fast Elevator Trip
When the elevator arrived, other people crowded into it; and Bill critically watched them push buttons for several floors. Bill figured that the elevator would stop at most floors at which it could stop. Therefore, noting that another elevator was approaching, he decided to get onto it instead; for he would share it with fewer passengers while it made far fewer intermediate stops on the way to his appointment. Avoiding the intermediate stops was worth the wait.

Secret Fuel
Marvin's neighbor had recently bought an extravagant sports car and bragged about it constantly. Hoping to quiet him down, Marvin poured a gallon of fuel into its fuel tank every few nights. After the neighbor began to boast about his new car's outstanding mileage, Marvin knew that his plan would work: merely add fuel quietly, then stop and let the neighbor wonder why the mileage suddenly deteriorated just as the warranty expired.

by Edward J. Harshman

Night Blindness Cure
1. Do you get night blindness only when driving your car?
2. When did you last clean and aim your headlights?

Ballpark Befuddlement
The nine men were practicing golf swings on a driving range.

No Television Trouble
A portable television set was on the dashboard, and it was off. Stuart was listening to an audio recording of his favorite show's theme music.

Down With Average
Being lost in the woods. Very bright children can learn and follow instructions regarding what to do if lost, or at least climb a tree to see and be seen. Cognitively limited children don't know any better, so they usually stay put until rescuers find them. Children of ordinary intelligence are the ones most likely to get lost further as they try to find their way.

Sound Reasoning
He had recently been cited for playing music too loudly. Because the police had not taken the precaution of impounding his car, he quickly changed the sound system so that, by proving it could not play music loudly, he could get the charges dropped.

The Marble
The electrician had just installed a stove and was about to level it so that grease would not pool at the side of a skillet during frying. But he had forgotten his level. So he put the borrowed marble on a large pan on a stove burner and adjusted the stove legs so that the marble would not roll.

The Predictable Cold
He was an actor on a soap opera. His boss threatened him by ordering the scriptwriters to give his character a minor illness, adding that he would either recover or, if he continued his irritating ways, his character would become critically ill and die—losing

him his job.

Canned

For fire safety, students were instructed not to lock their room doors at night. But Adam had withdrawn a large amount of cash for his trip. To protect the cash against theft, he stacked the soda cans in front of his door, as a makeshift burglar alarm, before going to sleep.

Easy as Pi

The capital letter Π helps one remember where to put the tape when hanging a poster. It has an approximately rectangular shape, with free ends at the sides of the top corners and at the bottom of the lower corners. If you tape a poster on a wall by placing the tape at the sides of the upper corners and the bottom of the lower corners, then it may eventually start to fall from the wall as the tape gives way. But the shear forces are such that the poster will not rip as it falls. Any other way of applying tape across the corners risks making the poster rip if it eventually starts to fall.

Suitcase Stress

"Well, officer, I did stop for a cup of coffee on the way to the airport," Sam explained at check-in. "So my suitcase was unattended for a minute or two, and the cabdriver seemed a little creepy. I think we'd all feel better if you search it." They did, and found a large stack of counterfeit foreign money that, if first seen in the country where Sam landed, would have thrown Sam in prison for years.

The Worrisome Guarantee

The part was an air bag; and the customer noted that it could be guaranteed to last a lifetime only if it killed, or let die, the driver. It would thereby last a lifetime by being guaranteed to shorten the life of the driver, exactly what the customer did not want.

Fast Broke

This puzzle is based on a true incident. Crazy Kate was driving at night, and there was very little traffic on the highway. When the alternator belt broke (rattling briefly as it shook free of the pulleys and fell to the ground), the electrical-system failure light on the dashboard came on. She knew that, without the battery's being charged by the engine, the headlights would run it down in a few hours. She therefore drove as fast as possible, hoping to get to a repair station before being stranded. By driving in the center of the highway, straddling both lanes, she could speed up and could compensate for the loose steering.

He Wanted the Copy

The tape was a VHS videotape copy of a foreign movie that was not available in the USA. He had to copy the tape from the European (PAL) format to the USA (NTSC) format with a special rented video cassette recorder (VCR) before he could see it on his own VCR. Most video stores in the USA do not buy or sell videotapes in the PAL format; USA videotapes (and DVD's) use the NTSC standard not the PAL standard that is used in, for example, Europe and South America.

He Didn't Mean to Kill

The car was a hearse, and the passenger had been previously killed in an unrelated incident.

Another Bad Check

He wrote VOID on the check with latent ink, which would become visible shortly after the creditor accepted it.

There's a Fly in my Soup!

Anticipating that the waiter would remove the fly but not replace the soup, the man put lots of sugar in it. Tasting the soup when it was returned, he knew that it had not been replaced.

She Hated Leftovers

Sally shaped the six hamburgers long and thin, like hot dogs. She bought two packages of hot dog rolls (16 total), and put each hamburger and each hot dog into one hot dog roll.

Wrong Answers are Plentiful
FULL.

The Crooked Headlight
The car had four headlights, two low-beam and two high-beam. A low-beam headlight burned out. The man re-aimed the high-beam light on the same side of the car so that it would work like a low-beam light. He also unplugged the high-beam light on the other side of the car. That procedure gave him two working headlights, one on each side of the car, that acted like low-beam headlights. He could then drive safely until he could get another headlight bulb.

The Mail is In!
Oscar impatiently awaited receiving whatever he sent for. Of course, it was unrealistic for him to expect a mail carrier to deliver the merchandise exactly when the order form was collected. But that is what Oscar did. He noted that a package pod that had a key in its lock the previous evening, when he mailed the order form, no longer had its key and therefore must contain a package. Although Oscar may have inferred wrongly that the package was for him, he

correctly inferred that the mail was delivered because only the mail carrier could have removed the key from the pod.

One Way to Liberty

Two spiral staircases, sharing the same center axis, are wrapped around each other. While climbing, you can look directly overhead and see the bottom of stairs that are used for descending.

Trials of the Uninvited

The nanny and kids were goats, and Ron was trying to convince John to buy them from him to keep John's lawn trimmed.

Tied Up In Knots

Fasten one rope end to itself, making a loop, then pass an end of the other rope through the loop and fasten it to itself also. Interlocking bowline knots are commonly used to fasten different-sized ropes together.

Sprayed at the Lawn Again

The electrical power had been off for about an hour. Henry would have seen that clocks and electronic devices that monitor the time (microwave ovens, for example) would have had to be reset.

Bad Directions

Ethan realized that, on the way home, he would be driving at night and at risk for getting lost, because signs and landmarks are hard to see at night. After getting directions, he studied them. Then he turned over the paper and wrote down how to drive home again. Unfortunately, he tried following the return-trip directions while driving to his relatives; for he was reading from the wrong side of the paper. He lived on Main Street and so did they, and he followed the return-trip instructions easily when they told him to leave the driveway and turn onto that street. Only when he tried to leave the Main Street near his home town did he get lost.

Defying Gravity

He had been painting the ceiling of a doll house, and he had turned it upside down to keep paint off its walls.

Unsolved Robbery
The two men are in a prison. The second man robbed the bank and was not identified, but he was promptly arrested for another crime and given a long sentence for it.

Brian Braggart and the Ant
Brian was describing the preserved remains of a theoretically impossible creature. Ants, like all insects, receive oxygen not through lungs but through breathing tubes. The tubes circulate oxygen by diffusion, without aid from a heart, a diaphragm, or any other pumping device. Diffusion works well only for small distances. Therefore, a large ant would suffocate. Also, if an ant doubles in every linear dimension, then the cross-section area of its legs increases to four times its original area. This, of course, increases the ant's legs' strength fourfold. But every part of the ant increases in three dimensions. Each part of the ant, therefore the entire ant, increases its weight to eight times its original weight. Doubling the size of an ant, therefore, increases its weight twice as much as its strength. A sufficiently large ant, by using similar reasoning, would be too weak to stand and may even promptly collapse on itself.

Supposed to Kill?
A scene was being filmed for a movie. For the protection of actors, it was universally agreed that anyone on the receiving end of a firearm had to load it personally with nonhazardous "blanks". This particular actor had forgotten to load the gun, and the scene had to be refilmed.

The Test Question
Emergency vehicles with sirens and flashing lights are allowed to run red lights when responding to an emergency. Henry was preparing to enter the police force.

The Late Train
During the night, which was in early spring, the time was advanced from standard time to daylight saving time. The engineer gained

fifteen minutes during the night, but the train was still late when Amanda got off it.

The Nonstop Elevator Trip

The floor was at the top of one range of floors served by one group of elevators. Jill instead used the adjacent group of elevators, going to the lowest floor served by them, which was one floor above her floor. Then, after her nonstop elevator ride, she merely walked down one flight of stairs.

Short-Lived Writing

Erasing colored chalk. Yolanda is a teacher and sometimes draws diagrams on the blackboard with colored chalk. Erasing such diagrams leaves colored smudges on the blackboard. Yolanda discovered that scribbling over the colored smudges with white chalk and erasing the scribbling helps remove the colored smudges and, unlike wiping the blackboard with a wet rag, permits immediate re-use of it.

The Debtor Paid

He went to small claims court, got a judgment, and donated the loan, with its judgment, to a racist extremist group with an ethnic background different from that of the customer. The extremist group was happy to receive the right to harass legally someone of its least favored race, exceeded the limits of the law in its enthusiasm, and scared the debtor into paying. Laws that restrict collection agents, those who are hired to collect money on behalf of someone else, do not apply to creditors directly. Selling a judgment at a heavy discount or giving it away outright can therefore be a prudent business practice, for it bypasses the collection-agent restrictions and may scare other debtors into paying promptly.

A Headache of a Problem

The doctor, making a house call to investigate intractable nausea, developed a headache while in the patient's house that cleared as soon as he stepped outside. He inferred a problem with the furnace, with improper ventilation, which might have been otherwise very hard to identify.

Too Much Money

The investor was going to be a limited partner. Someone who invests in a company as a limited partner does not have the right to manage the company, not even partial or voting rights. Such an arrangement is common and completely legal and ethical. Without management authority, the investor wouldn't be concerned about losing control to other investors; for he would have none to lose. What worried him were the personal finances of the people who were going to manage the company. They could have invested all of their money in it, but didn't. If they had a lot of money outside the company, then the investor feared that they expected the company to fail.

Ouch!

Being beaten, as by muggers. You are trying to make them think they have already injured you seriously, hoping that they will let you alone and not really do so.

Airplane in Flight

When an airplane is on the ground, its body supports the wings. When it is in the air, the wings support the body. Metal, though strong, is not completely rigid. Therefore, as the weight of the airplane shifts onto the wings during takeoff, they are bent upward slightly by the air pressure beneath them. When the pressure is released during landing, the wings bend downward slightly. You can see this wing motion during the takeoff and landing of a large commercial airplane if you look carefully.

Forgiven

Mary had an out-of-print book, that she liked, and wanted several copies to give away as Christmas presents. It turned out to be very hard to find. So she sent a photocopy to the publisher and convinced its editors to reprint it. They were grateful because it sold well.

Plastered

Fannie wanted some chairs, with wooden seats, that would be

by Edward J. Harshman

comfortable to sit in. To learn the best contour for them, she sat in plaster so that she could have the resulting shape carved into the wooden seats.

Mysterious Moon

A telephoto lens, which makes things look bigger, is farther from the camera film than a standard lens. Similarly, with the human eye, when its lens is farther from the retina, objects will look bigger than when it is closer. Gravity pulls the lens slightly closer when someone is looking up than when looking straight ahead, thereby causing the illusion of a difference in size, because the eye is not rigid. This effect is virtually unnoticeable because, perhaps by changing the shape of the lens itself, the eye maintains good focus.

Silly Goose

The priest did not ascertain the identity of the goose's rightful owner. Having stolen a goose, the man got explicit permission from its former owner to keep it, for the goose had been stolen from the priest!

Unfare Increase

The author actually made this proposal at a Transit Authority hearing in 1992. Mark and number parking spaces in residential neighborhoods, then auction annual leases for them to the highest bidders. A parking space leaseholder would be able to park easily, and a non-leaseholder would know that no parking space was available and would use public transportation instead of driving. Either way, driving slowly to seek parking spaces would stop. Money would be available to the Transit Authority from the leases. And many owners of single-family townhouses could park their cars at the curb in front of their houses if they wished to do so.

The One-Penny Contribution

The penny was a 1909S VDB or other rare coin and was worth well over a thousand dollars.

Mess on the Rug
The powder was an absorbent and was scattered to absorb a liquid that had just been accidentally spilled. Diana took off her shoes and tried to mix the powder in with the rug fibers as thoroughly as possible, intending to vacuum the powder and thereby remove the spilled liquid too.

He Made a Killing
Scott, anticipating restrictions on the manufacture and importation of high-capacity firearms, bought all he could afford. As he expected, the new laws permitted existing assault firearms to be owned and traded. They became more valuable, because of anticipated scarcity. Nancy thought of their presumably intended use, killing, and winced.

Heavy-Footed Harry
Harry is a horse.

The Clock was Right
It was 11:01 P.M., as shown on a digital display clock. The digits 1101 in base 2 translate to 13 in ordinary decimal notation. Intense study of binary numbers for the preceding several hours could easily have confused Al momentarily, especially if he was working very late.

The Inferior Car Rental
Sally planned a trip to more than one place. She first drove to one destination, then from it traveled by airplane to a second destination. Finally, she traveled by airplane to her home city. Obviously, she did not want to drive her own car to the distant airport and not be able to get it back easily.

The Mail Must Go Through
The stake was directly between the dog and the front door and was only 15 feet from the door. The dog, therefore, could easily get to the front door and attack the mail carrier.

The Switch of Mastery

Late at night, in a rural area without nearby neighbors or street lights, the mother could turn off the main light switch and effect complete darkness. Then, they would all be master of all they see because they could not see anything.

Time in Reverse

The man was a hairdresser and wanted a clock where he could see it and tell time easily, but where his customers could see it and tell time, too. He did not want a small clock on his counter, because counter space was so limited. He was not allowed to mount anything on the large mirror that was in front of his customers. Therefore, he wanted a backwards clock for the rear wall, so that it would appear correct to customers who looked in the mirror. He knew that he could learn to tell time from it after a little bit of practice.

Old-Time Digital

A player piano has the notes and the times at which they are played encoded on a piano roll. By the salesman's definition, it is a digital sound reproduction device. Older player pianos are powered by a vacuum that is generated by large foot pedals. Another digital sound reproduction device is a wind-up music box.

No Help

The other man was blind. He would have got lost if he had left his seeing but injured companion.

Silent Murder

The shotgun was used to club the victim to death, not used to fire a shell or bullet. There was no gunshot sound.

Destructive But Useful

As the sun ages, it is likely to expand, eventually heating the earth and destroying its life. A black hole that orbits the sun and loops through its outer edge, slowly depriving it of luminous matter, may postpone or prevent that process.

The Noble Lawyer

"Hold on there," the lawyer said to the miser when the latter started to leave. "You engaged my legal services in front of all this witnesses, and you know that I make my living from law practice. My fee, if you please." Claiming a consultation fee, a trial appearance fee, and extra charges for a short-notice legal action and for appearing outside of the town courtroom, he obtained a good sum of money from the miser, used part of it to pay the poor widow's back rent, used some to pay the landlord's henchmen to put her things back in the apartment, and gave the rest to the widow herself.

Taking Turns

Lisa was in England, and Ronnie was in the USA. Because they drove on opposite sides of the road, they disagreed about which kind of turn is across oncoming traffic and is therefore more difficult.

Exceptionally Vague

It was a label attached to a key to the politician's other campaign office. Keys are best labeled cryptically or so as to mislead, so that they will be easily used legitimately but will be worthless to someone who should not have them. Jerry insisted that the key to the other office, which was at the river, be labeled "River Bank And Trust."

Recycled Salt

Bread recipes customarily call for small amounts of salt. By vigorously kneading bread dough and working up a sweat, one can add previously eaten salt to the dough so that it will be eaten again.

Crossed Vision

If you cross your fingers, then there will be creases at the joints that will allow a small amount of light to pass between your crossed fingers. By looking at objects through the gaps between your fingers, you will expose your eye to only those rays of light that went through one small space. By doing so, you will see a sharply focused image even without wearing eyeglasses. This fact is unimportant except to people who need strong eyeglasses, but who are not wearing them at a particular time.

Secret Business

The men were planning a big business deal, and they were pretty sure that their telephones were tapped. They used a simple scrambler that could easily be obtained by an eavesdropper. But before the telephone conversation, they wrote a script for a fake conversation in which they discussed doing the opposite of what they really planned to do. They wanted eavesdroppers to anticipate the wrong plans and lose money, which the two men would gain. A secure scrambler would not have allowed eavesdroppers to hear the staged conversation and would not have helped the two men.

Calisthenics for Neighbors

A bird loose in the room. Scaring the bird and keeping it in flight is discourteous to the bird, but will provoke it to keep flying, eventually out a window. Closing the doors protects other rooms in the house. A badminton racquet can be used to agitate the bird and is intended by its manufacturer to swing at a "birdie."

The Wall-Mounted Sink

First, a wheelchair-bound patient cannot get to the sink if a pedestal or cabinet is under it. Second, a cabinet, or less effectively a pedestal, provides a hideout for cockroaches, which together with bug sprays can provoke allergies. Third, a sink the correct height prevents awkwardly leaning over it, an important consideration for a patient with a weak back who is taller than average, and is impractical for a pedestal or cabinet-mounted sink without additional carpentry.

The Ice Water

Richard worked in a restaurant kitchen, unloading china dishes from a conveyor-belt style dishwashing machine. Rubber gloves would not sufficiently protect his hands from the uncomfortable heat as he removed and stacked the hot dishes. Therefore, he dipped his hands into a bowl of ice water every few seconds to cool and protect them.

Artistic Appreciation
The artist had the painting put on display at a popular art gallery and called it "Portrait of a Dirty Rotten Scoundrel." The rich man had to pay a large sum to remove the painting from public view.

Smash and Destroy
Unhappy about the presence of vagrants who messily raided trash for saleable goods and sold them from street corners, activists urged the destruction of everything that is thrown away so that the vagrants would not be supported in their neighborhood.

Costly Borrowing
It was a license plate from Tim's car. Jim was a bank robber and borrowed a license plate from a car that looked like his own and was in a long-term parking lot, so that identifying him as he made his getaway would be more difficult. He later quietly returned the license plate, implicating Jim further, to hide the fact that it had been stolen at all.

License Unlost
William had cheated many people and wanted to move to another state. He would have to turn in his old driver's license and get a new one for the new state. Although he was interested in evading debts, he remembered one person who owed him money and was to pay him in a few months. He decided that he would later pick up a check from that person and cash it at the bank from which it was drawn, so that bank endorsements could not be used to locate him. But he knew that he would need identification at the bank. The old license would identify him to a teller, but would not give anyone the ability to locate him easily because it had his old address on it.

He Voted
This was a primary election. Ellery wanted the best possible candidate to win the (subsequent) general election and eventually take office. He would have been overjoyed if Lee could win the general election. But he knew that most voters disliked Lee and

feared that if Lee won the primary, then someone in the opposing party would win the general election. Ellery thought the candidates in the opposing party were not only less desirable than Lee but also less desirable than Ramona. He therefore preferred having Ramona win the primary and have a good chance of winning the general election. He did not want Lee to win the primary, for he would be very likely to lose the general election to a very undesirable candidate.

Cheap Silver
The silver was part of fillings in her teeth, and the fillings had induced heavy-metal toxicity. She had to have a dentist remove them, silver and all, and replace them with nontoxic fillings, which made her feel physically much better.

Carried Away
The woman had a heart attack, and her husband called for paramedics. One of them intubated her, and the other quickly pasted electrocardiogram leads on her chest after exposing it.

Beat the Water Shortage
When a long-awaited rainstorm was forecast, she was ready with soap and sponges. Then she washed her car using falling rainwater. Authorities noted a technical violation of the law, but did not prosecute because of the obvious lack of waste. (Note: Discovered during a true water shortage, the process of using falling rainwater is the quickest way to wash a car and is worth considering for that reason even when there is plenty of water available.)

Don't Break the Scale
First, she weighed the ruler. Then, she figured out how to put one end of the ruler on the scale and hold the other end on her finger so that the scale would register half the weight of the ruler. Finally, she carefully balanced the package on the middle of the ruler. She then doubled the weight shown on the scale and subtracted the weight of the ruler to get the full weight of the package.

Truckers and No Toll Money

When Hank left the restaurant, he forgot his wallet. Frank picked it up for him. He did not want to announce that fact on the CB, for Hank would then be known by state troopers to be driving without his license. He told Hank to get directly behind him when he got in line for the toll, and he paid his own toll from his money and also paid Frank's toll from Frank's money. The attendant, having been paid the toll for both trucks, let them through. Frank later returned Hank's wallet.

The Critical Student

This incident really happened, to the author. No one mentioned or asked which of the drugs were available in oral liquid form, so that they could be easily swallowed. The student, noting a unanimous failure to ask that question in the context of a swallowing difficulty, wondered about that hospital's standards of intelligence. At that time (1996), no calcium channel blockers (the preferred kind of drug for achalasia) were available in oral liquid form. A few years after the first book containing this question was published, oral calcium channel blockers became available. Coincidence? The answer to *that* question, alas, is not in this book.

Mowing the Pool

Leaves fell from the trees and landed on the pool deck. The draft from the mower was strong enough to push those leaves away from the pool, so that they would not later be blown into it. Using the lawn mower was faster than raking the leaves.

Sprayed at the Lawn

When standard time was replaced by daylight saving time, Henry forgot to advance the timer on the sprinkler. Relative to his daylight-saving work schedule, the sprinkler started an hour later than before. Unfortunately, that time was exactly when he was walking on the lawn.

Towing the Car

If the owner, having legally parked the car on a street or in another public place, is disabled by a sudden illness or accident, then the police will sometimes move the car to a safe place. This action protects the owner from damage to the apparently abandoned car and from parking tickets if the parking space is legal only during certain times of day.

Dancing

He felt the vibrations in the air and in the flooring. They gave him enough of a sense of rhythm to enable him to dance despite his being deaf.

Robbing the Bank

The organization was the local police force, and the numerous officers who were standing in line to cash their paychecks easily captured all of the would-be robbers.

A Token Wait in a Token Line

Smart Stephanie observed that most commuters bought tokens as they entered the subway from the street. She merely bought tokens as she left the subway, when few other commuters did so.

Another Mystery Fax

The executive, aware of how easy it is to communicate with outsiders for undesirable purposes, warned employees that calls would be monitored. A subordinate, aware of the difficulties of monitoring a fax message, bypassed the monitoring by faxing instead of speaking his personal messages. The metal siding of the building made mobile phone use unrealistic.

Dots on the I's

A small I includes one dot. A small I with a dot over it, therefore, actually has two dots, one above the other. Timmy took a pen and put two dots on his forehead, one over each eye.

A Sweet Problem

Diabetic skin ulcers. According to some alternative-medicine practitioners, sugar is a good medicine to apply to skin ulcers, blisters, and other open sores.

Gas-Station Glitch

The man whom George paid was not an employee of the station, but a con artist who got a uniform, asked everyone in line for ten dollars, and left quickly.

A Phony Call

Someone else, irritated at late-night wrong-number telephone calls from those two people, jotted down the numbers from the caller-ID display and, a few nights later, called them both at the same time from a 2-line telephone and connected them together.

Water in the Attic

The homeowner wanted filtered drinking water not only in the kitchen, but also in the bathrooms—including one upstairs. Because the pressure of the filtered water was not very high, the homeowner did not expect water to flow upward from it and, therefore, insisted on putting the filter and its tank as high up as possible.

Wooden Walls, Rubber Checks

Rick is hiding his income from the tax authorities and likes to be paid in cash. But sometimes, his customers prefer to pay by check. So he has the check written payable to the lumberyard instead of himself. The checks are usually insufficient to pay his lumber bills, and Rick pays the difference in cash. Sometimes, because a customer makes a mistake, a check bounces. Rick cheerfully pays the bank charges because they are less than the taxes he saves.

Water Under Pressure

If food is spilled on clothing, and blotted quickly with a napkin, then the lower end of the straw is a perfect device for putting a small amount of water on the spill so that it can be blotted further, with the napkin, before it has a chance to set permanently.

Cool Car and the Wire

Hiram was trying to save Calvin's windshield-wiper motor. Calvin's car had wipers that, when off, receded below the path of their up-down cycle. Snow that fell on the windshield would be pushed to its bottom and get squashed hard. Then, when the wipers were turned off, the motor would try to bring them to their normal off position; but the hard snow would get in their way and strain the motor. Hiram wanted to unfasten the wire that powered the motor after the wipers were turned off. Calvin would then have to turn them off exactly when they were near the bottom of the windshield, a nuisance; but the motor would not be strained.

The Five-State Golf Drive

Moe could hit the golf ball off a bridge into a railroad car that carried gravel or coal across the country. He could also hit it into a piece of driftwood that was floating in a major river.

They Love Each Other

Pat was a parrot. Not all parrots talk.

Ski Through The Tree

The expert skier, familiar with parallel skiing (in which the skis are kept parallel at all times), could ski while wearing only one ski. He made the tracks on two different runs, first passing the tree on one side and then passing it on the other.

The Terrified Mother

The baby, soon after being born, had been kidnapped and almost given, with a forged birth certificate and adoption papers, to a childless couple that wanted a son. Police intervened and restored him to his rightful mother. Still afraid of losing her baby, and having persistent nightmares about abduction, she carefully dressed him in clothing that did not identify his sex.

Won't Stop Ringing

A security check. The button was an alarm switch, located inside the house but near the front door. It was wired to trip the alarm, also to send a signal that would alert the police, if pressed.

Mystery Gate

The gate is there to block access not to the hotel, but to an exclusive fully gated luxury housing community adjacent to the hotel. The very rich residents of that community often patronize the restaurant and other facilities of the hotel, and they sometimes have the hotel provide lodging for their friends and relatives. The gate, therefore, is a convenience for the community's residents, who, in turn, control access through it.

He Called the Police

Once inside the house, he fell, breaking his leg. Pulling a telephone down from a table, he called an emergency police number for help and, though arrested, received treatment for his leg.

The Empty Wrapper

She had her two-year-old son with her. When her son got hungry, she got permission from a store manager to buy a sandwich at the delicatessen counter, give it to her son, and pay for it later at the checkout counter with the rest of her merchandise.

An Earful

The veterinarian spayed and neutered stray cats for free, but insisted on being paid when spaying and neutering pet cats. To protect against losing his fee to dishonest pet owners who pretended that their cat was a stray, he altered their appearance, knowing that a pet owner would object to such a disfigurement but that a stray cat would be unharmed by a notch in its ear.

Positions, Everyone!

Falling a great distance into deep water. These actions minimize damage from surface tension, protect pelvic structures, and assure that, if you must hit the bottom violently, your legs and not your neck take the blow.

Inefficient Elevators

Perhaps as a carryover from the days when elevators were operated by people, the prevailing practice is to summon an elevator then, after getting inside it, select the floor at which one gets off. But it is possible to program the elevators so that, when summoned to one floor, they are alerted to where the person wants to go, by putting the floor-select buttons at the landings and not in the elevators themselves. This feature would be easy to see, as Joe knows, and would greatly streamline elevator travel during rush hour and other busy periods by eliminating duplicate trips between pairs of floors. Modern high-speed computer processors can easily manage to direct a group of elevators this way if programmed to do so.

Self-Portrait

Instead of using one mirror, he used two. He fastened the edges of two mirrors together and set the angle between them at exactly 90 degrees. Then, when he looked at the pair of mirrors, he saw his double, unreversed, reflection. (Try it with a couple of pocket makeup mirrors.)

Not a Purse Snatcher

He shouted, "Hey, lady! You dropped your purse!" and returned it to its grateful owner.

No Littering Summons

Nancy's car had a sudden electrical system failure at night. Fearful of a collision, and being unable to drive off the road due to heavy traffic, she had to stop the car in the middle of the road. At first opportunity, she scattered everything available behind her car so that other drivers would see debris and drive around it. She could not turn on emergency flashers, for they did not work.

Does This Bulb Work?

Cal used clear-glass bulbs.

A Gift To Share

Laura had earlier lost an arm in an accident, and the prize was an expensive pair of gloves. She knew of a woman with one arm, the opposite arm, and with the same glove size; and she planned to give her the glove that she herself could not use.

A Shocking Problem

Louie and Lucy each put a plug on the end of the cord; neither of them added an outlet. They each plugged in one end of the cord, into separate outlets connected to the same wall switch. By chance, the plugs were inserted so as to connect the opposite sides of the electric circuit together, shorting the circuit and tripping the circuit breaker. Louie did not tell Lucy that he was going to install a plug and that she should install the outlet.

Poker Assault

The dealer was cheating. He had picked up the face-up cards in a careful order so that he would get a good hand; he had only pretended to shuffle the deck, and he had bent the bottom card before cutting the deck and handing it to the player on his right, who would probably cut the deck so as to put the bent card back on the bottom. But his arrangement of good cards was not perfect; he also wanted the very top card to be in his hand. The first five cards, therefore, were not from the top of the deck; they may have been from the bottom. Because he dealt from two different decks that had been mixed together, the other players got suspicious when the back of the top card stayed the same and the first five cards dealt did not all have the same back. That discrepancy proved that the dealer was cheating, and the observant players reacted accordingly.

The Unused Jacket

They were African-Americans, with dark skin. He wore a business suit, of dark fabric. She wore a dark dress and a black coat. He exposed his white shirt for safety so that motorists could easily see them.

Long Walk for the Disabled

He injured his neck and could no longer turn his head far enough to drive backwards easily. Therefore, he favored parking spaces that he could enter and leave without driving backwards, even if they were a long walk from his destination. To warn away children when he was forced to drive backwards, he installed a warning-tone device on his back bumper and wired it to his backup lights.

by Edward J. Harshman

Immovable Car

The car is in a garage, and its electrically operated door is closed and immovable due to a power failure. The garage has no other entrance.

The Bad Letter

Her friend was an author and was looking for a publisher. Some publishers ask for expense advances from authors, in exchange for a larger percentage of royalties. Unfortunately, some of these publishers are dishonest and don't do much except keep the money. Sally wrote to one, pretending to be an author, and hoped to be told she was not good enough to publish, which would have been encouraging for her friend. Had Sally received an enthusiastic reply, she would have warned her friend that the publisher was dishonest.

Shot Down

Fortunately or otherwise, his plane could fly faster than the bullets that emerged from its machine gun. He test-fired the gun, changed course somewhat radically, got in the bullets' way, and shot himself down. Oops!

Give Me a Dollar

Though a beggar, the man had compassion for the new storeowner and wished him success. With more small change than he really needed in that form, he happily handed some to the owner and took paper money in its place. The owner, whose store was in front of a bus stop where the exact fare was needed, underestimated the need for coins in his cash register and was happy that the beggar could help him.

Pierced Ears

He was familiar with Exodus 21: 2-6 and Deuteronomy 15: 12-17, which show that having a pierced ear is a sign that one is willing to be a lifelong slave.

THE END

Index

Puzzle name, puzzle page, clues, solution:

Puzzle name, puzzle page, clues, solution

Puzzle name, puzzle page, clues, solution

by Edward J. Harshman

Puzzle name, puzzle page, clues, solution

Puzzle name, puzzle page, clues, solution

by Edward J. Harshman

Puzzle name, puzzle page, clues, solution

Puzzle name, puzzle page, clues, solution

by Edward J. Harshman

Puzzle name, puzzle page, clues, solution

Puzzle name, puzzle page, clues, solution

Puzzle name, puzzle page, clues, solution

Puzzle name, puzzle page, clues, solution

Printed in Great Britain
by Amazon.co.uk, Ltd.,
Marston Gate.